TWICE SHY

What Reviewers Say About Aurora Rey's Work

The Last Place You Look

"This book is the perfect book to kick your feet up, relax with a glass of wine and enjoy. I'm a big Aurora Rey fan because her deliciously engaging books feature strong women who fall for sweet butch women. It's a winning recipe."—*Les Rêveur*

"The romance is satisfying and full-bodied, with each character learning how to achieve her own goals and still be part of a couple. A heartwarming story of two lovers learning to move past their fears and commit to a shared future."—*Kirkus Reviews*

"[A] sex-positive, body-positive love story. With its warm atmosphere and sweet characters, *The Last Place You Look* is a fluffy LGBTQ+ romance about finding a second chance at love where you least expect it."—*Foreword Reviews*

"If you enjoy stories that portray two gorgeous women who slowly fall in love in the quirkiest way ever coupled with nosy and well-meaning neighbors and family members, then this is definitely the story for you!"—*Lesbian Review*

Ice on Wheels—*Novella in* Hot Ice

"I liked how Brooke was so attracted to Riley despite the massive grudge she had. No matter how nice or charming Riley was, Brooke was dead set on hating her. A cute enemies to lovers story."—*Bookvark*

The Inn at Netherfield Green

"I really enjoyed this book but that's not surprising because it came from the pen of Aurora Rey. This is the kind of book you read while sitting by a warm fire with a Rosemary Gin and snuggly blanket."
—*Les Rêveur*

"Aurora Rey has created another striking and romantic setting with the village of Netherfield Green. With her vivid descriptions of the inn, the pub, and the surrounding village, I ended up wanting to live there myself. She also did a fantastic job creating two very different characters in Lauren and Cam."—*Rainbow Reflections*

"[Aurora Rey] constantly delivers a well-written romance that has just the right blend of humour, engaging characters, chemistry and romance."—*C-Spot Reviews*

Lead Counsel—*Novella in* The Boss of Her

"*Lead Counsel* by Aurora Rey is a short and sweet second chance romance. Not only was this story paced well and a delight to sink into, but there's A++ good swearing in it and has lines like this that made me all swoony because of how beautifully they're crafted."
—*Lesbian Review*

Recipe for Love

"*Recipe for Love* by Aurora Rey is a gorgeous romance that's sure to delight any of the foodies out there. Be sure to keep snacks on hand when you're reading it, though, because this book will make you want to nibble on something!"—*Lesbian Review*

"So here's a few things that always get me excited when Aurora Rey publishes a new book. ...Firstly, I am guaranteed a hot butch with a

sensitive side, this alone is a massive tick. Secondly, I am guaranteed to throw any diet out the window because the books always have the most delectable descriptions of food that I immediately go on the hunt for—this time it was a BLT with a difference. And lastly, hot sex scenes that personally have added to my fantasy list throughout the years! This book did not disappoint in any of those areas."
—*Les Rêveur*

Autumn's Light

"Aurora Rey has a knack for writing characters you care about and she never gives us the same pairing twice. Each character is always unique and fully fleshed out. Most of her pairings are butch/femme and her diversity in butch rep is so appreciated. This goes to prove the butch characters do not need to be one dimensional, nor do they all need to be rugged. Rey writes romances in which you can happily immerse yourself. They are gentle romances which are character driven."—*Lesbian Review*

"Aurora Rey is by far one of my favourite authors. She writes books that just get me. ...Her winning formula is Butch women who fall for strong femmes. I just love it. Another triumph from the pen of Aurora Rey. 5 stars."—*Les Rêveur*

"This is a beautiful romance. I loved the flow of the story, loved the characters including the secondary ones, and especially loved the setting of Provincetown, Massachusetts."—*Rainbow Reflections*

"[*Autumn's Light*] was another fun addition to a great series." —Danielle Kimerer, Librarian (Nevins Memorial Library, Massachusetts)

"Aurora Rey has shown a mastery of evoking setting and this is especially evident in her Cape End romances set in Provincetown. I have loved this entire series..."—*Kitty Kat's Book Review Blog*

Spring's Wake

"[A] feel-good romance that would make a perfect beach read. The Provincetown B&B setting is richly painted, feeling both indulgent and cozy."—*RT Book Reviews*

"*Spring's Wake* has shot to number one in my age-gap romance favorites shelf."—*Les Rêveur*

"The Ptown setting was idyllic and the supporting cast of characters from the previous books made it feel welcoming and homey. The love story was slow and perfectly timed, with a fair amount of heat. I loved it and hope that this isn't the last from this particular series."—*Kitty Kat's Book Review Blog*

"*Spring's Wake* by Aurora Rey is charming. This is the third story in Aurora Rey's Cape End romance series and every book gets better. Her stories are never the same twice and yet each one has a uniquely *her* flavour. The character work is strong and I find it exciting to see what she comes up with next."—*Lesbian Review*

Summer's Cove

"As expected in a small-town romance, *Summer's Cove* evokes a sunny, light-hearted atmosphere that matches its beach setting. …Emerson's shy pursuit of Darcy is sure to endear readers to her, though some may be put off during the moments Darcy winds tightly to the point of rigidity. Darcy desires romance yet is unwilling to disrupt her son's life to have it, and you feel for Emerson when she endeavors to show how there's room in her heart for a family." —*RT Book Reviews*

"From the moment the characters met I was gripped and couldn't wait for the moment that it all made sense to them both and they would finally go for it. Once again, Aurora Rey writes some of the steamiest sex scenes I have read whilst being able to keeping the romance going. I really think this could be one of my favorite series and can't wait to see what comes next. Keep 'em coming, Aurora."—*Les Rêveur*

Crescent City Confidential—*Lambda Literary Award Finalist*

"This book blew my socks off. ...[*Crescent City Confidential*] ticks all the boxes I've started to expect from Aurora Rey. It is written very well and the characters are extremely well developed; I felt like I was getting to know new friends and my excitement grew with every finished chapter."—*Les Rêveur*

"This book will make you want to visit New Orleans if you have never been. I enjoy descriptive writing and Rey does a really wonderful job of creating the setting. You actually feel like you know the place."—*Amanda's Reviews*

"*Crescent City Confidential* pulled me into the wonderful sights, sounds and smells of New Orleans. I was totally captivated by the city and the story of mystery writer Sam and her growing love for the place and for a certain lady. ...It was slow burning but romantic and sexy too. A mystery thrown into the mix really piqued my interest."—*Kitty Kat's Book Review Blog*

"*Crescent City Confidential* is a sweet romance with a hint of thriller thrown in for good measure."—*Lesbian Review*

Built to Last

"Rey's frothy contemporary romance brings two women together to restore an ancient farmhouse in Ithaca, N.Y. ...[T]he women totally click in bed, as well as when they're poring over paint chips, and readers will enjoy finding out whether love conquers all." —*Publishers Weekly*

Visit us at www.boldstrokesbooks.com

By the Author

Cape End Romances:

Winter's Harbor

Summer's Cove

Spring's Wake

Autumn's Light

Built to Last

Crescent City Confidential

Lead Counsel (Novella in The Boss of Her collection)

Recipe for Love: A Farm-to-Table Romance

The Inn at Netherfield Green

Ice on Wheels (Novella in Hot Ice collection)

The Last Place You Look

Twice Shy

TWICE SHY

by

Aurora Rey

2020

ISBN 13: 978-1-63555-737-4

This Trade Paperback Original Is Published By
Bold Strokes Books, Inc.
P.O. Box 249
Valley Falls, NY 12185

First Edition: October 2020

Credits
Editors: Ashley Tillman and Cindy Cresap
Production Design: Susan Ramundo
Cover Design By Tammy Seidick

Acknowledgments

In the acknowledgments for *The Last Place You Look,* I said, "I have a running joke that, when you read one of my books, you're getting a glimpse into what was going on in my life the year before." It makes me feel like I should lead with a disclaimer: No affairs with exes went into the making of this book. I do have a couple of great exes, though, and I owe a lot of who I am to the relationships we had and continue to have.

So much love, respect, and gratitude to everyone at Bold Strokes Books. You've helped me grow as a writer and as a person and I love that you care about both the art and business of books. Ash, you remain at the top of the list. Thank you for indulging me but also not hesitating to call me out.

Finally, thank you to everyone who has given me the gift of buying and reading my books, and for the kind words and encouragement along the way. You've given me more joy than you know.

Dedication

For all the iffy decisions that help us get where we need to be

Chapter One

How long have you been waiting for this?"

Amanda Russo regarded her best friend and did a mental calculation. "Ten years? Pretty much since the divorce."

Erin nodded. "Fucking Mel."

She snickered. It was Erin's stock reply anytime anyone referenced Amanda's ex. Even though she and Mel were on good terms at this point, she appreciated the loyalty. "But if she hadn't left, we might still be together. Just think how wretched that would be."

It was her standard answer, a reminder to herself as much as an attempt to soften the insult.

"So wise. So mature. So you." Erin bowed, her way of conceding the point. "Enough about her. Tell me everything."

Amanda took a deep breath and looked around the small eating area of her bakery. It held exactly five tables, each with two chairs. Another five chairs lined the wall and could be squeezed in here and there. But if they all happened to be in use, things got uncomfortably tight. Okay, fire code capacity tight.

Not for long. She'd bought the building so she could expand into the empty storefront next door, meaning more seating than she could possibly need and twice as much kitchen space. The prospect thrilled and slightly terrified her. "I'm meeting with the architect tomorrow."

Erin clapped her hands together and rubbed them in a way that did double duty for enthusiasm and maniacal plotting. "Boy or girl?"

Amanda made a face. "Are we twelve?"

"I act twelve and you act eighty. We balance out to sassy middle age."

"Hey, now." She had to protest, even if it was true.

"Well?"

"She. Quinn Sullivan. Based in Ithaca. Came highly recommended by Rob over at Fairmount Ridge Winery."

Erin hummed her approval. "Excellent. Age? Orientation? Is she hot? Single?"

"I'm hiring her, not hooking up with her."

"You say that like it can't be both."

Erin dated. Amanda did not. Pretty much ever at this point. Not that she was opposed. She just had plenty of other things to occupy her time. And her last attempt a few years prior had left her disappointed, if not completely jaded. Much like her opinion of Mel, Erin's thoughts on Amanda's celibacy were singularly focused. Like with Mel, Amanda had a stock answer. "I'm not looking to hook up. Certainly not with someone I'm working with."

"You should consider being a little less picky."

"Because lowered standards are the key to happily ever after?"

Erin wagged a finger. "Nobody said anything about ever after. We're talking about the here and now. And if a hot woman shows up tomorrow, you have no reason not to invite her over for dinner and take her to bed."

"I couldn't possibly." The mere thought sent a tingle of nerves through her.

"You could. It's the would, or maybe the won't, that's tripping you up and I think it's high time you got over it."

Amanda shook her head again but laughed. "I'll take it under consideration."

"Good. Now, tell me about your plans."

"That's what I was trying to do when you hijacked the conversation with sex talk."

"Sex"—Erin poked her right in the chest—"is the conversation. And maybe you should consider being hijacked. It would be good for you."

Instead of arguing, she launched into her ideas for the bakery. The added seating would make Bake My Day a place where people could sit and enjoy, rather than just pick up, their favorite treat. She planned to start lunch service in earnest. She'd dabbled in soup and sandwiches but wanted to add more options. Salads. Quiche, perhaps.

It also meant she'd have a dedicated space for decorating cakes. As weddings and bachelorette parties and birthdays got fancier, the demand for high-end cakes grew exponentially. New space would mean she could frost and fondant without disrupting the baking that gave her the cakes to frost in the first place. It was a lot to take on, but she was ready. At least that's what she told herself every time she had a moment of what the hell had she been thinking.

Erin nodded and tutted her agreement. "I love it. So, this architect, Quinn, is going to design it? Or do it? I'm not sure I know what an architect does."

She hadn't either, beyond designing buildings from the ground up. But Rob assured her it was worth it to hire a pro and she trusted his judgment. "She's going to assess the space, assess what can be done, and hopefully come up with something that doesn't look like I knocked down a wall and hoped for the best."

"Fun."

"And hopefully she has contractors she works with because I really, really don't want to deal with contractors."

Erin lifted both hands. "Preach."

They'd both had less than stellar experiences—Erin with a bathroom remodel and Amanda with an update of her kitchen. "Rob swears she saved him money in the long run."

"Even if she doesn't, saved headaches are priceless." Erin sipped her coffee and looked up at the ceiling. "Hot and fuckable would be bonus."

"Erin." She hadn't meant to use her scolding mom voice; it came out of its own volition.

Erin shrugged, unfazed. "I'm just saying. Anyway, what time is she coming? Maybe I can time my morning coffee to snag a look."

"You realize that makes me less likely to tell you the truth, right?"

"I'd behave." She fluttered her eyelashes, all innocence.

"I love you like a sister, but no, you would not."

"It's why you love me."

That part was true. Erin had fewer filters, fewer inhibitions, and a bigger taste for adventure. And wine. Between that and being a decade younger, Erin managed to keep Amanda from becoming too much of a stick in the mud. "It is."

She sighed. "I don't want to go to work."

"But if you don't, who will keep the streets of Kenota safe?"

"Yeah, that pack of raccoons has really been terrorizing folks."

"Easy for you to say. They've not upended your garbage twice in the last week and a half."

Erin pressed her lips together. "Tragic."

Amanda stood and smacked her on the arm. "Get out of here. I've got work to do."

"Fine. Do I want a donut for the road or a croissant?"

"Um." It was a rhetorical question, but she couldn't help but think on it. Erin, who ate like a linebacker and never gained an ounce, had already inhaled a muffin with her coffee.

Erin waved her off. "What am I saying? I'll take both."

Of course she would. "I'm going to leave you in Mei's capable hands."

Amanda gave her a hug and headed back to the kitchen. She found her assistant Tanya filling a row of cake pans. "I've got one more batch after this and the table is yours."

When she'd opened the bakery fifteen years prior, the kitchen had felt massive. Compared to her home kitchen, where she'd baked cakes and cookies as a side hustle to her job at the Statler Hotel, it was. Even if she had moments of frustration with her current situation, outgrowing her space was a very satisfying problem to have. "Take your time. I'm going to make modeling chocolate and start the gum paste flowers for next weekend."

"When are you meeting with the architect again?"

She laughed. Tanya's interest might be even keener than Erin's, but it had nothing to do with whether or not the architect was hot. Or single. "Tomorrow."

Tanya slid pans into the convection oven. "Not a moment too soon."

❖

Quinn studied the front of Bake My Day. She'd been there a handful of times, mostly with Lesedi. They'd spend Saturdays meandering the Seneca Lake wine trail and would stop in for coffee or a fortifying treat after sampling one too many local vintages. It somehow felt like a lifetime ago and just last week. Was that standard protocol for life a year after divorce?

Inside, the question evaporated with the aroma of donuts, muffins, and God only knew what else. She closed her eyes for a second and breathed it in, letting her sweet tooth momentarily rule her imagination. She'd get something, or maybe several somethings, to take home. And perhaps a cup of coffee. The smell of fresh espresso and the hiss of steam coming from the machine tempted her almost as much as the pastries. Almost.

She had an idea of what Amanda looked like from her photo on the website. Well, that and they'd technically met a couple of the times she'd been in. Since she was nowhere to be seen, Quinn joined the queue. It wouldn't be rude to bring a latte into her meeting, would it?

When her turn came, she offered the woman behind the register a smile. "Good morning. I have a meeting with Ms. Russo."

The woman, whose name tag read Tanya, gave her a quizzical look. "Is this about a cake?"

She was tempted to make a joke about wishing it was, but a number of people had joined the line after her and it felt rude to take more time than was necessary. "No, no. I'm her architect."

Tanya's eyes got big. "Right. That's today. Oh, we're so excited. Can I get you something while you wait?"

Memories of her marriage or not, she liked this place. "That would be fantastic."

Tanya called her coffee order to the guy working the espresso machine. "Something to eat? The donut of the week is strawberries and cream."

She should decline. She was about to take a business meeting. And she already had plans to bring things home. "Sold."

Tanya grinned and nodded her approval. "You go make yourself comfortable. We'll bring it over to you and I'll let Amanda know you're here."

Quinn pulled her wallet from her back pocket, but Tanya waved her away. "Amanda would have my head."

The choice of phrase gave Quinn pause. Was she kidding or was Amanda a tyrant? She'd figure out one way or the other soon enough. She'd barely settled at a table by the window before her coffee and donut appeared. "Thanks."

Tanya poked her head into the kitchen. When she emerged, she looked Quinn's way. "She just needs to clean up. She'll be with you in a few minutes."

Quinn didn't mind waiting in general, but especially when she had a gorgeous sugar bomb in front of her. She took a sip of her coffee—even better than she remembered—then dove in. The donut was fried to perfection and dusted with powdered sugar. The filling, though, put it over the edge. Fresh strawberries surrounded by a heavenly concoction somewhere between custard and whipped cream. It oozed onto her fingers. She licked it away, not wanting a drop to go to waste.

"Quinn?"

She looked up, thumb still in her mouth. Amanda was prettier than Quinn remembered, her features softer. And, because that's how her life worked, here she was looking like an idiot. She grabbed a napkin and wiped her fingers as she stood. She extended her hand, glad it wasn't the one she'd been licking. "Ms. Russo. Yes, hi."

Amanda shook her hand, an unreadable smile on her lips. "Amanda, please. Thank you for offering to meet me here."

"Of course. I'd want to see the space sooner rather than later anyway."

Amanda took the seat across from her. She bit her lip in a way that might be flirtatious. Could Amanda be flirting with her? Either way, it bumped Quinn's pulse up a few notches. Even if she had no business flirting with a client. "So, let's start with your big ideas and then we can get into the nitty-gritty."

"You, um…" She trailed off, leaving Quinn to wonder if maybe she made Amanda nervous.

Quinn offered her most reassuring smile. "I what?"

"You have some powdered sugar on your nose." Amanda bit her lip again, and seemed to be stifling a laugh.

Quinn's stomach dropped. She grabbed a napkin and wiped it across her face. "Did I get it?"

"Not quite." This time Amanda did chuckle. She picked up another napkin and leaned across the table. "May I?"

Mortified, all she could do was nod.

"There."

"Thanks." Quinn swiped her hand over her face. She didn't think Amanda would lie at this point, but it was like having a spider crawling up her arm. The phantom tickle got the better of her and probably would for the rest of the morning.

"I really did get it. Sorry. I figured you'd rather know than get in your car and realize it had been there the whole time."

The sincerity of Amanda's voice lessened her embarrassment, at least a little. "I appreciate it. Really."

"Considering it was one of my donuts you were enjoying, I take it as a compliment."

"That's nice of you to say." It was. Under normal circumstances, it would break the tension and be the end of it. Too bad she'd interpreted the whole thing as flirting.

Amanda clasped her hands together. "So, let's talk about why you're here."

She appreciated Amanda's ability to shift the conversation away from her gaffe so smoothly. "Yes. Right. You're expanding."

Amanda's eyes lit up then, enthusiasm radiating from her. "That's the plan. I'm taking over the space next door."

"Aha." She'd noticed the empty storefront when she parked. It looked like a mirror of Bake My Day, only she hadn't been able to tell what it was before and had no memory of ever setting foot inside. "Has it been vacant long?"

"About a year. It was an inspirational gift shop."

That would explain why she hadn't been inside. "And it's similar in size to what you have here?"

"Identical, only they didn't take half the floor space for a kitchen. There's only a small storeroom in the back."

She could work with that. "And what's your vision?"

Amanda let out a small sigh. She'd clearly been thinking about this for a long time. "I'm hoping to completely reconfigure the major equipment in the kitchen. I need more work space, mostly for assembling and decorating wedding cakes, but I think it makes sense to improve the overall flow."

Quinn opened the notebook she'd brought and started scribbling notes. "It shouldn't be difficult to combine the spaces and create something more efficient."

"I was hoping you'd say that. The other big thing is more seating. We started offering lunch a few months back and people have to take it to go because there's nowhere to sit."

Quinn hadn't sampled the lunch offerings, but if they were half as good as everything else, it would follow that business was booming. "But you don't want it to feel like an add-on."

"Yes. Exactly. I don't want customers to feel like they're at the kiddie table in the living room for Thanksgiving dinner."

She chuckled at the analogy because of just how well she could relate. "We'll have to see how much of the wall can go without having to put in new beams."

"I should say up front it's the part I'm willing to splurge on. It's that important."

It was hard to say which she liked more—Amanda's willingness to splurge or the fact that she cared about such a key architectural feature. "Then that's what you'll have."

"I was hoping you'd say that, too." Amanda smiled again. This time, it was all enthusiasm. Which Quinn didn't mind. This was, after all, a professional arrangement.

"Have you taken over the lease of the other space? Can we get in and walk through now?"

"One better. I bought the building."

One better indeed. They wouldn't have to worry about any approvals beyond the usual permits and things. "Fantastic."

"Shall we?"

"Please."

Amanda led her next door. She could already see the wall gone. They could add a second display case, another register. More lighting and, as Amanda mentioned, more seating. Probably three times as much as she had now. It wasn't hard to imagine the bakery going from a place to grab a quick bite to a destination. She'd make a point of coming more often for sure. For the food, of course, but also to maybe spend time with the beautiful owner, without powdered sugar on her face.

"Why do you look so worried?" Amanda's question cut through the haze of her imagination.

Quinn cleared her throat. "Not worried. Getting a little ahead of myself. I have that tendency sometimes."

"I imagine it's a good trait in your line of work."

Work. Right. That was the point. Not her fantasies of spending mornings working at one of the new tables and chatting up Amanda when she emerged from the kitchen. "It has its perks I suppose."

They spent a few minutes discussing next steps: measurements, initial blueprints, a visit from a structural engineer. Quinn scheduled an appointment to return the following week and bid Amanda a good day. But not before snagging a few cupcakes and another one of those strawberry donuts for the road.

CHAPTER TWO

Amanda walked into the house to the sound of gunfire and explosions. Fortunately, they were the digital kind and coming from the basement. She headed downstairs and found Cal and Zoe playing *Fortnite*. "How was the AP exam?"

Cal paused the game and they both looked her way. "Brutal."

Zoe rolled her eyes. "He's being dramatic. We're both pretty sure we got at least fours."

She looked at Cal. He made a face. "Yeah. What she said."

She wasn't worried. Physics was like a second language to Cal and he spoke it more fluently than she ever did. English, on the other hand, not so much. "Good. I assume you two are blowing off steam before your last stretch of studying for tomorrow?"

"Mom, if I write one more rhetorical analysis essay, I might literally die."

Zoe shook her head and looked at him with a mix of exasperation and pity. "Your misuse of the word literally begs to differ."

He turned his attention, along with a withering glare, her way. "I was being hyperbolic."

"Nice recovery. I withdraw my insult."

It was their usual banter—sarcastic and a bit brainy—but still made her smile. Zoe had been Cal's best friend since preschool. She'd come out as trans just as they hit puberty and Amanda had worried the combination of hormones and middle school angst might pull them apart. Cal never wavered, though, remaining so loyal she then wondered if maybe he'd developed a crush on her. But by all accounts, she was wrong on that front, too. They remained inseparable and, she was pretty sure, had similar taste in girls. It baffled her at times, but seemed to make perfect sense to them.

"Can Zoe stay for dinner?"

"Yes, but that doesn't mean you can play video games until it's ready."

Cal sighed, but said, "Okay."

Zoe, a lit nerd as much as a physics nerd, beamed. "I made Quizlets."

Cal groaned and Amanda chuckled. "I'm going to take a quick shower and then I'll get chicken on the grill. Sound good?"

Zoe asked, "Would you like help?"

"I've got it. I'll let you two tackle dishes."

Another groan from Cal, but there wasn't any feeling behind it. "Thanks, Mom."

She pointed at the television. "Go ahead and finish this round or whatever it is. Just don't blow the next hour on it."

They nodded and Amanda left them to finish saving the world. Or were they destroying it? She could never keep track.

She climbed the stairs to the main level, then up to her room. She peeled off her work clothes and headed for the shower, scrubbing off the powdered sugar that seemed to seep into her pores when she spent the day making frosting and rolling fondant. Thinking of powdered sugar made her think of Quinn. It was a good thing Erin hadn't stopped by because she'd never let Amanda hear the end of it. Because despite what Amanda might say about not having a stake one way or the other, Quinn was crazy good-looking. The dusting of sugar on her nose had only intensified that fact, adding a layer of adorably approachable to what might have been an intimidating level of hotness.

Not just general hotness, either. In gray pants and a white oxford, Quinn was rocking butch business casual hardcore. Her salt-and-pepper hair was cut short, with enough on top to enjoy running her fingers through. Not her fingers, obviously. One's fingers. Quinn's. Or someone she was dating.

Attempting to back out of the thought proved worse than the thought itself. Being in the shower didn't help. Amanda shook her head and scrubbed her arms with renewed vigor. She was being ridiculous. And she didn't do ridiculous.

After cutting the water and toweling off, she slipped on her robe and padded to her dresser. She had no business thinking about Quinn and her hotness. She was a grown woman with near-adult children and Quinn was her colleague. Or employee. Or something. Whatever the word was, it had professional in the definition, which made Quinn squarely off limits.

She got dressed and pulled her hair up in a clip. Working together or not, she wasn't in the market, so on or off limits didn't even matter. She could appreciate an attractive woman. That could—would—be the end of it.

After the meeting at the bakery, Quinn spent the rest of the day in her office, working on the plans for the Trumansburg Library expansion and trying her best not to think about Amanda. Or how badly she'd embarrassed herself when they met. She'd eaten enough donuts to know better. Such a rookie mistake.

Amanda had been gracious, not that she would have expected anything else. But it was more than that. She had this energy Quinn couldn't quite put a finger on. An easiness. Or maybe more accurately, Amanda put her at ease.

Given her recent track record with women, it was saying something. She'd been on probably twenty dates in the last year, and most of them had been first dates. Her sisters, her co-workers, and even her hiking buddies had attempted to set her up. They were so damn enthusiastic about it, she didn't have the heart to turn them down.

It wasn't like the women she went out with were awful. Okay, a couple of them had been awful. But most were nice, successful, attractive. A few were divorced, like her, but some were still looking. Maybe that was the problem. Women in their thirties and forties looking to get married didn't feel like her speed at this point. She'd sort of been there, done that. Which said nothing of the ones who wanted to have kids. At fifty, any desire to go down that path was long gone.

Quinn shook her head. It was all a bit more than she could handle. Or maybe more accurately, wanted to handle. She could handle all sorts of things, but God, it was exhausting.

"Do you have a minute?" Arti's head appeared in her doorway.

"Of course." Hopefully, whatever it was would take her mind off women.

"How'd the meeting at the bakery go?"

Amanda immediately popped back into her mind. "Really well. Have you been there?"

Arti made her trying to remember something face. "What's it called again?"

"Bake My Day." Every time she said the name, it made her smile.

"I think so. Kenota, right? Near the wine trail."

"That's the one. The cupcakes are to die for. Well, everything is to die for in my opinion." She grabbed the box from the console behind her desk. "I'd planned to eat all these myself, but I'll share."

Arti eyed the contents of the box. "I don't think those are paleo."

"No, but if cavemen could have eaten them, they would have."

"What the hell." She picked up the chocolate one with peanut butter frosting. "All in moderation, right?"

"Absolutely." Even if her version of moderation and Arti's were vastly different.

She thought Arti might take the cupcake back to her office for later, but she dug right in. "Oh, my God."

"I know."

"I'm glad this is your project and not mine. I'd probably gain twenty pounds over the course of the build."

Quinn chuckled. "I'm kind of worried for myself."

"Sugar coma aside, how was it?"

She gave Arti the overview of her meeting with Amanda and the scope of the project. "It's not earth-shattering, but I think we can make it something special."

Arti licked frosting from her fingers. "These cupcakes deserve something special."

The cupcakes had nothing on the woman who made them. "Exactly."

"Do you need help? I could spare Frida."

"I think I'm good." She didn't add it was because she didn't want the intern lurking around every time she met with Amanda.

"Well, you know where to find her if you change your mind."

Quinn experienced a pang of guilt. "I mean, I can bring her in if she doesn't have anything else."

Arti stuffed the last bite of cupcake into her mouth and waved a hand. "No, no. I'd love to have her on the Tompkins Trust job, but I don't want to monopolize her time if you could use the help."

She was probably more relieved than the situation warranted. It was her tendency to say yes to things even when she wanted to say no. She really needed to get that under control. Next time. "We're good."

"Fantastic. I'll catch you later."

Arti left and Quinn forced herself to focus. She made good progress, even if Amanda hovered at the periphery of her thoughts most of the time. She called it a day just after five, locking up the office and heading to her little apartment on the west side of town.

Quinn let herself in and sighed. It was a perfectly nice apartment and more than suited her needs. Still, she couldn't help but feel uninspired every time she walked in the door. Maybe it was time to start looking for a house in earnest.

She set down her things and wandered to the kitchen. As tempted as she might be to have cupcakes for dinner, she should have something other than sugar first. She opened the fridge, only to be greeted with a tub of hummus, a few beers, and the makings of a rather feeble salad. Talk about uninspiring.

Would it be wrong to have takeout again? Thai maybe, which she wouldn't cook for herself even if she were attempting to cook for herself. And more nutritional value than cupcakes.

Satisfied with the rationale, she grabbed her phone. *If you haven't ordered takeout yet, come over for dinner.*

She chuckled at the accuracy of the invitation. Her sister knew her too well. *What are we having?*

Shrimp tacos.

Hard to turn that down. *I'll be there in 20.*

Fab. Bring wine.

She grabbed her keys and headed back to her car. Too bad she hadn't thought to get enough cupcakes to bring over. Next time. She'd be spending quite a lot of time at the bakery, so that wouldn't be a problem.

She pulled into Kiera's driveway a few minutes later. Before she could grab the Sauvignon Blanc from the passenger seat, the door opened and Grace came running down the walk. She got out of her car just in time for Grace to launch herself into her arms. Quinn embraced her, her day suddenly ten times better. "Hello, gorgeous."

"Beauty is a social construct."

She didn't disagree, but hearing the assertion from a six-year-old had her biting back a smile. "You're right. How are you, Grace?"

"I'm good. I couldn't tie my shoelaces, but now I can because I persisted."

"Persistence is a very good trait to have." She carried her niece up the walk and into the house. "You can accomplish all sorts of things with persistence."

Kiera emerged from the kitchen. "Are we talking about shoelaces again?"

Quinn laughed. "How did you guess?"

Before they could catch up in earnest, Kiera's wife, Xinxin, arrived home from work. Grace abandoned her to relay the big news of her day and Quinn turned her attention to her sister. "Anything I can do to help?"

"Nope. I was waiting to throw these on the grill."

Xinxin dropped her bag and shed her jacket. "Please tell me we're having tacos."

Kiera picked up a platter of shrimp lined up on skewers and sent her wife an air kiss. "Be right back."

She headed out to the grill and Quinn pulled out the corkscrew to open the wine. In a matter of minutes, the four of them sat around the table on the back deck. Quinn polished off her first taco and licked a drop of sour cream from her thumb. "Thank you for saving me from takeout."

Kiera shook her head. "You realize you could make these yourself, right? It's literally five ingredients."

Quinn grinned. "Maybe I'll attempt them one day, but today wasn't going to be that day. And since I didn't have takeout tonight, I can have it tomorrow and not feel bad."

Kiera rolled her eyes. "You're impossible."

"It's a lifestyle choice," Xinxin said.

Quinn could always count on her to be magnanimous. "Exactly. Besides, I prefer hopeless."

"Speaking of hopeless, I have someone for you to meet."

Quinn groaned and Xinxin laughed. Quinn glared at her. "You're not helping."

That only made her laugh more, which got Grace giggling, even though she had no idea what they were laughing about.

"Her name is Lisa and I met her at yoga."

"Regular yoga or goat yoga?" It didn't really matter, but it sort of did.

Kiera scowled. "Goat. Is that a problem?"

The real problem was her sister's obsessive need to set her up. Hell, everyone's apparent need to set her up. Not only did it usually go badly, the whole concept was beginning to make her feel incompetent and borderline pathetic. "Deal breaker."

"She's a director of HR, not some hippie."

"I don't have anything against hippies. Or HR directors."

"So you'll meet her?"

The thing was, saying yes would let her off the hook for at least a month. And it wasn't like she was opposed to meeting up with a woman for coffee. And if she was a director of anything, chances were good she was at least forty. Which, in her book, was a bonus. "Maybe."

"She moved to Ithaca a few months ago. She could probably use new friends as much as dates."

Quinn wasn't clamoring for new friends, but she could appreciate trying to navigate a new place. "Are you sure she's a lesbian?"

Kiera huffed out a breath. "That only happened one time."

"But I'm still scarred," Quinn said. Kiera swore up and down she had no idea how the wires got so crossed, but the woman in question had not been any degree of queer. Nor had she been gracious about it.

Xinxin, who refrained from getting involved for the most part, angled her head. "Do you want to be dating?"

Such a loaded question. One the people trying to fix her up rarely bothered to ask. She didn't not want to date, which was maybe a hair shy of actually wanting to date. The bigger issue was she didn't seem to click with any of the women she went out with. Whether it was her, or bad luck, or maybe not being ready to wade into those waters, she wasn't sure. "I don't know."

Kiera visibly deflated. "I'm sorry."

Her own discomfort evaporated and the desire to smooth feathers kicked in. "Don't apologize. I know your heart is in the right place."

"It is." Kiera cringed. "I may have already told Lisa I'd set something up."

Quinn scrubbed a hand over her face. "Okay. I'll go out with her. But maybe you could lay off for a while."

She perked up. "Deal."

Xinxin shook her head, but looked at Kiera with affection, then at Quinn. "And I'll do my best to hold her to it."

"Thanks."

"Can we talk about me now?" Grace asked with her mouth full.

Quinn turned her attention to her niece. "I think that sounds like a fantastic idea."

CHAPTER THREE

As much as Amanda hated leaving work early, she wanted plenty of time to shower and put herself together before making the drive to Rochester. Not that she didn't always want to be put together, but Mel and Bella run-ins required full armor.

Tonight would be just that. Her daughter's final recital of the semester meant she'd be seeing her ex and her ex's wife. Close to ten years of practice made it easier to be in the same space, but it didn't mean she was ever comfortable with it. Or that she managed to tune out entirely the fact that Bella was twenty years younger, a professional powerhouse, and could have been mistaken for a supermodel. Ugh. She was so not in the mood.

Instead of moping, Amanda did what she did best: she pulled herself together and got on with it. Forty-five minutes later, she was dressed, hair done, and putting on lipstick. Not model material but more than presentable. And as the mother of a college freshman, it was exactly the look she was going for.

She headed downstairs, pleased to see Cal dressed and with a duffel bag slung over his shoulder. "Ready?"

He nodded. "We're going to eat first, right? I'm starving."

"Yes. Our reservations are for five so your sister can come too and we'll have plenty of time to get her to the concert."

"I guess I can wait that long."

"Didn't you eat something after school?"

He groaned. "I did, but that was like an hour ago."

What he referred to as a snack, she jokingly called second lunch. Oh, to have the metabolism of a teenage boy. "Horror. Why don't you grab a granola bar to tide you over?"

"I had one after my burrito."

Of course he did. "Then I'm thinking you'll survive."

"Fine. But I'm having an appetizer. And dessert."

He said it like she ever denied him either of those things. Well, dessert, sometimes. But even that was rare. "Deal."

They got in the car and headed north. The drive took less than two hours, but she'd reserved a hotel for the night so they could move Daniella out of her dorm the following day. Not having to make two trips, or drive home at ten at night, made the splurge more than worth it. She was pretty sure Mel had made the same plan, which meant they'd be able to pack up everything at once. Aside from having to see Bella twice in two days, it was perfect.

"Can I stay over with Daniella tonight?"

Amanda raised a brow. "You're going to give up a private bathroom and a bed to yourself to sleep on the floor of your sister's dorm room?"

Cal lifted a shoulder and looked away. "Yeah."

"Where's the party?"

He rolled his eyes and let out an exasperated sigh. "Mom."

"I'm not saying you can't go, I just want to know the specifics."

He sighed again. "It's Daniella's roommate's boyfriend. Wait. Girlfriend? What do you call a non-binary person you're sleeping with?"

"Um, partner?"

Cal wrinkled his nose. "That sounds super old."

Amanda pulled through the toll booth and got on the thruway. "Maybe not the thing to say when you're asking me for something."

"I didn't mean you're old. I meant it sounds like what adults do. Are. You know."

She did. Giving him a hard time felt like both a right and a responsibility, though. It kept him in line, but it also gave them rapport, the kind of rapport that would hopefully become the cornerstone of their relationship as he became an adult. "I do. So, where do they live?"

"On campus in one of the apartments. It's going to be super chill."

She wasn't sure she'd go that far, but she preferred it to off-campus or, worse, a frat house. "And how will you get back to Daniella's dorm after?"

"We can walk. It's all on campus and there are those blue lights everywhere."

She knew the answer, but wanted to make sure he did, too. "All right."

"All right I can go?"

He'd be in college on his own soon enough. He might as well get a taste of it under the wing of his serious older sister. "You may. But we're still leaving at nine and all her things need to be packed up. I have a wedding cake to finish and deliver tomorrow night."

Cal leaned across the seat and gave her a kiss on the cheek. "You're the best."

It was her turn to sigh. She didn't want to turn back the clock, but moments like this gave her a tiny pang of they grow up so fast. "I know."

He pushed the button to turn on the radio. "In honor of your awesomeness, you get to pick the music. What'll it be?"

She smiled. Control of the radio in the car was a big deal. She'd lost track of the number of fights through the years. It said something that he offered after she'd already said yes. "Yacht rock all the way."

He groaned but laughed, then sang along with her to Hall & Oates and Michael McDonald. And in that moment, all felt right with the world.

After picking up Daniella, they headed to the restaurant where she'd made reservations. They hadn't been seated two minutes when her phone pinged. Mel.

Any chance you're doing dinner before the concert?

Amanda frowned at the screen. *Just sat down. Why?*

Flying solo and would love to join you.

She closed her eyes. Not exactly how she wanted to spend her evening, but not having to see Bella at all would be a perk. And while family dinners had become increasingly rare as the kids grew up, both Daniella and Cal loved it when they all sat down together. *Roux. We'll add a chair and order appetizers.*

❖

Amanda basked in parental pride while her kids talked nonstop. The recital had been perfect, with Daniella looking poised and confident as part of the ensemble performance and during her brief solo. Sure, it wasn't at the caliber of what the music majors put on, but the fact that her daughter could do it while also studying molecular biology? Well, it was more than any mother could ask for.

She dropped Daniella and Cal off with promises to stay safe and be ready to go in the morning, then headed to her hotel. Maybe she'd order a glass of wine and take it to her room. Now that she wasn't bunking with Cal, she could take a bath and lounge around in one of those cushy robes. It shouldn't, but it made her feel better to know Mel would be spending the night alone, too.

Mel. She'd been so weird at dinner. The concert, too. Charming and deferential. Hell, she'd been attentive. Amanda couldn't remember the last time Mel had been attentive to her. Long before the divorce, that's for sure. She couldn't decide whether to enjoy it or be suspicious of it.

When she pulled into the garage at the hotel, Mel was waiting, ostensibly for her. Next level weird. Not to mention the sort of gesture that made Amanda fall for her in the first place all those years ago. At this point, she had to wonder if Mel was having a rare moment of sentimentality or wanted something. Probably the latter. Sentimentality didn't seem to be in her DNA. Angling? Absolutely.

"Everyone make out okay?"

Amanda shrugged. "I think so. Daniella won't get into trouble and she'll keep an eye on Cal."

Mel frowned. "You think Cal would get into trouble on his own?"

She didn't. Not really. But new situations and wanting to be cool could inspire all sorts of shenanigans. "I'm glad they'll be together."

"This is why you were always better at the parenting thing than me. You know when to tie them down and when to let them free range."

Classic Mel—shirking responsibility because Amanda was better at it. It was exactly the kind of statement that would have driven her up a tree during their marriage and the first few years of their divorce. Now that she didn't have to depend on Mel for anything, it didn't bother her as much. "Still working the helpless angle, I see."

Mel slapped a hand to her chest. "You wound me."

Amanda raised a brow. "I think you'll live."

Mel grinned. "You always did know how to keep me in my place."

She chuckled, more amused by the banter than she would have expected. "Someone has to."

"Would you like to grab a drink? It's early still." Mel looked at her with hopeful eyes. Like an eager puppy—cliché but irresistible.

"You and me? At a bar?" Just saying it aloud felt like a bad idea.

"Come on. We're friends at this point, aren't we?"

Friends. She wasn't sure she'd go that far, but it was one of those umbrella words that offered shade to all manner of connections. "All right."

Mel held the door as they entered the hotel. In the ten or so steps it took to get to the bar, she rested her hand in the small of Amanda's back. Strange. Or, maybe, strange of her to notice.

The bar was dim, elegant rather than seedy. Small candles flickered on dark wood tables. Couples got cozy on leather love seats and in high-backed booths. Amanda cleared her throat. That had bad idea written all over it. "Why don't we sit at the bar?"

Mel chuckled but didn't argue. "Old-fashioned?"

Amanda smiled in spite of herself. Mel forgot their anniversary at least half the years they were married, but she always remembered the little things. Like Amanda's favorite drink. "Yes, please."

They took a pair of stools at the end of the bar. Not quite as intimate as one of the tables but not far off. Mel snagged the attention of the bartender and ordered. She still took her bourbon neat.

When their drinks came, Mel raised her glass. "Here's to making a couple of fantastic kids."

It would be impossible not to toast that. She tapped her glass to Mel's. "Cheers."

Mel sipped her drink. "How are you?"

"You know, I'm good." She realized how nice it was to mean it and not just say it. "What about you?"

Mel sighed and shook her head. "Bella and I are doing a trial separation."

"Oh. Oh, Mel, I'm sorry." There might have been a time when she'd have wished doom on their marriage, but it was a long time ago. "What happened?"

Mel shrugged, seemingly at a loss. "We've been fighting nonstop. We're trying to take a breather, let the dust settle."

That explained why she was by herself. And clingy. "What's causing all the tension?"

"Well, I don't think the fertility treatments are helping." She rolled her eyes and laughed.

"Fertility treatments?"

Another shrug. "Bella wants kids. I didn't feel like I could deny her because I'd already done the parenting thing."

Amanda pressed her fingers to her eyes. "You know that's a terrible reason to have kids, right?"

"Yes, right after having them to save a marriage." Mel nodded, seemingly aware of the absurdity of what she was saying.

God, this was so none of her business. "Look, I'm not about to tell you—"

Mel raised a hand. "Don't worry. We've hit the pause button for now."

Relief spread through her. She didn't stop to analyze whether it had more to do with bringing a baby into a failing relationship or the idea of Mel having a baby with another woman. Because, again, it was none of her business.

"Let's change the subject, shall we?"

Normally, she hated when Mel did that. This time, though, she was in total agreement. "Let's."

"What's going on with you? Tell me all the things."

It was strange and more than a little satisfying to be the one with exciting goings-on. "I had my first meeting with the architect about the addition to the bakery."

"Oh. Do tell."

The thing about Mel was, for all her faults, she knew how to work a conversation. Being the center of her attention felt like being the center of the universe. It had been years since Amanda experienced it, but the pull was no less potent.

After the bakery, Mel asked about the house and the garden. She dismissed questions about her own work, calling it too boring to warrant mention. One drink became two. Amanda knew she'd regret the third—or was it the fourth?—but she couldn't remember the last time she'd let loose. Her kids were off doing their thing and it wasn't like she had to drive. The jazz in the background was soft and the company, whether she wanted to admit it or not, was good.

Maybe her vision started to blur a hair. Maybe she put a hand on Mel's arm. Maybe Mel's hand landed on her thigh. Maybe it inched up in a way that felt familiar but exciting at the same time. Maybe Mel kissed her in the elevator on the way up to their respective rooms.

Maybe she didn't make it to her own room at all.

CHAPTER FOUR

Amanda blinked open her eyes. Sunlight poured through the windows. Odd that she hadn't pulled the curtains. She moved her head and winced at the pain that ricocheted like a pinball in her skull. The reason for the headache hit her one second before the other details of the night.

Oh, God.

Slowly, she turned her head the rest of the way, hoping for something—anything—other than what she knew would be waiting for her. Mel's face, with that half smile of sleep, mere inches from hers. Mel's naked torso a confirmation of the hazy memory.

Oh. God.

What had she done? And for the love of all that was good and holy, why?

As if sensing her awakeness, or maybe her panic, Mel opened her eyes. "Well, good morning."

The laid-back confidence was almost too much. If she didn't think sudden movement might make her vomit, Amanda would have hauled herself out of bed and away from Mel faster than she could have uttered the word regret. Since vomiting remained a very real possibility, she covered her eyes with her hands. "What did we do?"

Mel propped her head in her hand. "We had an amazing time."

"You're married."

"Separated."

Right. They'd discussed that somewhere between Daniella's summer plans and tearing each other's clothes off. "Trial separation. You're still living together."

Mel shrugged, clearly unbothered by the specifics. "I'm not cheating on her. We agreed we could see other people. Is that what you're worried about?"

It was on the list, for sure, but by no means the only thing freaking her the fuck out. "I can't even begin to articulate all the ways this is wrong."

Mel looked at her earnestly then. The same eager puppy eyes as last night. "But think how much history we have. That has to make it at least the tiniest bit right."

That was the problem. Yes, Mel was her college sweetheart. They had close to fifteen years together and two smart, beautiful children. They also had years of fighting, Mel's affair with the woman who was now her wife, and a rather nasty divorce. They'd finally settled into something resembling friendship. And now they'd gone and ruined it.

"I can see your wheels turning. You're overthinking this, trust me."

"Well, at least one of us needs to be thinking."

Mel closed the distance between them and pressed her lips briefly to Amanda's. "I'm thinking you're incredible, even more so than I remembered."

Damn it all to hell if a giddy flutter didn't make its way up her spine. She shook her head, as though denying it might vanquish the weakness before it showed on her face. The movement reminded her she was hungover, and the hangover somehow reminded her of all the reasons having a hangover today was the worst possible thing. "What time is it?"

Mel lifted her head and glanced over Amanda's shoulder. "Quarter after eight."

"Damn it." She climbed out of bed as quickly as her throbbing head and queasy stomach would allow. "Don't look at me."

She ignored Mel's comment about not being able to keep her eyes off her and dragged herself to the bathroom. The hot shower made her feel semi-human but also drove home how much sex she'd had. Her thighs ached and, well, between her thighs did, too. As the water sluiced over her, she gave herself one minute—one single, solitary minute—to bask in how good it had been. Or maybe how long it had been. One of those things.

She was in the middle of that minute when Mel knocked on the door. "Care for company?"

A tiny part of her wanted to say yes, to invite Mel in and do it all over again. To savor being wanted and touched by someone who knew her better than anyone, who knew exactly what and where and how she liked to be touched. Fortunately, the sane and rational part of her brain was bigger. "Don't even think about it."

She wrapped herself in a towel and looked for her toothbrush, only to remember she was in Mel's room, not hers. No toothbrush. No ibuprofen. No clothes. She yanked open the bathroom door. "This isn't my room."

Mel had pulled on a robe, but didn't bother to tie it. Amanda couldn't stop her eyes from drifting down to the curve of her breast peeking out. "It's not."

"All my things are in my room."

"Would you like me to go get them for you?"

Walk of shame in a hotel where she didn't know anyone or getting ready side by side with Mel. Those were her choices. "No, no. I'll just pull on my clothes from last night."

"All right." Mel smiled.

"Don't you want to," she gestured to the bathroom, "go in there?"

"I'm in no hurry."

Rather than arguing or cajoling, Amanda scooped up her clothes from the various places they'd been discarded and returned to the bathroom herself. She got dressed and ran her fingers through her hair a few times in an effort to tame it. A shadow on her neck caught her attention. A hickey. She had a fucking hickey.

She emerged to find Mel sitting on the corner of the bed in the robe and a pair of silk boxers. It was unfortunate smug looked so good on her. "Don't smile at me like that."

"I can't help it. I'm happy."

Amanda slipped into her shoes and shook her head. "The sex has addled your brain. This was a terrible idea."

Mel got up and crossed the room with purpose. She placed a hand on each of Amanda's shoulders. "Being with you is never a terrible idea."

Amanda laughed in spite of herself. "This isn't your classroom, Professor Stein. Just because you declare it doesn't make it true."

The insult didn't stick for even a second. "You don't have to admit it, but I'm right about this."

"Well, I don't have time to argue, so there you go."

"I'll take it." She winked, then kissed Amanda on the cheek. "I'll meet you downstairs to check out and drive over to Daniella's."

Right. That. Crap. "Give me fifteen minutes."

Mel offered a playful salute. "Yes, ma'am."

She hurried to her room, happy not to bump into anyone along the way. She changed, packed up her things, and cast a parting glance at the bed she'd not even touched. When she walked into the lobby, Mel was already there. She couldn't remember the last time Mel was somewhere waiting for her and now it had to go and happen twice in twenty-four hours.

"I texted the kids and let them know we were running a few minutes late."

Amanda handed her key card to the man at the desk and tamped down the flash of panic. It made perfect sense for Mel and her to coordinate. It wouldn't give away spending the night together. Surely, the kids wouldn't pick up on it. "You didn't tell them, did you?"

Mel offered her a flirtatious smile. "Tell them what?"

"I'm serious. It would only confuse them. And potentially freak them out." Hell, she was confused and freaked out and she was the one who'd done it.

That seemed to make Mel relent. "I was kidding. Of course I'm not going to say anything to them."

"Good. Thank you."

"It doesn't mean I'm not interested in doing it again."

Amanda told herself Mel was joking about that, too, even though her expression was serious. "I can't have this conversation with you right now. We need to go."

"Yes, ma'am."

It was the second time Mel had used the phrase. Much like the waiting, it stirred up all sorts of memories from the early years of their relationship. Memories of Mel teasing her about being bossy everywhere but bed, of Mel finding it sexy she was so driven and goal-oriented. Memories she'd not suppressed, exactly, but had set aside so she could get on with the business of her life. But just like the conversation about doing it again, she didn't have the time or the energy to go there.

They parted ways at the garage and drove to Daniella's dorm. Both Cal and Daniella sat on a bench out front and made a point of twiddling their thumbs to show they'd been ready and waiting. Amanda reminded them how many times she'd sat around waiting for them.

Between the four of them, they had both cars loaded in under an hour. Daniella opted to ride home with Mel, while Cal piled in with her. She started the trek home, wishing she'd taken some ibuprofen before getting in the car.

"Are you all right? You seem, I don't know, dazed." Cal regarded her with concern.

She waved her hand. "I'm fine. Didn't sleep well. You know how I am in hotels."

He seemed to take her answer at face value. "Yeah."

It felt in that moment like she was keeping a secret from him. Not the sort of private detail a parent would obviously keep from a teenage son. More like something he maybe should know but she was ashamed to disclose. Ugh. "I'll be fine after a night in my own bed. Tell me all about the party."

Cal launched into one story after another. Him sharing so much confirmed her hope the party would be relatively tame. He chatted most of the way home and, when conversation lulled, she gave him control of the music. He sang along and didn't ask any more questions, and she'd never appreciated angsty white guys with guitars quite so much.

❖

Quinn lingered over coffee, reading the paper and taking a stab at the crossword. For some reason, weekend mornings hit her the hardest. Probably because it was one of the few true rituals she and Lesedi had. Fighting over the different sections, taking turns refilling their cups, passing the puzzle back and forth until they'd conquered it.

She no longer yearned to share those moments with Lesedi, fortunately, but she yearned to share them with someone. Even as her brain reminded her she wasn't ready for another serious relationship, her heart longed. A condition she'd come to think of as the divorce paradox.

Knowing she could slip into a state of moping that would haunt her all day, she hoisted herself up and got dressed. After packing a lunch into her cooler bag, she went outside to load her kayak. Sunshine and a paddle would do her good. It would also let her off the hook for going to the gym—total bonus.

Although Cayuga Lake was closer, she decided to mix things up and drive over to Seneca. She could put in at Watkins Glen and paddle up the east side a ways before circling back. And if she found herself on the route that would take her past Bake My Day on the way home, well, it wouldn't be such a bad thing.

She got to the lake before the picnickers descended and unloaded without crossing paths with another soul. A breeze gave the water a hint of chop, but she didn't mind. It kept her cool and gave her arms something to work against. She wouldn't have to feel bad about skipping the gym. She kept close to the shore, assessing and occasionally admiring the grand lake houses and tiny cottages along the way. It bugged her when the designs were clearly high-end but lacked anything resembling finesse. Some people clearly dropped money into things that did little more than show off their money.

She pulled into a cove to cool off with a swim and have lunch, then paddled back to where she'd started. After loading her kayak and exchanging hellos with a few of the folks coming and going from the launch spot, she remembered her plan to stop by the bakery. She ran her fingers through her hair and glanced in the rearview mirror. Perhaps she shouldn't have taken the swim.

No worries. She likely wouldn't see Amanda anyway. And if she did, well, it was a compliment to her cupcakes that Quinn couldn't resist them. Disheveled or otherwise.

For a tiny town, Kenota was bustling. She parked a few blocks away, telling herself it was to get a feel for the surrounding architecture and not to give her hair a few extra minutes to dry. Couples and families strolled along, eating ice cream and popping in and out of the handful of shops. She'd not been to the newest addition—Rustic Refined—but had heard good things. She'd have to check it out when she was less soggy.

At the bakery, a handful of customers occupied the few tables but no one waited in line ahead of her. She focused her attention on the contents of the case and not the fact that there was no sign of Amanda. It was relief spreading through her, not disappointment.

She'd almost convinced herself when Amanda emerged from the kitchen. Unlike the day of their meeting, she wore a crisp white chef's coat with the bakery logo embroidered on it. Her sandy hair was pulled back into some sort of twist, leaving a few loose strands to frame her face.

Quinn cleared her throat. Her pulse definitely didn't kick up a notch and she absolutely didn't get a flutter of butterflies in her stomach.

"I'm about ready to load up. Do you need anything before I go?" Amanda said to the woman at the register.

Was it bad form to stare if the woman she was staring at hadn't even noticed her presence?

"We're all good here. Are you coming back or calling it a day after you deliver?"

"I think I'm going to head home. I've had a very full twenty-four hours."

The woman behind the register nodded. "Good. I hope you put your feet up and have a glass of wine."

Amanda turned back toward the kitchen. Quinn sighed. Not being noticed at all wasn't a relief, no matter how hard she tried to convince herself.

But then Amanda paused. She turned and looked back, like she was doing a double take. Quinn raised a hand in greeting. "Hi."

Recognition gave way to alarm. "Quinn. We don't have a meeting today, do we?"

She probably shouldn't notice, much less enjoy, the way Amanda said her name. She glanced down at her casual, not to mention damp, appearance. "If we did, I'd hope to be a bit more presentable."

Amanda laughed. Quinn liked that sound even more. "Oh, good. What brings you by?"

It was nice that her primary motivation wasn't hoping to run into Amanda. She hated lying, even over silly things. "Cupcakes."

"Well then, you're in the right place."

"I mean, I took my kayak out on Seneca Lake, so I was sort of passing by. I didn't come all the way here just for cupcakes."

"Ah." Amanda raised a brow, making Quinn realize her defense came out like a backhanded compliment.

"Not that your cupcakes wouldn't be worth the trip. I just like to think I have slightly more restraint."

Amanda lifted both hands. "You don't need an explanation, one way or the other."

Was that a trace of teasing in her voice? It sounded like it. How did Amanda manage to be so easy to talk to, even when Quinn seemed hell-bent on making an ass of herself? "Thanks." She could leave it at that, but she didn't quite want the conversation to end. "You look very fancy today."

Amanda tugged at the hem of her coat and patted her chest. "I try to look the part when delivering wedding cakes."

Quinn found the hint of self-deprecation endearing. "It's definitely working. You could bark out orders like Gordon Ramsay and I have no doubt you'd send a whole room scurrying to do your bidding. Myself included."

The woman behind the register—Tanya?—chimed in. "Maybe don't give her ideas."

Amanda rolled her eyes. "Right, because I'm so prone to yelling."

Quinn squinted at the name tag on her apron. Yes, Tanya.

Tanya shrugged. "I don't want you getting any ideas."

Quinn tried for a playful smile. "Sorry."

"Mm-hmm. Likely story," Tanya said.

Amanda crossed her arms. She might not yell, but she looked plenty fierce without it. "Not that I wouldn't love to stay and be harassed by the two of you, but I do have a wedding cake to deliver."

"Sorry. Really. Don't let me keep you." Quinn meant it that time.

Amanda's smile told her she wasn't really mad. "We're meeting next week, right?"

She conjured the image of her calendar. "Yes. Tuesday."

"Fantastic. I'll see you then."

"I'm looking forward to it." Quinn sighed. In more ways than one.

"Same. Enjoy your cupcakes."

Amanda left and Quinn felt silly stopping in for cupcakes without any real occasion to do so. Of course, she'd feel even sillier leaving empty-handed. She turned her attention to Tanya. "So, what do you recommend?"

Tanya regarded her with a trace of suspicion. "You know I didn't mean anything by that. Not really."

Although unnecessary, she appreciated the sentiment of the disclaimer. "I take it as a healthy working relationship when employees can give the boss grief." She lifted a hand. "Good-naturedly, of course."

Tanya nodded slowly and her smile returned. "Of course."

She had no way of knowing how close Amanda and Tanya were, or if Tanya would have any involvement in the project. But it certainly couldn't hurt to be on her good side. "Glad we cleared that up. Now, really, what do you recommend?"

"Are you bringing them home to the family or are they for you?"

Was she fishing? Or judging? "Does it matter?"

Tanya's eyes narrowed. "Maybe."

Whatever the reason, Quinn decided Tanya taking a personal interest in her was a good sign. Of what, she couldn't say. But it gave her a good feeling. "Just me."

The answer seemed satisfactory. "If you like chocolate, I'd go with mocha or the German chocolate. If you're fruity, the blueberry-lemon has local blueberries in the filling."

They all sounded fantastic. "Yes."

"Yes to what?"

"All of them. And add a fourth. Surprise me."

Tanya picked up a box but pointed at Quinn before she started to fill it. "I appreciate a woman with a sweet tooth."

"Oh, good. I was afraid you might be judging my life choices."

She loaded the cupcakes and closed the box with a sticker. "I don't know you well enough for that. We'll see."

Quinn laughed as she pulled out her wallet. "Fair enough."

Tanya waved her off. "On the house."

"You really don't need to—"

"You're working with the boss, you're treated like family. Or staff. Same difference."

"Thank you." Quinn accepted the box. "That could be dangerous, but thank you."

Tanya smirked. "You enjoy those and we'll see you on Tuesday."

"I have no doubt I will. Have a good night."

"You, too."

Quinn returned to her car, setting the box carefully on the seat next to her. She started the drive home, resisting the urge to dig in. She wanted to savor each and every one. Instead, she replayed the conversation, both with Amanda and her assistant. Although sidekick might be a more accurate description.

She hadn't gone in with expectations, but the interaction managed to be not at all what she would have expected. Not bad, of course. Just unexpected. She had a lot of the unexpected in her life these days. Perhaps this project would fall into the category of pleasant surprise. And wouldn't that be nice for a change?

CHAPTER FIVE

Amanda moved around the kitchen, completely in her element and utterly content. Okay, mostly content. Content save the giant cloud of what the fuck was I thinking following her around the last few days. Content aside from wondering what the hell to do next or how to respond to the flirty texts Mel had taken to sending during the day.

Erin sniffed the air. "I love it when dinner is at your place."

"Hey." Jack's and Julia's protests came out in unison.

"You're both amazing cooks, but Amanda cooks and bakes." She put the emphasis on "and."

Amanda pulled the pan of chicken picatta from the oven. "It's not a competition."

"It's okay." Jack wandered over and gestured to the pan. "I don't mind losing to that."

Julia nodded. "Yeah."

Amanda brought the pan to the table out on the deck, then returned to the kitchen for the salad and roasted potatoes. "I don't care who cooks. I love all our dinner parties."

"Hear, hear." Julia lifted her glass and everyone clinked a toast.

She'd lucked out in the friend department. An unlikely crew in a way, but they clicked and it just worked. At this point, there was nothing she didn't share with them. Well, practically nothing. She remained undecided re the whole Mel situation. She wanted to. They'd tease her but come through with support and wisdom and maybe a knock upside the head. The problem was, telling them made it one hundred percent real. Once she confided, there would be no pretending it didn't happen.

Not that Mel and her texts were letting her do much pretending. She should probably get it out there so she could process it and get on with her life. Because that's what she wanted, right? To accept it for what it was and go back to life as usual. Why did the idea make her sad?

She shook off the question and the emotions and everything else. Maybe she'd try to get a handle on things first. She picked up the salad bowl and turned, almost running into Jack.

He narrowed his eyes and looked her up and down. "You had sex."

"What?" Her reply pitched higher than she would have liked. She cleared her throat. "What?"

He pointed at her and moved his finger up and down to indicate the length of her. "You had sex with someone. I can tell."

"What can you tell?" Erin appeared behind him as if on cue.

There went any notion of getting a handle on the situation. "Nothing."

At the same time, Jack said, "Sex."

"Wait, wait, wait. We can't be discussing sex and nothing at the same time." She lifted her chin at Amanda. "Unless it's the fact that Jack and Julia are getting lots and you and I aren't getting any."

"What am I getting lots of?" Julia stepped into the kitchen behind Erin.

"Sex," Jack and Erin said in unison.

Julia let out a contented sigh. "Yeah."

Jack waved a hand. "This isn't about your bliss. This is about Amanda having sex."

"Amanda's having sex?" Julia looked her way, a mixture of confusion and accusation in her eyes. "You're having sex and you didn't tell me?"

As an only child, she didn't have a lot of experience being ganged up on, but that's definitely what was happening. "I might have had sex. And I might be willing to discuss it. Can we sit down, though? Dinner's ready."

Her friends mumbled and exclaimed an assortment of questions and opinions, but they did as she asked. Amanda took her time refilling her wine glass. Not stalling, exactly, but okay, stalling. She'd waffled but was already relieved to have it out in the open. There'd be judgment, for sure, but maybe advice, too. Lord knew she could use some of that.

She took her seat, put some potatoes on her plate, then passed the bowl to Jack. He let out a dramatic sigh but took it from her. Dishes were passed and, when everyone had a full plate, Amanda took a long sip of wine. Yep, stalling.

"Well?" Erin asked.

All eyes fixed on her.

"I may have had a hookup." Even saying the word hookup made her feel ridiculous.

"May have?" Julia asked. "I think that's a pretty definitive yes or no kind of thing."

"When?" Jack added.

"With whom?" Erin demanded.

No going back now. "Friday. In Rochester." She closed her eyes. "With Mel."

The entire table erupted in a cacophony of disbelief and demands for details. Amanda methodically cut a bite of chicken. She put it in her mouth and chewed slowly. Eventually, the questions and commentary died down. She was left with three people staring at her expectantly. She took another sip of wine.

"Well?" Erin asked again.

"Well." Amanda set down her glass and launched in. Bella not coming and why. Having dinner. Cal wanting to stay with his sister. Drinks at the bar. Good conversation. More drinks. She got to the after drinks part, skimming over the more explicit details. Even the closest friendships had their boundaries. Or, maybe more accurately, she had her own boundaries when it came to kissing and telling.

"When I woke up and she was right there, naked, I just about had a heart attack. And then I had to put on my clothes from the night before and do the walk of shame back to my room."

They stared at her, wide-eyed. No one spoke. Amanda took, not a sip, but a gulp of wine. At the rate she was going, she was going to be hammered before dessert.

"What did Mel say? The next morning, I mean. After." Jack quirked a brow.

Amanda blew out a breath. "That it was amazing and we shouldn't overthink it. Oh, and we should do it again."

Jack let out a low whistle. "Yeah, she did. You're so much hotter than Bella."

Amanda waved the compliment away. "You're biased."

His finger wagged. "Oh, no. Don't even think about going there with me. You're gorgeous and she's plastic."

"Yeah," Julia added, just as Erin said, "Exactly."

"Well, it's not like it matters one way or the other." They weren't in a competition. At least not anymore.

"No?" Erin asked.

"No." Her answer held more conviction than she did.

Julia frowned. "But what does it mean? Or, I guess what I'm asking is, what do you want it to mean?"

Erin smacked her arm. "It doesn't have to mean anything."

Jack made a sweeping gesture with his hand. "Unless she wants it to mean something."

"Agreed." Erin nodded.

They all looked at her again.

"I don't know what it means or what I want it to mean. That's the problem." She hadn't thought about Mel in that way in so many years. Going from zero to sex in one night was enough to give her whiplash.

"Okay." Erin's voice held all the authority of a woman used to being in charge. "So, that leaves two questions."

"Okay." No authority on Amanda's part. Just apprehension.

"One. Was it good?"

She looked around the table. Based on their faces, the question was clearly on everyone's mind. No point in being anything but honest. "Yeah."

There was a gasp. And maybe a squeal.

"What's the second question?" Jack asked.

Erin's smile was slow and full of mischief. She looked at Jack, then squarely at Amanda. "Are you going to do it again?"

God. She'd been so worried about what a terrible idea it was, she'd not given serious thought to repeating it. "No."

Julia laced her fingers together and gave Amanda a look of concern. "Why not?"

"Because it's a terrible idea." Wasn't it? And Mel might not have even meant it when she said she wanted to do it again. It was the sort of thing she'd say in the moment and not want to be held to later on, a lesson Amanda had learned the hard way.

Jack's face softened. "I'm not necessarily disagreeing with you. God knows I am not a fan of Mel's."

"Thank you." She didn't need the vindication at this point, but it didn't mean she couldn't enjoy it.

"But." He lifted a finger.

Sigh. There was always a but. "But?"

"Are you saying no on principle, because you feel like that's what you're supposed to do, or because you don't want to do it again?"

Sometimes, it was a real pain in the ass to have insightful friends. Even if it kept her honest. "I don't know."

No teasing in Jack's eyes this time, just understanding. "That's what you have to figure out."

"Right." Moments like this reminded her how little practice she had focusing on what she wanted instead of what was best for everyone else.

Julia nodded. "Right."

Erin shrugged, but then nodded as well. "Right."

Amanda closed her eyes, grateful for her friends but so done with this conversation. She opened her eyes and looked around the table with purpose. "We should eat now."

"You've had enough, haven't you?" Erin asked with a grin.

"Yes, but the food's going to get cold. You know how I feel about that. And I made cream puffs for dessert."

Jack picked up his fork and made a point of piling a massive bite onto it. "Oh. Well, then."

They made it through dinner, serving dessert, and pouring coffee without incident. Jack filled them in on the most recent foster kid he and Chris had been assigned. Julia asked about Cal's graduation party and lamented losing him at the store when he started college in the fall. And Erin regaled them with her latest exploits in the wilds of dating. Now that Julia had fallen hard for Taylor, Erin was the only one of them actively on the market.

Of course, that somehow managed to turn the conversation back to her.

"So, are you back on the market?" Jack asked.

"What? No." The thought of subjecting herself to that made her skin crawl.

"Maybe you should be," Erin said with a wink.

"Julia, a little help here?" Surely, her misadventures before Taylor would make her an ally.

"I don't know. I learned a lot. And I think there's something to be said for getting back in the saddle. Keeps you on your toes and keeps all the parts working."

Amanda pressed her fingers to her temples. "It's not like I've been completely celibate."

Jack folded his arms. Erin laced her hands together and set them on the table. Julia pressed her lips together and made a show of looking around.

"Oh, stop. It's not that bad."

No one moved. No one spoke.

"Okay, fine. I've maybe been neglecting it more than I haven't. I'm busy. It's simply not a priority."

Still nothing.

She knew they were doing it on purpose but couldn't seem to stop herself. "So, I should sleep with Mel again? Is that what you're saying?"

"It doesn't have to be Mel," Erin said.

"It might be better if it isn't," Jack added.

Out of nowhere, Quinn's face popped into her mind. Well, not exactly nowhere. She'd seen her the day before. And even if she knew she shouldn't be thinking of her in that way, Amanda couldn't seem to help it. She wasn't quite ready to give her friends that fodder, especially given Erin's teasing before their first meeting. "I'll take it under advisement."

"I could show you the app." Julia lifted a shoulder and offered a perky smile.

She'd tried online dating briefly a couple of years after her divorce. It had been the single most demoralizing experience of her life. "No, thanks."

"Come on." Erin stuck her hands out. "Tanya met Kofi that way."

She didn't believe online dating never worked. She'd simply had enough traumatic experiences that it didn't seem worth the risk to life and limb. Or ego. "I love you, but I'm a hard no."

Julia smirked at the phrase, but then sighed. "I'd love to stay all night, but I should probably head home."

Jack rolled his eyes. "You'd think she was the one with the kid."

Amanda shook her head. "Don't begrudge her the honeymoon phase."

"Yeah." Julia lifted her chin. "Don't begrudge me."

Amanda stood. "Go on. Get laid. At least one of us is."

Erin got up, too. "You don't get to say that when you're rocking the ex with benefits."

"What she said." Jack stood and stretched.

"You three are a thorn in my side, but I love you."

"Ditto." Jack gave her a hug.

Erin and Julia echoed the sentiments and took turns giving her a squeeze. "I've got cream puffs for you to take home."

"Of course you do." Erin rubbed her hands together. "And I won't even have to share mine."

"There's plenty for everyone," she said.

She handed out the boxes she'd put together earlier and bid her friends a good night. She put on music and tried not to think too much about being on the market—for Mel or Quinn or anyone else, really. It wasn't that she was too old. She simply wasn't interested.

Even if her body had yet to stop humming. Even if she felt that perfect combination of sore and limber that only came with good sex. Even if it felt like she'd flipped a switch that had been in the off position for too long and she wasn't sure she wanted to flip it back.

Between being kind of turned on and more than a little confused, her plan not to think failed miserably. But Cal and Daniella came home while she was still cleaning the kitchen, providing her favorite distraction of all. "What have you two been up to?"

Cal opened the fridge. "Dinner with M."

She looked at him with amusement. "Did you not manage to eat dinner at dinner?"

Daniella rolled her eyes. "He ate plen—wait. Are those cream puffs?"

The next thing she knew, she and her kids were sitting around the table with a plate of pastry, talking about everything and nothing. With Daniella starting her summer job as a camp counselor in a couple of weeks, there wouldn't be many more evenings like this, save holidays. Rather than dwelling, she reminded herself to enjoy it. The rest could be sorted out later.

CHAPTER SIX

Quinn shook her head. The eccentricities of old buildings came with the territory of her work. She accepted that. Most of the time, she embraced it. She prided herself on finding creative ways to work with the existing structure, not against it. It was the cornerstone of her brand when it came to retrofitting spaces for new purposes.

Why, then, was she dreading having that very conversation with Amanda?

Because Amanda had a clear picture in her mind of what she wanted for her bakery. Because Quinn had given her every indication it would be a simple and straightforward job. Oh, the hubris.

But it was more, if she was being honest. She was already more invested in Amanda than she would normally be in a client. Not the kind of professional investment that came with big, influential clients, either. No, her interest in Amanda was personal. She wanted Amanda to be pleased with her.

Quinn sighed. She wanted Amanda to like her.

How was it possible for her to go on date after date and feel pretty much nothing—nothing good at least—and then find herself all stirred up by a client? Because she'd lost her mind, apparently. Or the universe had singled her out for bad luck. Maybe both.

She shook her head again. She needed to deliver bad news and a list of options and here she was lamenting finding Amanda attractive. Maybe she was bringing the bad luck on herself.

Enough. She grabbed a pencil and sketch pad and got to work. Once she had a rough idea drawn out, she opened Revit and started a more detailed rendering. She had no idea if Amanda would go for something so far from what she initially wanted, but it made her feel better to have multiple options to present. Especially since this one wouldn't blow the budget they'd initially discussed out of the water.

"I didn't even realize you were here."

"Gah." The sound escaped and her body reflexively jerked.

"Sorry. Didn't mean to startle you." Arti smirked from the doorway, looking not at all sorry.

Quinn rolled her shoulders. Her muscles protested the movement. How long had she been hunched over her computer? "I was caught up in something."

"I'll say. It's two o'clock and you didn't even come out for lunch. That's why I figured you weren't here."

"It's two?" It wasn't unusual for her to get lost in a project, but not four hours kind of lost.

Arti nodded. "What's got you in genius-at-work mode?"

"Um." Her stomach rumbled. Now that her concentration was broken, her body was all about missing lunch. She stood and stretched, working out some of the kinks that had settled. "The bakery. All the roofing joists are being supported by the center wall."

"Oh." Arti let the word drag out, understanding clear.

"The building is old, but not that old. Maybe I should have expected it, but I didn't."

"You never know what passed muster back in the day, especially in tiny towns where the guy approving the build could have been the cousin of the guy doing the build."

"Yeah."

Arti came the rest of the way into the office, plopped in the chair across from Quinn, and folded her arms. "So, what are you going to do?"

"I'm going to present three options."

She grinned. "Of course you are."

Quinn shrugged. Not every job required that, but when the initial concept went sideways, she'd learned it was always better to present three options instead of two. Especially if the two were what the client wanted, but at an exorbitant cost, and something within budget, but clearly not what they'd envisioned.

"I assume it's number three that's got you all amped up."

She chuckled at the description. "I wouldn't go that far."

Even in the most generous of terms, amped up rarely, if ever, fit the bill. Generally, she was okay with her calm and steady demeanor. But she couldn't help but wonder what kind of energy Amanda might be drawn to. Ridiculous.

"Okay, okay." Arti lifted both hands in concession. "Focused, then. I take it the mystical third option is what inspired your laser focus."

Quinn nodded, both at the new description and Arti's read of the situation. "She might hate it."

"You always say that."

"Yeah, but she had pretty specific ideas and this is completely different, both visually and in terms of flow."

Arti clicked her tongue a couple of times, then let the silence sit for a moment. Eventually, she asked, "But is it better?"

"Eh?" She wasn't overly modest when it came to her professional skill. The reality was that better was relative. People instinctively liked something or they didn't. It was impossible to predict. She didn't say any of that, but Arti drummed her fingers on the table like she knew. Quinn let out a sigh. "Yes. It's better."

"Was that so hard?"

"I want her to be happy and I'm worried she isn't going to be."

"Are you worried she won't like the design or won't like you?"

Quinn propped her elbows on the desk and pressed her thumbs to her temples. "Yes."

"Well, there's your problem. It doesn't matter if she likes you or, really, even which design she picks. As long as she's happy with the final design."

She knew this. She wasn't an idiot. She also knew having any kind of personal investment in Amanda, romantic or otherwise, would be a bad idea. But knowing something and making it so weren't the same thing. "You're right."

Arti frowned. "You don't have to look so glum about it."

"I'm not glum." Maybe a little. But it had less to do with Arti being right than realizing she'd just upped the ante of her relationship woes. Not only did she have to keep going out with women she didn't click with, she had an inkling she might very well click with one who was off limits. What was wrong with her?

"Come on. Talk to me."

No way was she turning her office into a therapy session. Even if she and Arti were as much friends as business partners. She had a real therapist for a reason. Okay, lots of reasons. "The snag was unexpected. It threw me is all. It'll all be fine." Arti didn't look convinced, so she scrambled for more. "Oh, and I'm sure my blood sugar is low. I'm starving."

Whether Arti decided to let her off the hook or her hangry argument proved convincing, she couldn't say. But Arti seemed to relent. "I'm ordering Ethiopian. You want in?"

Normally, she found it vexing that Arti didn't want lunch until mid-afternoon. Today, she was grateful. "Oh, yeah."

"Fantastic. I'll go order and then you can show me what you've come up with."

Without waiting for a reply, Arti vanished in the direction of her office. Quinn stared at what she had so far. Since there was a decent chance Amanda might dismiss it out of hand, she didn't want to take it much further. Even without all the details, the concept came through. It made the whole space feel more intentional. It also created a more structured flow for customers to peruse their options, order, and pay. From a design standpoint, it really was better.

She hoped Amanda saw it that way and chose it. Because it was a sound business decision. Obviously. Personal anything had nothing to do with it. Nothing at all.

Quinn pulled out a chair and sat. She felt guilty that Amanda had a latte and a cupcake waiting for her. Not guilty enough to refuse it, but guilty. God, she hated this part of her job. "I'm afraid I have some bad news."

"Why do I get the feeling having your architect say that is second only to having it come from your doctor?"

"Or your mechanic?" Quinn offered a sheepish smile and tried not to think about the fact that her news might cost Amanda more than a new car. A cheap new car, but still.

"Well, don't hold me in suspense."

She took a deep breath. "Although you don't have much of an attic, the entire load of it is supported by the center wall. It appears it never occurred to the original builder that someone might want to combine the spaces."

To her credit, Amanda didn't swear or even scowl, really. The only tell of her displeasure was a thin line between her eyebrows. "Does it mean my design is impossible or just a hell of a lot more expensive?"

Quinn couldn't help but chuckle at the question. "You seem to understand how this works. I thought you said it was your first reno."

Amanda raised one brow, erasing the line altogether. "First one here. And I've watched my share of HGTV. Tell me how bad it is. Don't sugarcoat."

"Okay. Nothing is off the table design-wise. Cost, as you guessed, is another matter. I've worked up some options."

She hadn't gotten the sense Amanda would be impossible to work with, but the small smile made Quinn more optimistic than when she'd arrived. "Let's see them."

She pulled the rubber band from the roll and laid out the blueprints. "The first is your original design. It would require a steel I-beam and new support beams at either end of the building. Given the size and span, along with new roof joists, you're looking at about twenty grand more than the original budget."

Amanda regarded the plan and nodded slowly. It was impossible to tell if she was considering it or bidding farewell to the vision she'd had for who knew how long. "And the second?"

Quinn rearranged the pieces of paper. "The second creates one opening in the kitchen, essentially giving you a separate room for decorating and storage."

"And the front?"

"A slightly larger opening. A double doorway, if you will."

"I see." There was definitely a scowl now.

"The upside of this is it would actually bring the work under budget."

Amanda sat back in her chair, folded her arms, and sighed. "I know that's supposed to make me happy, but it doesn't."

She'd been afraid of that. "Which is why I took the liberty of creating a third option."

"A third?"

It was so unlike what they'd initially discussed, Quinn debated even showing it to her. But she'd already put in the work on her own time, so it wasn't like she had anything to lose. And as she'd told Arti, objectively, it was the best of the three. "It's a very different concept."

She brought the final plan to the top of the stack. Amanda angled her head one way, then the other. She narrowed her eyes and did it again. Eventually, she tapped the page. "You moved the counter."

"I did."

"And added a bar."

"That, too."

"It's like a completely different space."

"It is." For some people, that would make it all the more appealing. For others, it was a dealbreaker. She didn't know Amanda well enough to have a sense of which camp she fell in.

"It's…" She trailed off this time, not giving Quinn much in the way of clues.

"It's completely okay if you don't like it. It's not at all what you asked for when we sat down together."

"But…"

"It might feel like not your bakery anymore. You were looking to expand, not reinvent."

Amanda sighed. She looked up from the plans and into Quinn's eyes. Quinn seemed worried, like maybe she regretted showing this version. Not like she'd been looking to strike a nerve, or a chord, or whatever it was she'd just struck. "Maybe a reinvention is exactly what I need."

Quinn's eyes went from worried to alarmed. "I hope I didn't give that impression. It certainly wasn't my intention."

Amanda smiled. "I'm not saying it's a bad thing."

"But, still. Perhaps I overstepped. I—"

"You're a genius is what you are."

The statement seemed to confuse, rather than reassure. "That's definitely an overstatement."

Amanda studied the plans again. Instead of working against the center wall, the design worked with it. The opening between the spaces, the same double-door width, now looked intentional. Even better, the shift created a flow for customers to place orders and pick them up. If business grew half as much as she hoped it did, that would make a huge difference. "No, I think it's completely true in this case."

Quinn's face finally softened. "I'm glad you like it."

"Wait. Did you think of this the first time we met?"

She lifted a shoulder. "Not concretely."

Amanda shook her head. "If we hadn't run into a snag, you never would have mentioned it."

"You were very clear on what you wanted. It wasn't my place to change your mind."

"I can't decide if I should commend you or smack the back of your head."

"How about neither?" Quinn looked honestly horrified.

Amanda laughed. "You don't have kids, do you?"

"I don't." Quinn frowned.

"I was having a mom moment. I promise I would never actually smack the back of your head. Or my kids, for that matter. Although I have been tempted a time or two."

"Oh." Quinn mimed the gesture of a head slap, then laughed. "I get it."

"Maybe you should consider being pushy more often."

Quinn leaned back in her chair and put her hands on either side of her waist. "Have you been talking to my therapist?"

Amanda laughed. "No, but I think our therapists might be kindred spirits."

Quinn shrugged. "Or maybe we are."

She said it lightly, with a hint of a smile playing at the edges of her mouth. Still, Amanda couldn't help but take it to heart. A novel concept, especially given her recent run-ins with Mel.

"I'm sorry if that was too forward," Quinn added before she could respond.

She felt herself smirk. "Apologizing isn't helping your pushy quotient."

"Oh, God. You're so right." Quinn shook her head and laughed. "It's a good thing you aren't talking to my therapist or I'd never hear the end of it."

Amanda tried not to notice the way laughing brought out the lines at the corners of Quinn's green eyes, or how the self-deprecating humor stirred something inside her. "Your secret is safe with me."

"Phew." Quinn wiped her eyes and seemed to remember the reason they were meeting in the first place. "So, this one. You'd seriously consider it?"

She was well beyond considering it, but she didn't want to overplay her hand. "Talk to me about cost." She took a deep breath. "And time line."

"I thought you'd never ask."

By the time they wrapped up the meeting an hour later, Amanda's head was spinning. In a good way. She had a remarkably detailed understanding of how the project would unfold, including approximately when and for how long she'd need to close.

She'd only have to take the kitchen offline for about five weeks, which she could do with her current wedding cake schedule. She'd just have to commit to the time frame and turn down any requests that came in. Difficult, but doable.

"Tell me about the contractors you work with." She'd done some research ahead of time, but it seemed like Quinn's firm worked with a number of companies.

"For this project, my first choice would be Bauer and Sons. They're based in Ithaca. I'll need to see if we can get on their calendar. I penciled us in after our first meeting, so it shouldn't be a problem."

Amanda frowned.

"Is something wrong? I can't imagine you've heard something bad about them."

"No. I trust your judgment."

"But?"

She sighed. "I had this fantasy of hiring a woman-owned business."

Quinn grinned. "This is close."

"Really?" She imagined this swarthy older woman with a brood of strapping young men doing her bidding.

"Joss Bauer is one of the 'and sons,' even though she's technically a daughter. Or maybe it's granddaughter. It might be third generation by now. Anyway, she's the one I work closest with. She's great and has a ton of experience rehabbing older buildings."

The description made her smile. "I can't wait to meet her."

"I'll set something up before work gets started for sure."

"Perfect." She considered leaving it at that but thought better of it. "I really can't thank you enough for putting in the time on an idea you weren't sure would fly. It's so much better than what I could have imagined."

"I'm glad I took a chance, and I'm even more glad you like it."

Again, Quinn's words struck a chord. She wasn't one for good omens, but this certainly felt like one. "I'm glad you took a chance, too."

"Now that I know we're on the same page, I'll do full renderings. I'd like to run them by you again before taking them to the zoning and code officers. Especially the kitchen layout."

"Makes sense."

Quinn pulled out her phone and poked at the screen. "How's Friday?"

"It's good. I can come to you if that's easier. I feel bad you always drive out my way."

Quinn grinned. "But you have cupcakes."

She did. And it really was easier to meet at the bakery. It meant she only had to step away from her work for as long as the meeting took. "Well, if you don't mind, I'll happily provide you with all the cupcakes you can eat."

"Both a delightful and a dangerous proposition." Quinn stuck out her hand. "Deal."

The handshake was a friendly gesture, practically a joke. It shouldn't have sent a spark buzzing through her. But that's exactly what happened. Amanda cleared her throat and stood. "I'll look forward to seeing you soon."

Quinn didn't seem to pick up on the abruptness of the move. "Me, too. And not just because of the cupcakes."

Quinn left and Amanda returned to the kitchen. She'd no sooner finished the first batch of cake batter when her phone buzzed in her pocket. Mel. She'd ignored the last couple of texts. Still. There was always the chance something was wrong. "Hello?"

CHAPTER SEVEN

Amanda lay sprawled in her bed, completely naked in broad daylight. She covered her eyes with her hands. Why did it feel like she was doing that a lot lately? Oh, because she was. "We have to stop doing this."

Mel rolled onto her side. "Does your brain kick back on literally the second after you orgasm?"

"One of us needs to be thinking rationally." And when it came to Mel, the task fell to her. Always.

"You're giving thinking too much credit." Mel trailed a finger down her arm. "I think there's something to be said for letting go."

"Until you have to deal with the consequences."

"What consequences? We are two consenting adults with a long history and a deep fondness for one another. We're enjoying each other's company and having sex, which at our age, is good for both our mental and physical health."

Amanda rolled her eyes. "You sound like such a professor right now."

Mel kissed her shoulder. "Be honest. You like it."

God help her, she did. "Maybe."

"Aside from last week, how long has it been?"

She so didn't want to answer. "Not the point."

"Amanda." Mel's tone was stern.

Rather than making her bristle, it reminded her of the playful push and pull of the early years of their marriage. Like when she lusted after exorbitantly expensive equipment for the bakery or when Mel wanted to buy a lake house before getting tenure. Before the kids and before their arguments took on an edge. Before they—okay, mostly Mel—started doing whatever they wanted without consulting the other at all. She gave Mel a poke. "It's none of your business."

"No?" Mel rolled until she was half on top of Amanda and started tickling her.

Amanda squealed and squirmed. "Stop, stop, stop."

Mel obliged but didn't roll away. "How long?"

Amanda lifted a shoulder and looked away. "Three years."

Mel shook her head. "Too long."

"It's not a priority." It wasn't, and she was okay with that.

"You are a beautiful woman still in her sexual prime. There is no reason on earth you shouldn't be having amazing sex all the time."

"I've spent the last decade raising two teenagers and running a business. I've had a lot on my plate." Even as she defended her choices, she cringed. If one of her friends tried that line, she'd give them a lecture on all the reasons being a martyr was unhealthy, unfeminist, and unhelpful in raising self-sufficient children.

She expected Mel to argue or perhaps dismiss her assertion altogether. Instead, she cupped Amanda's cheek in her palm. The tenderness of the gesture caught her off guard. "You've done an incredible job. So incredible, it was easy to let you take on the lion's share of the work. I'm sorry for that."

Before she could stop them, tears pricked her eyes. How many times had she longed to hear those words? Not so much recently, but in the beginning, when lacrosse and piano lessons and karate and Girl Scouts had sucked up every spare moment. Amanda shook her head, unsure whether the emotions swirling in her were vindication or regret.

"Shh." Mel kissed one cheek, then the other.

She was long past the point of needing tenderness from Mel. Perhaps not needing it made it all the sweeter. Whether it was that or something else, Amanda didn't know. But she let herself sink into it. She let Mel kiss her way down her body and slip into her with something that felt a lot like reverence.

By the time they came up for air, Amanda was almost an hour late for work. "I really have to go."

Mel agreed but managed to talk her into having dinner together the next night. And showering with her. Which led to shower sex. She couldn't even remember the last time she'd had shower sex. When she pulled into work a full two hours after her usual arrival time, her limbs felt loose and her body hummed with the afterglow of multiple orgasms.

Since the bakery was already open, she went in the front door, letting herself imagine the new entry she'd have in a few months' time. Mei stood behind the counter arranging muffins on a cake stand. Amanda offered a wave. "Good morning."

Mei looked at her with concern. "Are you okay? We were expecting you hours ago."

"I let myself get distracted by a few things at home. Is something wrong?"

Before Mei could answer, Tanya pushed through the kitchen door. "Oh, thank God. We were about to call the cops."

"I know I'm rarely late, but that's a bit over-the-top, don't you think? All I have is the Chen anniversary cake."

Tanya's eyes got big. "And the Humane Society fundraiser."

Amanda's pulse tripped. "That's next week."

"It's tonight and you promised twelve cakes to be used as centerpieces."

She had. Twelve unique but complementary designs. Eight-inch cakes she could practically decorate in her sleep but wouldn't decorate themselves. "Are you sure?"

Tanya pointed to the poster she'd hung on the community bulletin board advertising the event.

"Oh, no."

"They're baked, but not filled. I can get started on that as soon as I finish the cookie order for this afternoon."

Amanda's mind raced. "I can't believe I mixed up the dates."

Tanya raised a brow. "It's so unlike you."

It was. "I guess I've been a little distracted."

This time Tanya folded her arms. "I'll ask again. Are you okay?"

Amanda nodded. "I am, I promise. Good distraction, if anything. You know, thinking about the expansion."

If her staff didn't believe her, they opted not to say so. She was usually pretty transparent with them, but things with Mel weren't usual by any stretch of the imagination. And since she still had no idea what any of it meant, the fewer people who knew the better.

She headed into the kitchen and donned her apron and cap. It was fine. It would be fine. She still had close to six hours. She'd pulled off bigger projects in less time. She'd be frantic, but she'd get it done.

Quinn pulled into the small lot next to Bake My Day. Maybe she'd been thinking about Amanda a lot in the last week, but she could just as easily argue she'd been thinking about the job. Not the biggest or even most complicated on her plate right now, but outside of her wheelhouse. And she was a sucker for anything that involved old buildings. Older building, quirky project, and a beautiful client? She'd be worried if she wasn't preoccupied.

But now was not the time for preoccupation. She had a meeting with that beautiful client, and she was here to discuss business. She grabbed the plans and headed inside.

At least a half dozen people waited in line ahead of her. Looked like lunch service was popular even without the new seating area. Since Amanda was nowhere to be seen, she waited, just as she had for their first meeting.

Instead of ogling the baked goods, she studied the chalkboard displaying the lunch options. Two salads, two sandwiches, and one soup. Limited for sure, but it all looked good. It probably rotated, so people could come again and again and not get bored. Would Amanda expand the selections when she expanded her kitchen? Would she have her hand in the cooking as much as the baking?

She'd have to become a regular customer and find out. Even if the bakery was a solid half hour from her house and close to an hour from her office.

"Hi. Quinn Sullivan. I'm here for a meeting with Amanda." The person behind the register was different from the one she met at her first meeting, so she didn't feel silly introducing herself again.

"One second."

She disappeared through the swinging door. Quinn could make out voices, followed by something clattering to the ground. She glanced at her watch to make sure she wasn't inconveniently early. Nope. Right on time.

A moment later, Amanda emerged from the kitchen looking harried. No, harried didn't do justice to the state she appeared to be in. Her hair was all tucked up in one of those chef's caps, her apron smeared with at least four different colors of frosting, and she had a streak of powdered sugar across her forehead. Really, though, it was her eyes. She had an almost frantic look in her eyes. "Quinn."

"Is everything okay?"

"I'm so sorry. I somehow forgot we had a meeting today and I'm literally drowning in cake."

"Oh." Not the end of the world. Deflating, perhaps, since she couldn't seem to chase Amanda from her thoughts, but Amanda didn't need to know that. "Um, it's all right."

"Is there any chance we could reschedule? I have two deliveries this afternoon and am nowhere near done."

"Of course." It happened to everyone at some point, right?

"I really am sorry. Can I text you tomorrow?"

"Sure."

"Mei, box up whatever Quinn wants, on the house." She tossed another apologetic look Quinn's way. "Thank you."

And then she was gone.

It would be silly to take the mix-up as anything more than a simple crossing of wires, the result of one too many things to do and not enough hours in the day. But even as Quinn told herself that, she struggled not to be disappointed.

"What can I get for you?" Mei asked.

Quinn sighed. Did it count as consolation if she'd planned to bring something home all along? She eyed the case. "Cookies, I think. I'll take one of each kind."

Eight cookies wasn't unreasonable if she didn't eat them all at once, right?

Mei smiled. "Excellent choice."

While she boxed them up, Quinn pulled out her wallet. "I don't mind paying, though. Eight feels like an abuse of the nice gesture."

"Nonsense. You came all this way."

She didn't really want to argue. And she had gone out of her way. "Thanks."

Quinn accepted the box. As she turned to leave, a loud crash came from the kitchen. She couldn't make out Amanda's words, but the tone was all expletive. She'd never wish Amanda, or anyone, a bad day, but she couldn't help but feel a little better that Amanda forgetting about her was perhaps tied up in an above average level of stress.

"Good luck with everything," she said to Mei, although she mostly meant it for Amanda.

On the drive back to town, she considered calling Joss to reschedule their meeting. They did have another project in the works, though, and it was always nice to connect face-to-face. And since she had no doubt she'd eat all the cookies if she brought them home, stopping by would give her the opportunity to share.

She pulled into the Bauer and Sons parking lot and cut the engine. Maybe she'd luck out and the baby would be in. Babies always lifted her spirits.

She'd no sooner opened the door to the office then Daphne called out a greeting. Not a neighborhood bar, but she appreciated being known by name. "Hey, Daph."

"Joss called to say she's running late, but she'll only be a few minutes."

Maybe it was something in the water. "No worries. How're you doing?"

"You know, living the dream."

"How are the kids?"

"Tyrants. Absolute tyrants."

"That bad, huh?"

She laughed. "Not really. But they're enough of a handful that I'm reminded daily two is enough. Which is good because every time Joss brings Charlotte to the office, my hormones try to convince me otherwise."

Quinn was past any such hormonal flutters, not that she ever had a burning desire for kids of her own. Still, she could appreciate the power of an adorable kid. "Is she walking yet?"

"Not quite, but any day I think."

Before she could ask more questions, Joss walked in, Charlotte in her arms. "Speak of the devil. Or maybe I should say angel."

"Hey, Quinn. Sorry to keep you waiting." Joss shifted the baby and extended her hand.

Quinn shook it. "I literally just got here. And getting to see Charlotte earns you all sorts of concessions."

Joss grinned. "I'll remember that next time we go over budget."

"Now, now. Let's not get carried away."

Joss handed the baby over to her sister, who seemed more than happy to set aside the stack of receipts she was entering. Quinn and Joss headed into Joss's office. She filled Joss in on the canceled appointment and they spent a few minutes commiserating the vagaries of working with clients. They debriefed the upcoming library project and spent a few minutes catching up on life.

"Any more setups?" Joss asked.

Quinn closed her eyes and shook her head. "Two last week. Why won't people give it a rest?"

"You know you can decline, right?"

She did. And she was going to have to start doing just that if she hoped to preserve her sanity, not to mention her faith in love. "People mean well, though. And they get so excited about it. I feel bad and I don't want to hurt anyone's feelings."

Joss leaned back in her chair and folded her arms. "Here's the thing."

Joss wasn't big on doling out advice, so Quinn was intrigued. "Yeah?"

"If you're not feeling it, you're wasting their time."

"Huh." She'd not thought of it that way.

"Assuming the women you're set up with are looking for a relationship, going out with you is keeping them from meeting the person who might be that relationship."

"Good point." And, in a weird way, took a whole lot of pressure off of her.

"Don't tell my wife I said so, but I'm pretty smart when it comes to women."

For the first time that day, Quinn laughed. Truly laughed. "I'm so going to hold that over your head the next time you won't do something I want."

Joss gave her a look of mild exasperation. "How often do I not do something you want?"

Quinn shrugged. "Rarely."

"Thank you."

"Speaking of Olivia, how is she?"

At the mention of her wife's name, Joss's features softened. "She's good."

"Tenured life treating her well?"

"It's not technically official until the board votes on it next month, but she says it's pretty much official at this point."

Quinn knew firsthand how life changing tenure could be. When Lesedi got it, the pressure of her work got cut in half. At least it had felt that way to Quinn. Those first few years after she got associate professor were some of the best years of their marriage. She sighed at the memory. "It's going to be fantastic."

Joss chuckled. "So I'm told. We can't decide whether to enjoy it for a year or start trying for baby number two."

She and Joss weren't super close, but they were definitely more than colleagues. She'd gone to her and Olivia's wedding and had been to their house for dinner before she and Lesedi broke up. Quinn sighed at that memory, too.

"You okay?"

"Yeah." She missed being married more than she missed Lesedi at this point, which felt like at least a minor improvement. "I think either sounds wonderful."

Joss got a dreamy look on her face. "Yeah."

Even with her own angst, she couldn't be anything but happy for her. Both of them, really. "And it's not like they're mutually exclusive."

"You've got a point." Joss grinned. "So, the bakery woman. Is she a flake?"

She'd managed to go ten whole minutes without thinking about Amanda, but the image of her all disheveled and apologetic popped right back into her mind. "I don't think so. Or at least I didn't. I'm hoping this was a fluke."

"Here's hoping."

Working with a scatterbrained and indecisive client could be as bad as working with an overly demanding one. Even with the events of the morning still fresh, she had a good feeling about Amanda. "I think it's going to work out fine."

Chapter Eight

A manda sat at the bar of Fig, a glass of pinot noir in front of her. The giddiness in her stomach left her feeling like a teenager going on a first date. Only this was all the good parts. No worries about whether or not she'd be cool enough or if the kissing would be any good. Going out with Mel had her remembering why dates were worth the bother in the first place.

She sipped her wine and angled in her seat to watch the goings-on around her. One couple sat at the bar, looking cozy, while a man on his own seemed as interested in his phone as he did his drink. Because the bar area was small, she also had a view into the dining room. It was more than half full, which was nice to see at six on a weekday.

She knew Nick, the owner, from some food service and networking events, and she'd delivered a wedding cake here only a few months prior. It had been his newish head chef getting married, so he'd closed the whole restaurant for the reception. Knowing that, and knowing small places in towns like hers could reinvent themselves and thrive, made her happy on so many levels.

Waitstaff moved efficiently around the room and she tried to snag peeks at the dishes coming out of the kitchen. At one point, the chef emerged in a white chef coat and hat not unlike the one she wore for deliveries. Drew made the rounds, chatting with customers. She imagined doing the same when her bakery had enough space for people to sit and enjoy their food. Even though it wasn't some fancy restaurant, she wanted her customers to feel appreciated, known.

When Drew glanced her way, she smiled. It was cute to see her face register recognition, then process and ultimately land on how they knew each other. She was glad she wasn't alone in needing a second sometimes. She didn't expect a conversation, but Drew crossed the dining room to her.

"Amanda, how nice to see you."

She shook Drew's extended hand. "Same. How's married life treating you?"

Drew's face softened and took on the look of someone blissfully in love. "Better than I imagined."

"Good."

"What brings you in tonight?"

Amanda hesitated. She felt silly saying a date, even though that's exactly what it was. Maybe it was who she was meeting and not the date itself giving her pause. Either way, weird. "Just meeting a friend for dinner."

"Nice. How about I send over a little something while you wait? We've got a garlic scape pesto bruschetta tonight."

As delicious as it sounded, she didn't want to be stuffing her face when Mel arrived. Nor did she want crazy garlic breath. Not that she could admit either of those things without outing herself as a liar. "I'm good, but thank you. I've already committed to saving myself for dessert."

Drew grinned. "A woman after my own heart. If you change your mind, you let Carlton here know and we'll hook you up."

She loved the local food industry for a lot of reasons, but this camaraderie might be the best part. "Thanks."

Drew returned to the kitchen. Amanda checked her watch and frowned. Fifteen minutes late wasn't the end of the world, but Mel running late gave her the sort of flashbacks she'd just as soon not have.

"Another glass of pinot?" Carlton asked as she started to stew.

She probably shouldn't, but sitting at the bar alone and without a drink made her self-conscious. "That would be great. Thank you."

He poured and she stared into the glass. Would Mel stand her up? Without a text of apology even?

Amanda glanced toward the door, willing herself not to ruminate on that very real possibility. When a familiar face walked in, she had an instinctive flash of delight before registering the details. It was Quinn, which on her own, might have been delightful. Only she wasn't alone. Hanging on her arm like some celebrity at a red carpet was a stunning brunette who couldn't be a day over thirty.

Amanda looked away, hoping Quinn hadn't noticed her. But of course the universe couldn't be that kind. When she stole another glance, Quinn was looking her way. Quinn raised her hand in a friendly wave, so she did, too. Then she pulled out her phone, hoping desperately Mel had texted her an *almost there.*

Her phone told her the time and gave her a glimpse of her kids smiling at her from the photo she'd set as her wallpaper. No message. No apology. Nothing.

"I'd say funny seeing you here, but I don't suppose there are that many places on this side of the lake."

She didn't have to look to know it was Quinn behind her. She schooled her face into an upbeat expression before turning. "Small towns."

Quinn, sans date, smiled back at her. "How are you tonight?"

Miserable. Annoyed. Humiliated. "I'm great. You?"

"Pretty good. Are you waiting for someone?"

Amanda tried for a casual shrug. "That's the plan. Although I'm starting to fear perhaps they were waylaid."

Quinn frowned with what appeared to be a mixture of pity and regret. "I'm stuck on a blind date or I'd ask you to join us."

Humiliation leapfrogged right over annoyance. "That would take the notion of being a third wheel to a whole new level."

Quinn's frown intensified.

"But thank you for the gesture. Really."

"Are you sure you're okay?"

"Absolutely. I have an in with the chef, so she'll take care of me either way."

Quinn's frown gave way to a sort of half-smile that brought out a dimple in her left cheek. It managed to make her look sexy and adorable at the same time. "I sort of wish I was here with you, instead."

The comment could be read a dozen different ways. Although tempted to tease it apart, she settled on it being a nice thing to say, even if it wasn't true. "Thank you for the sentiment, but please don't let me keep you from your date."

Quinn glanced over to the table where the woman waited. "I should probably go."

Amanda waved her away. "Have a good time."

Quinn excused herself, leaving Amanda alone at the bar with her wine. She looked at her phone again. A full hour late and not even a peep from Mel. She contemplated taking Drew up on her offer, of enjoying a nice dinner on her own. Normally, that wouldn't bother her. Tonight, though, tonight it made her feel pathetic.

She asked Carlton for her check and paid, leaving her second glass of wine half full. She slipped off the stool and headed for the exit, looking in the opposite direction of where she knew Quinn and her date sat. In her car, the sum of her evening hit her. Since no one was there to see, she let a couple of tears spill over.

So stupid. She wiped them away and drove herself home. Once there, she peeled off the dress she'd poured herself into and drew a bath.

Still nothing from Mel.

A twinge of worry played at the back of her mind. What if something terrible had happened? No way was she Mel's emergency contact, so she might not know about an accident or anything like that for days.

Even as anxiety took hold, she shook her head. How many times had Mel run late or not come home for dinner at all? Every time, Amanda's worry fought with her anger. So much so that even when she laid into Mel about it, relief tempered her wrath and she would be quick to back down. She didn't want to feel that wrath anymore, or that relief. And she wouldn't.

She slipped into the steaming, sudsy water and let the tension melt away. Whether it was the bath or her decision, she didn't know. Either way, the certainty of it felt good. Yes, it had been fun. She just didn't want to do it anymore.

❖

Without being obvious, Quinn had continued to steal glances at Amanda while her date perused the wine list. They'd no sooner settled on a local dry Riesling than she saw Amanda pay her tab and leave. What was that about? She was pretty sure Amanda hadn't eaten. Even if her friend canceled, why wouldn't she have dinner since she was already there?

She tried to convince herself the curiosity was more friendly concern than romantic interest, especially since she was here on a date. Even if it was a date she'd been hesitant to agree to in the first place. "So, how do you know Kiera again?"

"Yoga."

Right. The goat kind. "How did you get into that?"

They chatted about exercise, ordered wine. Over dinner, conversation hit the expected first date high points—hometowns and family trees and the best parts of upstate New York in the summer. Lisa was beautiful and charming and easy to talk to. But like so many of the women Quinn had been fixed up with in the last year, that was the end of it. No spark, no craving for more.

Maybe it was her. Maybe she wasn't ready. Maybe she'd never be ready.

When they finished eating, Quinn insisted on paying the check. In part, she was old school and preferred to when her date didn't mind. Really, though, it made her feel less guilty about not having her head, or her heart, in the game.

On the drive back to Lisa's apartment, conversation lulled. It felt like more of a comfortable silence than an awkward one. That might have been more wishful thinking than reality, but the jazz on the radio was nice and Lisa had mentioned liking Nina Simone.

It didn't take long for her thoughts to drift to Amanda.

It felt skeevy to be thinking about Amanda while driving another woman home from dinner. They weren't sexual thoughts, though, so it could be worse. Not that she hadn't had her share of sexual thoughts about Amanda since they'd met. But tonight was different. There was something in Amanda's eyes she hadn't seen before: vulnerability. Despite the casual conversation, it left Quinn longing to swoop in and rescue her. From what, she had no idea, but something about it triggered all her protective instincts.

She did her best to shake it off, and not only because her date was speaking. "I'm sorry. What?"

"I said you seemed distracted."

Quinn chuckled. "I think you're right, although I swear it isn't the present company."

"I don't take it personally. It's the tricky thing about fix-ups, isn't it?"

By all accounts, Lisa was a lovely woman: smart, attractive, funny. But she was thirty-five, close to fifteen years Quinn's junior and Quinn couldn't help but feel like a dinosaur around her. Lisa hadn't articulated it in those words, but Quinn got the sense the feeling was mutual. Or, at the very least, they were looking for different things. "People mean well, though, right?"

Lisa laughed, a true and lovely laugh. "Yes. But they're so bad at it."

Quinn chuckled. It was a relief to be on the same page. She'd gone into this whole dating process so worried she'd fall for someone who wasn't interested in her. It hadn't occurred to her the opposite might happen. Not fall for her full on, but have interest she didn't reciprocate. Letting people down gently was now officially her least favorite thing.

Lisa reached across the console and rested a hand on hers. "Oh, God. I didn't go too far, did I? I do think you're fantastic."

Quinn pulled up to a light and looked at Lisa. "No, no. You're fantastic, too. But not for me. I'm starting to think maybe I'm not ready to be dating after all."

Lisa offered her a reassuring smile. "It's okay if you aren't."

Quinn let out a sigh and realized how much tension she'd been holding. "And you deserve to find someone who is exactly what you want and who wants the same things as you."

"We should give our friends a good stern talking-to, shouldn't we?"

Quinn laughed in earnest then. "Agreed. Knowing two women who both happen to be single and lesbian should not be the sole criteria for matchmaking."

"Well, we're smart, too. And charming. It's not a total leap. Even if we're in very different places in our lives."

A thought occurred to Quinn and she cringed. "You didn't feel pressured to go out with me, did you?"

"It was Kiera. Of course I felt pressured."

She should leave it at that. After all, she'd felt pressured, too. Kiera could be very persistent. But as much as she feared the answer, she needed to know. "I meant me specifically."

God, she sounded so pathetic.

"You're nobody's pity date, if that's what you're worried about."

Relief lost ground to the embarrassment of asking in the first place. "I'm not sure if I should thank you or apologize."

"Neither."

She pulled into the lot of Lisa's building. "Thanks."

Lisa unbuckled her seat belt and shifted to face Quinn. "Thank you for dinner."

"Thank you for such lovely company."

"Maybe I'll see you around at yoga sometime."

If she got nothing else out of this date, she could pick up a few pointers on being gracious when it became clear a second date wouldn't be in the cards. There were worse consolation prizes. "I'm sure we will."

Lisa made to get out of the car. Quinn did the same, more out of habit than anything else, but Lisa waved her off. "I hope you find what you're looking for."

How classy. Quinn smiled. "You, too."

She waited until Lisa was inside, then backed her car out and headed home. Lisa's parting words played in her mind. Maybe her problem wasn't that her sisters and her friends didn't get what she was looking for. Maybe her problem was that she didn't know herself.

But on the heels of that worry came the image of Amanda sitting alone at the bar. With it, the attraction she'd been denying. She wasn't in the business of pursuing clients, but it was nice to know that part of herself—the part that felt immediately and intensely drawn to a woman—wasn't broken entirely.

Chapter Nine

Quinn pulled into Amanda's driveway and cut the engine. She'd been equal parts elated and conflicted when Amanda offered to make dinner for their rescheduled meeting. Elated because it meant time with Amanda, not to mention a home cooked meal. Conflicted because she worried Amanda felt obligated. Oh, and because she had no business being elated.

She took a deep breath and gathered up her bag and the revised plans she wanted to review before handing things over to Joss. For some reason, having them, having a reason to be there other than dinner with Amanda, made her calmer. She shook her head. That was the problem with so many iffy, if not downright bad, dates. They had her on edge about spending time with an attractive woman.

Work. She was here for work. Nothing more, nothing less. At least when it came to work, she knew what she was doing.

She repeated the sentiment to herself as she climbed the porch steps and rang the bell.

When Amanda answered the door in a pair of jeans, a paisley top, and flats, she relaxed. So not a date. Even if the smile Amanda offered was enough to make her wish it was.

"Hey. It's so good to see you. Come on in."

"Likewise. Thank you for inviting me." She took in the details of the entryway and living room—many of them the original craftsman design—and nodded her approval. "You've got a great place."

"High praise coming from an architect."

Quinn frowned. "I'm not a snob."

Amanda smirked. "Oh, I hope you are at least a little. I'm an incorrigible snob when it comes to baked goods."

The comment made her like Amanda even more. "I won't confess my Little Debbie habit to you then."

"And I won't tell you about the original molding sacrificed for my kitchen reno."

Quinn nodded. "Deal."

She followed Amanda down the short hall to the kitchen. It definitely had the look and feel of a recent high-end remodel. Still, it wasn't garish or modern or too out of step with the character of the house.

"I spend enough time in here that I let myself get exactly what I wanted."

"I find nothing to take issue with." She really didn't. It almost made her wish she cooked.

"Are you just saying that so I'll feed you?"

She chuckled at how close the question cut to her line of thinking. "Maybe."

Amanda laughed and even though they absolutely were not on a date, Quinn made a mental note to try to get her to do it again. And again after that. "Don't worry. I never promise to feed someone then take it back. I think it's part of the mom code."

"Oh, good." Quinn set her things down on the table. "Still, I hope you didn't feel obligated to make me dinner."

"Does wanting to do something nice count as feeling obligated?"

She sure hoped that wasn't the case. "Not necessarily."

Amanda lifted a shoulder in a way that might be flirtatious. "I don't bail on meetings, especially if someone has gone out of their way to show up at my bakery. This feels like the least I could do for making you reschedule."

Quinn offered a shrug of her own. Any lingering disappointment was overshadowed by the dinner invitation. For the dinner as much as the company. "It happens to the best of us."

"It's kind of you to say so."

"It's easy to be generous when a beautiful woman is making me dinner." Her cheeks flushed. Did she really just say that?

Amanda bit her lip but didn't seem to mind the compliment. "I'll remember that."

A bolder woman would take it as invitation. Quinn wasn't quite that, at least not these days. "So, what are we having?"

"Coq au vin. It can simmer while we go over the plans, which I figured we should do first."

She had a point, especially since that was the reason for meeting in the first place. "Sounds perfect."

"Can I pour you a glass of wine now?"

The offer of wine made her think maybe Amanda didn't consider this strictly a business meeting. "Only if you'll join me."

"Well, if you insist." Amanda pulled a bottle from the fridge and poured two glasses.

Quinn accepted her glass and lifted it. "Here's to rescheduling in style."

Amanda touched her glass to Quinn's. "I'll drink to that."

They sat at the table and Quinn unrolled the plans. After getting Amanda's approval on her more radical design, she'd worked out a more detailed plan. Still, she wanted Amanda's input, especially on the layout for the kitchen. "I've done a handful of kitchen spaces, but none with your exact uses. I did some scouting for best practices, but I think you should drive the process since you actually spend time there."

"You say that like it's unusual."

"For the owner to also be the head chef? Yes, it's unusual."

Amanda gave her an exasperated look. "It's not some Michelin starred restaurant. I'm not a head chef."

Quinn studied her, looking for something unspoken. "I wouldn't have pegged you for false modesty."

"My cakes could make a grown man cry they're so good. It has nothing to do with modesty."

The retort came with a straight face and not a second of hesitation. Had she not found Amanda attractive before, it would have tipped the scales. "Point taken."

They talked through Amanda's ideas for the different work spaces—baking, decorating, and the new lunch service. It was good she asked because it wouldn't have occurred to her roasted garlic should never share the same work surface as modeling chocolate. She made copious notes and penciled things directly on the plans. Amanda did, too. In under an hour, they had enough ironed out to take the plans to Joss and the zoning board.

Quinn rolled up the oversize sheets of paper, securing them with rubber bands. "Do we get to eat now?"

"Hungry?"

"I wasn't, but I've been smelling that chicken for the last forty-five minutes and let's say I'm pretty happy with myself for not drooling on your blueprints."

Amanda laughed. God, she really did have an incredible laugh. "You could have said so sooner."

Quinn shook her head. "No, work before pleasure. I'm super boring like that."

"Is work done, then?"

"Done."

It was a special thing when food tasted even better than it smelled. Amanda's chicken was that and more. The homemade bread helped. As did the second glass of chardonnay. Or maybe it was the company. Probably a combination of everything. Whatever it was, it was the best meal she'd had in as long as she could remember. She said as much to Amanda.

And then Amanda whipped out this torch contraption and burned the sugar on a pair of crème brûlées. Like, literally, right in front of her. Her spoon did that satisfying crack when it broke the shell and the custard underneath might have been the most delicious thing she'd ever put in her mouth.

"Wow."

"Like I said, it's the least I could do."

"Could you forget all our meetings? Please?"

Amanda chuckled. "Couldn't I just agree to make you dinner again?"

"But what would I do to repay you?"

She considered. "Well, you are giving me the bakery of my dreams."

Quinn made her face serious. "Um. I'm sorry. Maybe we weren't fully clear. You're going to have to pay for that."

The sound that came out of Amanda was more of a snort than a laugh. Not as sexy, but so genuine and uninhibited. Quinn couldn't decide which she preferred.

They finished dessert and Amanda refused all offers of help cleaning up. Quinn was sorry to see the meeting end, to be honest, but they were going on three hours. Probably best to make a graceful exit.

Amanda walked her to the door. "Thank you again for being so accommodating."

"I feel like I should be the one thanking you. Dinner was fantastic."

"You're easy." Amanda folded her arms.

Quinn raised a brow. "Sometimes."

"I'll remember that next time I want something from you."

She held Amanda's gaze even as her pulse ticked up a notch. "Or you could ask."

"Maybe I have a hard time asking for things without offering something in return."

"I could give you a lecture, but it would be a pot and kettle situation." And true of her personal life as much as her professional habits.

"It's nice to know I'm not alone," Amanda said.

The flush that rose in Amanda's cheeks made her feel bold. Made her feel like herself. "I liked talking about more than work, too, if I'm being honest."

"Same."

"So, I think we should do it again."

Amanda swallowed and felt a flush creep into her cheeks. Was Quinn asking her out? "I'd like that."

"Maybe with no talk about work at all."

Aha. All right. She'd thought maybe Quinn was flirting with her, but couldn't be sure. But that was way more than friendly. "I'd like that, too."

Amanda opened the door, but Quinn didn't immediately step through. The hesitation made the air between them feel electric, like the moment before a first kiss. Amanda braced herself for it— excitement and anticipation buzzing through her. Quinn looked at her mouth, then into her eyes.

A car pulling into the driveway broke the moment. The tension or spark or whatever it was dissipated. Amanda glanced over. "That would be my son."

"Ah." Quinn's expression turned sheepish, like she was processing what it would have been like to be caught. Amanda couldn't help but find it endearing.

"I'll just catch him so he can let you out."

"Great. Thanks."

Amanda stepped onto the porch and waved in Cal's direction. He put down his window. "What's up?"

"Could you pull in behind me so Quinn can leave?"

He offered her a playful salute and repositioned his car.

Since a kiss was completely out of the question now, she walked Quinn down the sidewalk. When Cal reached them, she said, "Quinn, this is my son, Cal. Cal, this is Quinn Sullivan. She's the architect working on the bakery expansion."

Quinn and Cal exchanged greetings, then Cal headed inside. Quinn seemed unbothered by the interruption. "Still in high school or done?"

"Just finished. He's starting at Cornell in the fall."

Quinn smiled. "Congratulations. My nephew just finished his first year in the architecture program."

"Cal's planning environmental engineering. We'll see if it sticks."

"Yeah. I think Jacob is pretty settled, but who knows?"

While the almost maybe kiss had been nice, this conversation was much more her speed. For better or worse. "As long as he doesn't change his mind ten times, I think I'll be okay."

"Totally reasonable." Quinn seemed to hesitate again.

"Have a great night." It came out almost like a question and made her wish she wasn't so out of practice.

Quinn stuck her hands in her pockets and rocked back on her heels. "You, too."

Amanda walked back to the house as Quinn got in her car, but she turned to wave from the porch. All the while wondering if Quinn might have kissed her.

Inside, she found Cal with his head in the refrigerator. "Didn't you eat at Zoe's?"

"Yeah, but like two hours ago."

"There's coq au vin leftover from dinner if you want. Glass bowl with the green lid."

"Yes." He dragged out the word and snagged the bowl.

"There's salad, too."

He waved her off, scooped out a piece of chicken, and started eating it with his fingers. "I'm good."

"Don't you want that warmed up?"

"Nah."

She shook her head. "I suppose I should be grateful you're using a plate."

He shrugged. "Why was your architect over for dinner?"

"Because I forgot I had a meeting with her and felt bad."

"That's too bad."

"I know. She showed up at the bakery and I was frantically trying to finish an order."

"No, I mean it's too bad that's the reason."

She started cleaning the kitchen around him. "What do you mean?"

"I thought maybe it was a date."

She didn't discuss her love life in any great detail with her kids, but they often teased her about getting out more, getting a life. It was mostly that—teasing. Or at least she always figured it was. "We're working together."

"So? It's not like she's your employee."

Amanda frowned. She always deflected these kinds of comments, but she didn't want to this time. Not with Quinn. What was that about? "I know."

"Seriously, Mom. How long has it been since you've been on a date?"

Not counting Mel? God, if Cal or Daniella had a clue about that. She shoved the idea aside. They didn't and wouldn't. "A while."

"Exactly. You're going to have an empty nest soon. You should start living it up."

She got the image of a cozy night in with Quinn. Dinner, a fire, a kiss that would lead to more. "I'm pretty happy with my life, thank you very much."

"You know what I mean." He sighed and, for the first time, she wondered if maybe there was more to it.

"Are you worried about me?"

He rolled his eyes and she got the impression he wished Daniella was there to back him up. "Not worried worried. We just don't want you to be lonely."

Suddenly, the ripple effect of her choices came into focus. She'd always put her kids first, had wanted to as much as she'd felt like it was an obligation. But now she could see she wasn't modeling the sort of balance she always encouraged them to find. She crossed the room and wrapped her arms around him. "You don't need to worry."

He returned the hug, but then stepped back and folded his arms. The gesture reminded her so much of Mel she almost laughed. "And what's your answer when Daniella and I say that to you?"

Touché. "It's my prerogative to worry about you."

He lifted his chin with a trace of challenge. "Well, same goes."

"How'd I get so lucky in the kid department?"

He dropped his hands to his sides and shrugged. "Beats me."

And just like that, the emotional moment passed and her smart-aleck son was back. She loved that he had the capacity for both. She bumped his shoulder with hers. "Are you in for the night?"

"Yeah. I have to work early tomorrow."

She kissed his cheek. "Have a good night."

"You, too."

She started toward the stairs but paused when he called after her. She poked her head back in the kitchen. "What's up?"

"Maybe you should think about dating your architect. She's totally your type."

She shook her head but laughed. "Thanks for the advice. I'll take it under consideration."

His voice followed her up the stairs. "You should listen to me. I'm very smart."

CHAPTER TEN

Amanda heard the door swing behind her. Assuming it was Tanya, she didn't look up from the cake layers in front of her. "Did we make almond pastry cream yesterday? I didn't see it in the cooler."

"I don't know, but I sure hope there's some leftover for samples," Mel said.

She resisted a growl and turned. "What are you doing here?"

"You didn't answer my texts."

"Because I didn't want to talk to you."

Mel sighed. "I'm trying to apologize."

Amanda wiped her hands on her apron. "And I'm not interested."

"Bella and I had a huge fight. I wanted to be with you, but I couldn't walk out. I mean, we're trying to figure out whether or not to get divorced."

The irony of the excuse made her chuckle. "Oh, well then. That makes me feel much better."

"Don't be mad."

Amanda closed her eyes. "I'm not mad."

"Of course you are. And you have every right to be. Just tell me what I need to do to make it up to you."

She shook her head. "There's nothing to make up."

Mel folded her arms and gave her a look of exasperation. "Your mouth is saying one thing, but your body language is saying another."

"My body language is saying I don't want to do this with you anymore. It doesn't mean I'm angry."

Mel's expression changed. It was almost comical to see the recalibration of her switching tactics. "I want to see where this is going. Don't deny us the chance to find out."

Twenty years ago, the move would have worked. She'd always been inclined to kiss and make up. Even at her most frustrated, she'd have a soft spot for one or another of Mel's strategies and Mel was a master of working her way through them until she found the one that worked. But a lot had changed in twenty years.

The conciliatory smile gave way to full charm. Mel angled her head and, without words, managed to convey a sense of come on, you know you want to. "Foot massage."

It wasn't fair to tempt women who spent hours and hours on their feet with foot massages. Through the years, Mel had gotten away with a lot courtesy of her skill and willingness to give them. Only Amanda spent a lot less time on her feet than she used to. And she had the money and appreciation for self-care to get massages on a regular basis. "Not this time."

"So, next time."

God, she was relentless. Not to mention arrogant. To think she'd once found it attractive. "No next time. Please believe me when I say there won't be a next time."

Mel's shoulders dropped. "All right."

It wasn't like her to give in this easily, but at this point, Amanda wanted out of the conversation. "I need to get to work."

"Of course. I'm sure whatever it is will be delicious."

She didn't watch Mel go, the way she had so many times. Instead, she turned her focus to the cakes in front of her waiting to be split and filled and frosted. Because as much as she'd wanted to get rid of Mel, she also had a ton of work to do.

She'd just gotten the first one filled before Tanya burst through the door like the place was on fire. "What was that about?"

Amanda scooped frosting onto the cake and started the crumb coat. "Nothing."

Tanya's sniff came with hands on hips and head cocked to one side. "You can refuse to tell me, but don't lie to me."

Ugh. She really didn't have time for this. But she and Tanya had been friends for almost as long as they'd worked together. She knew the intimate details of Tanya's romantic ups and downs. Not reciprocating would be insulting. "Mel and I slept together, but I realized it was a terrible idea and broke it off and she's not happy about it."

"Wait, wait, wait. What?"

She should have known better than to think she could get away with such an abbreviated explanation. She slid the first cake into the cooler and gave Tanya her full attention. "Did you not hear me or do you not believe me?"

Tanya's mouth came open, then it closed. "The second one."

"I know." She took a deep breath and looked up at the ceiling. "I know."

"I demand you tell me everything. Literally everything."

"I promise. Just not now. We've got a wedding tonight and three tomorrow." Not an overly hectic few days, but she needed to be focused if she wanted to keep it that way.

"You have to eat. You can give me the broad strokes when I make you sit down and eat a real lunch."

She didn't skip meals, but she did have the bad habit of ten-minute lunches between tasks. "Deal."

"Do you need anything for now?"

"I don't think—wait." She remembered the question she'd accidentally asked Mel. "The almond pastry cream."

"Top shelf. All the way in the back." Tanya lifted her chin. "If I don't see you in an hour, I'm coming for you. Consider yourself warned."

"Noted."

Tanya disappeared the way she'd come and Amanda got back to work. Each cake got split in two; the resulting layers got sandwiched with filling. A thin coat of buttercream to seal in the crumbs and create a smooth surface for the second coat of frosting. By the time she finished the three smaller tiers, the two larger ones had chilled enough. She pulled one from the cooler and set it on her turntable. Since this cake would be covered in fondant, it didn't need to be perfect, but the smoother the frosting, the smoother the final result.

By the time she had all five frosted and ready to be covered and decorated, she'd used up most of the time Tanya had allotted her. Might as well take her break now. Once she was rolling fondant, she preferred to do it all at once.

Amanda washed her hands and headed to the front, only to find Julia and Erin chatting with Tanya. She made a show of spinning on the ball of her foot and going back the way she'd come. A chorus of "hey" and "get your ass back here" followed her. She did as she was told, not really looking to avoid them. If she could tell them all at once, she could save having to tell it multiple times. If only Jack was there.

He swept in, an infant strapped to his chest in a BabyBjorn. "Looks like I almost missed a party."

It wasn't unusual for her friends to converge on the bakery at once, but the timing of his arrival made her laugh. Julia grinned at the baby before looking at Jack. "Accidental party. We'd never have an on purpose party and not invite you."

Erin nodded and shrugged. "As accidental as bumping into each other at a place we all come several times a week can be."

Jack waved them off. "I'm not worried. I'm the life of your parties and we all know it."

"I love you, Jack, but you've got nothing on this beautiful girl." Julia had crossed the room and was now making silly faces at the baby, who giggled with delight.

Enissa was cute and had a way of pulling all the attention in the room. Maybe Amanda could let her. She could air her woes on a group text and avoid having to talk about it out loud at all. She knew better than to think she could get away with such a tactic, but it didn't hurt to dream.

❖

Quinn walked into the Advocacy Center charity breakfast, a knot of tension in her stomach. Lesedi would be there, but so would three hundred other people. She might have to see her across the room or, at worse, run into her at the raffle table. It would be fine.

Only her life didn't seem to work that way. She'd barely handed over her ticket before literally bumping into her. "Good morning."

Lesedi beamed at her. "Well, hello."

She didn't see any sign of Lesedi's new girlfriend, so that counted for something. "How did the semester treat you?"

Lesedi tipped her head back and forth. "Quite good. My last paper hit the *Journal of Consumer Behavior.*"

Quinn mustered a smile. "Not surprising at all. Congratulations."

Out of nowhere, or seemingly out of nowhere, Joanna appeared. She stuck out her hand like they were old friends and not like she'd stolen Quinn's wife right from under her nose. "Quinn, good to see you."

Quinn couldn't quite bring herself to reciprocate the sentiment. She accepted the handshake and wondered how quickly she'd be able to escape. "How've you been?"

"Good, good. Gearing up for the late summer term in Monaco."

Of course they were. They were both marketing professors at Cornell. Lesedi's area of specialty was consumer behavior, while Joanna's was luxury brand management. Teaming up on a research project was the start of the affair that ended her marriage. "Sounds exciting."

Lesedi's face softened. Whether it was guilt or regret, Quinn could never tell. Not that she was interested in either. "What about you? What do you have cooked up for the summer?"

As someone who wasn't an academic and didn't have kids, summer didn't provide the same kind of dramatic shift as it did for some people. Even people who were married to academics, which she no longer was. She didn't say as much because it would probably come out bitter. And honestly, she wasn't bitter. Disappointed, maybe. At worst, jaded. But not bitter. "Nothing major. I'll take the kayak out, spend as much time as I can on the lake or up at the cabin."

Lesedi smiled. "I'll miss the lake."

"I'm sure you'll make do with the Mediterranean."

Both Lesedi and Joanna laughed. Not an arrogant, in your face sort of laugh. More of a what can we do, we're so blissfully happy sound. Even without the ill intent, it cut.

"How're your sisters and the kids?" Lesedi asked.

She both loved and hated that Lesedi felt the need to ask about them. It was standard divorce protocol according to her friends and several of the self-help books she'd waded through on the matter, but it left a bad taste in her mouth. At least for now. Maybe that would fade with time. "Good, good. Kids are loving summer. Jacob finished his first year at Cornell."

"Oh, that's wonderful." Lesedi clapped her hands together. "Architecture, right? Following in your footsteps."

See, this was the problem. Lesedi wasn't a bad person. She was thoughtful and interested and all the other things Quinn valued in a woman—partner or otherwise. "Yep."

"I'm so glad. You'll have to make sure he emails me. I'd love to take him to lunch."

Quinn sighed. "I'm sure he'd like that."

"And work?" Joanna asked.

The worst part about Lesedi falling in love with Joanna was that Joanna had been a mutual friend as much as Lesedi's colleague. Hell, Joanna and her wife. Ex-wife. They'd done dinners and wine tours and even a trip to Provincetown together. It made hating her difficult for someone like Quinn, who had a dyed-in-the-wool tendency to assume the best of people. "It's good."

"Anything new and exciting in the hopper?"

Her mind flashed to Amanda and her little bakery out in Kenota. Hardly the stuff Cornell powerhouses would find exciting, but it sat pretty high on her list at the moment. "The Trumansburg Library expansion will break ground soon."

"That's great," Joanna said. They both nodded encouragingly.

Quinn nodded back but allowed her gaze to wander in search of someone—anyone—else she might know and urgently need to chat with. She'd made it about halfway around the room when her sights landed on the woman she'd just been thinking about. Bingo. "If you two will excuse me, I see a client I should say hello to."

"Of course." Lesedi reached out and squeezed her hand. "It's good to see you."

She no longer flinched when Lesedi did that. It still bugged her, but more in a vaguely awkward way than the patronizing pity she got right after the divorce. "You take care."

"You, too."

Quinn wound her way around the room, trying not to be obvious in making a beeline for Amanda. Quinn got to her as she dropped a handful of tickets into one of the raffle buckets. "So, you're an all in sort of woman."

Amanda turned her way, confusion apparent on her face. Fortunately, recognition quickly followed. "Quinn. Hi."

"I didn't expect to see you here, but it's definitely a pleasant surprise."

"Same. I've been coming for years, actually. Long-time supporter of the agency. You?"

"Only my second. My firm did the design for the new administrative spaces last year." Arti had pitched it as their big pro bono project for the year. Once Quinn understood the scope of the project and the mission of the organization, she'd taken the lead.

"Right, right. I remember the board president talking about it."

Not quite wanting the conversation to end, Quinn indicated the bucket. "So, as I was saying before, you're an all in sort of woman."

Amanda offered a playful smile. "I embrace a hybrid model."

They could be discussing sock-folding methods for all she cared, as long as it came with that smile. "Do tell."

"I buy twenty tickets. Ten go in the one I really want and then the other ten get spread around."

"Huh." She didn't put a lot of thought into raffles, but it was kind of genius.

"You think I'm silly. I can tell."

"Not at all." There were several words she was thinking that she'd just as soon Amanda not know, but silly was absolutely not one of them.

Amanda lifted her chin. "All right. What's your method?"

Quinn raised her hands. "I'm now embarrassed to admit I don't have one."

Amanda let out a tutting sound and shook her head. "Well, that won't do."

"Would it be bad form to steal your strategy?"

She considered for a moment. "Only if you put your ten in Cook's Night Off."

That particular item, a collection of gift certificates to local restaurants, was one of several dozen options. "Seems fair."

"Good. I'd hate to have to boo you if you won." Amanda smirked.

"Do you always heckle the winner if it isn't you?"

Amanda shrugged. "Only on the inside. I'm generally well behaved."

How was it easier to talk to Amanda than the majority of the women she went on dates with?

"You're making that judgmental face again." Amanda seemed to be kidding but still.

Quinn cleared her throat. "Sorry. My mind wandered. No judgment, I swear."

"I suppose I can take your word for it."

Before Quinn could reply, a voice came over the sound system encouraging guests to visit the buffet and purchase their raffle tickets in the next ten minutes. "I guess that's my cue."

"I'll see you next week, right?"

All the approvals were in place and they were officially closing the bakery to start construction. They had one final meeting to sign contracts and releases. "Absolutely. Are you excited?"

Amanda clasped her hands together, delight clear on her face. "I can't wait."

As sorry as she was to see the conversation end, she did need to buy her tickets. And get breakfast. And find her table. She offered Amanda a parting smile. "I hope you win."

Amanda chuckled. "You, too."

She joined the line at one of the ticket stations and studied the program for the raffles she should enter. She put her first ten in a wine of the month from Fairmount Ridge and sprinkled the remainder without thinking about it too much. She was sure, however, to avoid Amanda's bucket of choice. Because while she believed Amanda wouldn't literally boo her, when it came to staying on Amanda's good side, she found herself not wanting to take any chances.

CHAPTER ELEVEN

Amanda took a deep breath and looked around. Everything, including the appliances and the big worktable, had been packed up and put in storage. Even knowing it was temporary, seeing her kitchen so empty filled her with unease. It reminded her of a dream—nightmare, really—she used to have of this exact scene. Only, in her dream, Bake My Day had failed. She'd failed. And she was standing alone in the kitchen to say a final good-bye to everything she'd worked for.

She shook her head, as though the movement itself might shake off the anxiety that used to haunt her with more regularity. It was silly to feel that way now. Bake My Day wasn't merely keeping its head above water. It was more successful than she'd dared to hope for back in the early days. Back when Mel had been supportive on the surface but couldn't seem to keep herself from commenting on their dwindling savings. When every Saturday night cake delivery was met with a self-aggrandizing offer to babysit. Like taking care of her own children by herself was some grand gesture.

Her phone pinged with a text from Mel. *Big day! Let me know if you want company.*

The sense of dread crept back in, and it hit her. She wasn't feeling this way because of the bakery. She was feeling this way because of Mel. She dashed off an, *I'm good, but thanks,* annoyed but not wanting to start an argument.

She headed to the front of the bakery, which managed to look even more starkly empty than the kitchen. It didn't bring her down the way the kitchen did, though. Realizing the source of her angst had actually helped.

Joss was already there, giving directions to her crew. When she saw Amanda, she stopped mid-sentence and did introductions. A small thing, really, but the kind of personal touch Amanda appreciated.

"Do you need anything else from me?" she asked, already knowing the answer but wanting to linger a moment longer.

"No, we're ready to get started."

She nodded, not used to feeling unneeded. "Great."

"I have something for you, though." Joss handed her a white hard hat with the Bauer and Sons logo on it in deep green.

"Is this a souvenir?"

"No, it's so you can visit the site anytime you want." The answer came from Quinn, who appeared in the doorway, hard hat already on.

She ignored the ripple of pleasure. "I didn't expect to see you today."

Quinn looked at her feet before making eye contact. "I had a feeling you'd be here, and I thought a little moral support might come in handy."

"Thank you." So similar to Mel's offer, yet utterly different. With one comment, Quinn had managed to make her presence all about Amanda.

"It's my pleasure." Quinn angled her head toward Joss. "Although, I should warn you, she's not above putting clients to work. It's how she met her wife."

Joss shot Quinn a look of mild exasperation. "That's not what happened."

Amanda looked from Joss to Quinn and back. "Why do I get the feeling this is a really good story?"

"Because it is," Quinn said.

The exasperation faded and Joss smiled. "Olivia, my wife, hired me to rehab the old farmhouse she bought. She had strong feelings about doing some of the work herself."

"Ah. That's sweet. Were you already together?"

"Oh, no." Quinn's answer came with a snicker. "They couldn't stand each other at first."

Amanda had only met Joss twice now, but she liked her. "Is that so?"

"It was mostly me." Joss shook her head. "I was an ass. Fortunately, she didn't hold it against me in the long run. And I promise I won't put you to work."

"That's good. I'm pretty sure I'd just be in your way." She sometimes wished she was handy, but not enough to risk ruining something.

Quinn narrowed her eyes. "Do you want to be put to work?"

"Um." She hadn't given it any thought.

"What about some demo?" Joss asked.

Quinn offered an encouraging smile. "Impossible to mess up. And a great way to work out aggression."

She thought about Mel and the idea of destroying something suddenly had a certain appeal. "Really?"

Joss and Quinn exchanged knowing looks. Quinn looked her up and down. "How do you feel about that outfit?"

She'd specifically dressed for a construction zone—jeans and a University of Rochester shirt with sneakers. "They're work clothes."

Joss grinned. "All right, then. Let's do this."

She put on her hard hat and Joss handed her a pair of gloves, then a sledgehammer. Quinn stepped to the side while Joss gave directions. The hammer weighed a lot more than she thought and the idea of trying to wield it with an audience made her self-conscious. "Maybe I shouldn't. I don't really know what I'm doing."

Quinn put a hand on her shoulder. A casual gesture, friendly at most, but it sent a shiver up her spine. "You can't mess it up."

Backing out now would make her look like a coward, which would be worse than looking like an idiot. "Okay."

Amanda positioned herself the way Joss instructed. She swung the hammer over her shoulder and into the wall. It broke through and lodged with a satisfying thud. Joss helped her free it and encouraged her to keep going. So she did. Again and again. She didn't picture Mel's face, exactly, but their recent interactions certainly fueled her.

When she stopped, a dozen holes covered the wall. Her arms ached and she was out of breath. "That might be my limit."

"That was amazing." Joss took the hammer from her. "You ever want to join the crew, you say the word."

Amanda laughed. "You're exaggerating, but thank you."

"You did better than I could have." Quinn's voice gave her a start.

She'd sort of forgotten Quinn was there, watching her. She felt her cheeks flush. "I'm not going to lie, it was fun."

"Right? Fair warning, though, your arms will probably be killing you tomorrow."

Despite the self-consciousness a moment ago, she couldn't help but smirk. "I lift a lot of twenty-quart bowls in an average day."

Quinn bowed slightly. "I stand corrected."

Amanda pulled off the gloves and handed them to Joss. "Thank you for letting me have a go. Now I'll get out of your hair so you can get to work."

"Don't feel like you need to keep tabs on things, but you really are welcome anytime," Joss said.

"Thank you for that, too."

"I'll walk you out," Quinn said.

In the parking lot, Amanda hesitated. She wasn't in a rush to leave but didn't want to keep Quinn from whatever she needed to be doing inside. "Was the hard hat your idea or Joss's?"

"It's something Joss will do when a client is interested. I suggested you might be one of those clients."

For some reason, Quinn thinking about her that way made her happy. She took off the hat and studied it. "I appreciate that. And you being here today."

"Of course. I confess, I had an ulterior motive. I wanted to see you."

Another shiver of pleasure. "You did?"

"Now that construction is underway, I thought we could discuss furniture."

"Oh." Of course Quinn would want to talk to her about the project. It was dumb of her to think otherwise. Even after that maybe almost kiss on her porch.

"I mean, I wanted to see you. I just also had a reason."

Did Quinn mean that or did she see the disappointment on Amanda's face and want to soften the blow? She had no way of knowing, which irked her. Why was this so complicated? "What about furniture?"

"You mentioned wanting to do antique tables and chairs."

"Do you think that won't work?"

"Oh, no. I think it's a fantastic idea. I wanted to know if you'd already been scouting them or were starting from scratch."

The few tables she'd had in the bakery were wrought iron. Cute, but not the most comfortable. She planned to set them up outside after the renovation. They'd only be usable a few months of the year, but better than having them go to waste. "I haven't started yet. Is that a problem?"

Quinn smiled. "I don't think so. I asked because there's this amazing antique show and flea market near Cooperstown. I thought maybe we could go together, make a day of it?"

Was this a date? Or the sort of thing architects did with their clients? "That sounds like fun. When is it?"

"This weekend. I thought, with the bakery closed, there might be a chance you were free."

It really did seem like a date. Didn't it? "I have one wedding cake Friday. I'm co-opting a kitchen in Trumansburg. I could go Saturday or Sunday."

"I think Saturday should be the better day, weather-wise. And the offerings are better the first day. How about I pick you up at nine? There's a great brewery and barbecue joint, if you're into that sort of thing."

She'd pretty much be into anything that involved Quinn, but didn't want to seem too eager. "Sounds good."

Quinn pulled into the grass lot at the edge of the fair, put her car in park, and cut the engine. "Ready?"

Amanda nodded eagerly. "I am."

It was hard to say which had her stomach doing nervous flips—Amanda's genuine excitement about hunting for old chairs or being on this pseudo-date with Amanda in the first place. Amanda had this effervescent personality, but it had substance underneath. She'd come to appreciate how rare that was. "We should be able to fit eight in the back and another four on the roof if you don't mind them being tied down for the ride home."

"If I find a dozen chairs today, you can tie me to the roof for the ride home." Her emphasis on the "me" made Quinn laugh.

"Fortunately, you take up less room in the passenger seat, so you're safe."

Amanda smirked. "Where's your sense of adventure?"

A harmless question, but it hit home as they wandered into town. Booths lined the main street, mostly crafts and food vendors. "All the serious stuff is in the field up ahead."

"Field?"

They rounded a small bend in the road and the main area spread out to their left, the size of three or four football fields. "I told you it was big."

"Yeah, but this." Amanda gestured in front of her, arms wide. "This is intense. How are we supposed to make our way through it all?"

"We aren't. We're going to be selective."

Amanda's brows furrowed in a way she found unreasonably charming. "But how do you even know where to start?"

"Easy. You come with someone who knows what they're doing." She grabbed Amanda's hand. Only after doing so did she realize what an intimate gesture it was. But dropping it would only draw more attention or, worse, give Amanda the impression she didn't want to hold her hand. She made a point of giving it a gentle tug as she steered them into the crowd. There, that made it seem logistical more than romantic.

They meandered the aisles, scoping out chairs, but pausing for vintage signs, antique milk jugs, and even a chicken coop. Amanda's commentary was smart with a hint of self-deprecating. If Quinn hadn't been smitten before, she was now.

Amanda found two pairs of chairs, letting Quinn haggle on the second set. She got the price down by twenty dollars, which didn't seem like much but thrilled Amanda. "That's it. I'm only going to flea markets and antique shows with you."

Sounded good to her. "I accept this right and responsibility."

After a couple of hours, the press of people and lack of shade started to take a toll, at least on her. She imagined Amanda felt the same. "Lunch break?"

"That sounds fantastic."

"The barbecue place is out of this world, but if that's not your thing, there are lots of other options."

"Oh, no." Amanda shook her head. "You put barbecue in my head and I've been thinking about it all week."

"It's that way."

The line was long but moved quickly. Before long, they sat side by side at a picnic table with a family of four.

"You're going to let me try that, right?" Amanda gestured to the pulled pork sandwich in front of Quinn.

"Assuming you're going to return the favor with the brisket."

"Want to go halvsies?"

Quinn chuckled, amused by the phrasing as much as the idea. "Sure."

"Don't feel like you have to say yes," Amanda said.

"Oh, I want to. I just don't ever assume people want to share. And my ex-wife is a vegetarian."

Amanda laughed. "I have kids. I've been sharing my plate for twenty years."

"Right." She cut her sandwich in half and offered it to Amanda. Amanda did the same. They ate leisurely, then resumed the hunt. By midafternoon, they'd hit their goal of twelve chairs. They circled back through to collect them and got them loaded.

After everything was secured, Amanda stepped back and planted her hands on her hips. "You've done this before, haven't you?"

"Once or twice." It was the sort of thing she and Lesedi used to do together. She hadn't realized how long it had been or how much she'd missed it. "I'm also good at spatial relations."

On the trek home, conversation lulled, but in a good way. It left Quinn feeling like they'd known each other longer, and spent far more time together, than they had. At Amanda's, they unloaded the chairs into the garage, then stood for a moment admiring them. Eventually, Amanda turned her way. "I can't thank you enough."

"It was my pleasure, really."

"I feel bad you didn't find anything for yourself, especially if it was so I could have all the room in your car."

She loved that Amanda would think about that, even if there was no need. "My apartment is too full already. So, if anything, you saved me from being a fire hazard."

Amanda's face took on a shadow of worry. "Were you sad to give up your house when you got divorced?"

Oh. That. "I was. It had great architecture. And, you know, fifteen years of memories."

Amanda touched her arm. "I'm sorry."

The last thing she wanted was to ruin the day with bad memories. "Thank you. It's fine, though. I wasn't crazy about the neighborhood. Full of Cornell professors."

Amanda snickered. "They're the worst, aren't they?"

Right. Because her ex was a Cornell professor, too. "They are."

She'd expected the day to end there, but suddenly she didn't want to leave. Too bad they were at Amanda's and not her place.

"Would you like to come in for a glass of wine?"

Well, that was easy. "Are you offering because you feel like you should?"

Amanda looked at the ground and then right into her eyes. "No."

"Then I'd love to."

Amanda poured glasses of Riesling and they sat on her porch. The perfect end to a pretty perfect day, not to mention the kind of thing she could imagine doing again and again. When their glasses were drained, Amanda offered to pour a second.

"I shouldn't, but thank you." Even if she wanted to.

Amanda sighed. "I probably shouldn't either. I promised my son dinner when he got home from work."

Quinn cringed inwardly. "You shouldn't have let me keep you."

She lifted a shoulder. "Maybe I liked being kept."

The comment wasn't suggestive, at least not really. That didn't stop Quinn's body from responding like it was. She cleared her throat and hoped her face didn't give away her thoughts. Amanda took her glass, leaving nothing to clear or help bring inside. Still, she hesitated. "Thank you for today. I had a really nice time."

"I did, too."

Before her brain could convince her it was a bad idea, she leaned in and brushed her mouth over Amanda's. She had a fraction of a second of thinking how perfect Amanda felt before her doubts came roaring to life. She pulled back. "I'm sorry. I meant to—I mean, I was trying to—"

Amanda didn't seem bothered. Maybe a little surprised, but in a good way. "Did you not mean to or not want to?"

If Amanda was interested in the difference, it couldn't be all bad. "Didn't mean to."

"So, you wanted to?"

Quinn blew out a breath. "I think I've wanted to since the day we first met to talk about the bakery."

Amanda nodded slowly. "I see."

"But we're working together and the last thing I want is to blur professional lines or make you uncomfortable or—"

Amanda didn't let her finish. She pressed her lips to Quinn's in the most perfect way. She didn't linger, but there was nothing accidental about it. "Do you want to go out with me?"

Quinn swallowed. "I do."

"And kiss me again?"

"I do. Very much."

Amanda tipped her head slightly. "Then you should ask me. I promise I'll say yes."

This playful back and forth of Amanda taking the lead but not turned her on in ways she couldn't quite put into words. She cleared her throat. "Amanda?"

"Yes?"

"Would you have dinner with me tomorrow night?"

Amanda's head moved back and forth. "No."

She felt her shoulders drop.

"But only because I have plans with my kids. Any other day this week would be perfect."

"You had me worried there for a second."

Amanda's brow lifted. "Seriously?"

She shrugged. "You could change your mind."

"Quinn?"

She so loved the way Amanda said her name. "Yes?"

"I won't change my mind."

Quinn nodded. "I'll remember that."

"Good."

Wanting to quit while she was ahead, she reluctantly wished Amanda a good night. Amanda seemed sorry to see her leave. It gave her an almost giddy feeling as she drove home. Plus she had a date, one she made with a woman she wanted to go out with. More than her attraction to Amanda, it made her feel like she was back in the driver's seat of her life.

She pulled into her usual parking spot but sat in her car for a long minute. It was a good feeling, this being in charge. It struck her, though. She'd not even realized how far away from it she'd let herself get.

Chapter Twelve

Erin topped off her wine glass, then handed Amanda the bottle. "So, how's operation Mel Be Gone? Is she still sniffing around your feet like a puppy?"

Amanda let out a snort of laughter, then coughed to cover it up. "I think the stern talk worked. She hasn't texted me in over a week."

Julia took the bottle after Amanda. "Good. I'm still sorry you had to do that, though."

Jack raised a shoulder. "I don't know. I'd have taken immense satisfaction in telling her off."

"Hear, hear." Erin clinked her glass to his.

Julia shook her head. "It's satisfying in principle, but it really sucks in the moment."

She offered Julia a sympathetic smile. She'd had a completely different sort of run-in with her ex a few months prior, but the theme of having to put her foot down was the same. And she was a fellow conflict avoider, so there was that, too. "Thank you."

Erin sighed. "Fair, fair. Plus you had to give up the benefits. And knowing you, it's going to take some cosmic shift before you get laid again."

"Ouch." Jack leaned over and smacked her arm. "Low blow."

"I'm saying she's stubborn. She's a total catch. That hasn't changed."

He lifted both hands. "I rescind. That's totally true."

Amanda made a point at glaring at both of them. "I'll have you know I have a date this week. And we've already kissed."

She had the satisfaction of watching her friends gasp, slap the table, and otherwise flip out. She couldn't make out what each person said, exactly, but the sentiments were clear. She tucked her tongue in her cheek and waited for the commotion to die down. This was more fun than confessing the whole Mel thing.

"Well?" Jack said, when everyone else had quieted.

"It's Quinn, my architect."

"I knew it." Erin's voice was full of vindication.

"Wait, wait, wait. What did I miss?" Jack asked.

"She hired a hot architect for the bakery and they've been dancing around each other for weeks," Erin said matter-of-factly. "Who finally made the move? Her or you?"

She closed her eyes for a second, reliving the kiss on the front porch. "She did, but then backed off. So I told her not to."

Jack made a face. "Not to make a move or not to back off?"

"Not to back off. She was worried because we're working together."

A chorus of "oh" surrounded her.

"And maybe that should have given me pause, or maybe it would have a couple of months ago, but I figured what the hell. I'm too cautious most of the time." If any good came of the Mel fiasco, it was that.

"Hallelujah." Erin threw both hands in the air.

Amanda smiled ruefully. She'd never been a wild child, but she had let herself grow downright timid through the years, at least when it came to relationships. "I think Mel helped me realize how much I'd been neglecting that part of myself."

"Are you going to slut it up?" Julia asked.

She laughed. That was how Julia described her approach to dating after her divorce. Before falling head over heels for Taylor. "Let's not get carried away."

"Can we go back for a second?" Jack raised his hand. "Why don't I know anything about Quinn?"

"Because you've been eyeballs deep in daddy mode," Erin said.

Julia reached over and squeezed his arm. "Which we love and respect, by the way."

Erin's eyes got big. "Yes. So much love. I didn't mean it in a bad way, I swear."

Jack sent her an air kiss. "I know."

Erin returned the gesture. "Before we dive into Quinnland, can I just say something?" She didn't wait before continuing. "I'm not giving up my loathing of Mel anytime soon, but I'm willing to give her a couple of points for her role in waking up your inner sex goddess."

"Yeah." Jack nodded. "That."

She didn't have hard feelings toward Mel at this point. Well, no really hard feelings. And no matter how ill-advised sleeping with her had been, it had reminded her there was more to life than work and parenting and being a responsible adult.

"You're thinking about being a sex goddess, aren't you?" Erin lifted her chin. "I can tell."

She laughed and shook her head. "I'm not sure sex goddess is ever going to be part of my identity, but I'll embrace the spirit of it. Maybe I can be like Stella and get my groove back."

"Oh, I like that," Julia said.

"A very reasonable compromise." Erin lifted her glass. "To Amanda getting her groove back."

Glasses clinked and a moment of quiet followed. Seconds ticked by. Julia had a wistful smile and Erin a satisfied smirk. She glanced at Jack, who regarded her with impatience. "Now can someone please fill me in on Quinn?"

Amanda laughed. She had a motley group of friends, but she loved them. "Well, she's my architect."

She spent the rest of dinner fielding questions about how much time they'd spent together, why she'd been keeping it to herself, and how many dates it would take before they slept together. After clearing the dishes, she showed off her new chairs and explained how they came to be in her garage. By the time she cut slices of chocolate tart, she couldn't help but wonder if Quinn's ears were ringing. And although she wasn't sure whether she really wanted to know the answer, she wondered if Quinn had spent half as much time thinking and talking about her.

❖

Quinn slept in, leaving her just enough time to do laundry and go for a paddle before Sunday afternoon dinner at her sister's. Well, paddle and a shower. Showing up in outdoor gear opened the door to her sisters teasing her about being that sort of lesbian. When she rolled into Alana's just after one, she was the last to arrive, but she looked more than presentable.

She let herself in without bothering to knock and headed straight for the kitchen. Kiera and Alana sat at the table with cups of coffee. "Greetings, siblings. Happy Sunday."

"The prodigal sister returns," Kiera said.

Quinn rolled her eyes. "I saw you like three days ago."

Kiera made a pouting face. "I figured you were avoiding me."

"I don't need to now that you aren't trying to set me up at every turn."

Kiera sniffed and Alana snickered.

Quinn shrugged. "Where is everyone?"

"Gary and Xinxin are out back with Grace. Jacob and Adam are in the basement."

With their parents on vacation in Greece, that was the whole clan.

"You look like you're considering your options. Too good to hang with your sisters these days?"

She laughed, knowing the jab didn't have any malice. Honestly, one of her favorite things about her family was that it didn't fall into the husbands club and wives club so many extended families did. Sure, it had as much to do with the fact that two of the three of them were queer and one had married someone from another country, but still. "Maybe I'm trying to figure out who will harass me the least."

Kiera let out a sarcastic "ha, ha," but Alana laughed for real.

"Hang with us. I promise I won't let Kiera be mean."

"I'm not mean." Kiera's tone was defiant.

She helped herself to a cup of coffee. "You're not. Just nosy. And maybe bossy."

Kiera scowled. "Am not."

Quinn slung an arm around her shoulders before joining them at the table. "Are too."

"It's a good thing I love you," Kiera said.

"And I you."

"Aw." Alana tipped her head to the side. "I love it when you two have a moment."

She was teasing but also not. She'd spent a solid two decades playing the peacekeeper between Quinn and Kiera. Not that they fought constantly, but the combination of being only a year apart and having completely opposite personalities had made for some serious bickering. They were mostly past that now. Mostly.

Kiera made a show of batting her eyelashes. "Since we love each other so much, do you want to be my plus-one at a Girl Scout fundraiser Thursday? Xinxin has a work thing."

"I can't. I have a date."

Kiera's shoulders dropped and she made a face. "If you don't want to, just say so. You don't need to lie."

"Kiera." Alana gave her a stern look.

"What? She gave me the lecture about fixing her up last week. She doesn't get to play the no more dates card, then pretend she has one."

"Maybe she's not pretending," Alana said.

Quinn folded her arms. "Yeah, maybe I'm not pretending."

Kiera raised a brow, completely incredulous. Alana looked from her to Quinn and wrinkled her nose. "Are you pretending?"

"I am not." It came out a little smug, but it wasn't like her sisters would take it personally.

"Well?" It was Kiera's turn to fold her arms.

"Well what?" Playing dumb was one of Kiera's top pet peeves and absolutely the reason she did it.

"What are we talking about?" Adam and Jacob filed into the kitchen and made a beeline for the refrigerator.

"Aunt Quinn's love life."

Jacob made a face. "Y'all talk about that stuff?"

"Not when I can help it." Quinn rolled her eyes. "What are you guys up to?"

"Not talking about our love lives, that's for sure." Adam pulled out two cheese sticks and handed one to his brother. "When's dinner?"

Alana shook her head. "Half an hour."

"Cool." Adam plopped himself on one of the stools at the island.

Jacob devoured his cheese stick in two bites. After throwing the wrapper in the trash, he lifted his chin in Quinn's direction. "So? Hot date?"

For some reason, having her nephews join the conversation made her more comfortable rather than less. Maybe because their presence would keep things PG. Which was ironic since they were probably the most sexually active ones in the room. "As a matter of fact, yes."

"All right." Kiera shot her a look of exasperation. "Who is she?"

"Her name is Amanda and she's a client."

"She's a client?" Kiera's voice pitched high.

Quinn flinched involuntarily. She'd made a stink about professional boundaries a few months prior when Kiera had tried to get her to ask one of her clients out. "This is different."

"How so?" Alana posed the question before Kiera could say anything else, her tone upbeat and curious.

"We've spent time together, become friends. I sort of kissed her by accident."

Kiera shook her head. "Only you."

"I did it without thinking."

Alana shrugged. "I think it's cute you got caught up in the moment. And I'm proud of you for going for it."

It might expose her to merciless teasing, but she loved her sisters and they'd been her confidantes and her champions through the sad saga of her divorce. "Going for it might be a bit generous. I mean, full disclosure, I apologized."

Kiera burst into laughter. Alana bit her lip, but only for a second before she joined in.

"Do chicks like that?" Jacob asked.

She'd forgotten they were part of the conversation. "Um, I think they appreciate sincerity."

"And you were sincerely sorry?" Poor Jacob seemed confused.

"Well, we'd spent the day together as friends, so I think it was unexpected. And I was worried I'd crossed a line."

Alana pointed at both boys. "That's a good lesson. You should only kiss a girl if you're sure she wants you to."

"But Aunt Quinn just said—"

Quinn lifted a hand. "That's why I apologized."

"And then what happened?" Adam, for some reason, seemed fascinated by the whole thing.

She closed her eyes for a second. "She asked if I wanted to kiss her."

"What did you say?" Adam asked.

Quinn shrugged. "I told her the truth."

"And?"

She hadn't paused for dramatic effect, but that's sort of what it felt like. "And then she kissed me."

"Wow." Adam nodded slowly. The level of his interest made her wonder if perhaps he was nursing a crush and strategizing what to do with it.

"I'm not sure it's the smoothest move." And she was probably the last person who should be giving dating advice at this point.

Kiera raised a shoulder. "Hapless and charming seems to work for you when you want it to."

She shook her head. "How do you manage to tease and compliment me at the same time?"

Kiera smirked. "It's a gift."

The back door opened and Grace came tearing in. Xinxin and Gary followed. The timer on the stove beeped and Alana got up to pull the ham and scalloped potatoes from the oven. In the bustle of getting hands washed and the table set, her pending date faded into the background. Which was fine by her. But when they all sat down at the table, Kiera snagged the seat next to her and leaned in. Quinn braced herself for, well, something.

"I'm happy for you, and I hope it works out."

"But?"

"But nothing."

Quinn regarded her with suspicion. "No, really. What's the catch? The fact that you're not the one who set me up?"

Kiera let out an exasperated sigh. "Stop. I'm not a jerk. No catch."

"I wasn't accusing you of being a jerk. I mostly appreciate that you don't let me off the hook."

"Aw, that's like the nicest thing you've ever said to me."

It was her turn to say, "Stop."

"Okay, fine. You've said nicer things. But I mean it. I'm happy you're interested in someone. And I'm glad you're doing it on your terms."

And this was why she loved her family. They could be the biggest pains known to man, but when push came to shove, they had her best interests at heart. And maybe even more importantly, they had her back. "Thanks."

"But don't think for one second you're going to keep the details to yourself."

Quinn laughed. "Noted."

Chapter Thirteen

Amanda sat at her vanity, taking extra care with her makeup. It had more to do with taking pleasure in the ritual than being nervous about her appearance. Quinn already knew what she looked like, after all. And had seen her looking less than her best.

No, tonight was about slowing down and remembering all the fun aspects of going on a date with someone. Just the right amount of anticipation without the worry of whether or not they'd hit it off. Not having to worry if it was ill-advised was nice too. And since she was pretty sure Quinn wasn't a first date sex sort of person, it was kind of a relief to have that off the table, at least for now. Maybe, though, maybe there would be a kiss. Or kisses, plural. She'd been thinking quite a lot about what it would be like to kiss Quinn again. Kiss her in earnest.

Her doorbell rang at seven on the dot, making her wonder if it was a fluke or if Quinn had arrived early but waited. Either prospect had a certain charm. She grabbed her purse and opened the door, only to find Quinn clutching a bouquet of irises. She couldn't suppress the girly sigh that escaped. "Hi."

"Hi." Quinn smiled. "Roses seemed presumptuous for some reason. But I didn't want to come empty-handed."

Amanda raised a brow. "A floral compromise?"

Quinn chuckled. "Yes, exactly."

The little dance of forward and back, bold and timid, made her like Quinn even more. "They're beautiful."

Quinn handed over the bouquet. "I'm glad you think so."

"Give me a second to put them in water."

Quinn followed her to the kitchen. "How are your kids enjoying summer?"

"Daniella is a counselor at a music camp up in Rochester and Cal is working at Rustic Refined so he doesn't have to get a job on campus first semester. They're both lamenting how much adulting it all is."

"Sounds rough."

Amanda laughed. "You and your ex don't have kids, right?"

"Correct. We decided to do the doting aunt thing. Or at least I did. She was never one for kids."

Something in the phrase struck her. "Did you want them?"

Quinn considered for a moment, like she was choosing her words carefully. "I thought I did. Lesedi, that's my ex, wasn't completely opposed. She would have considered them, for me."

"Sounds like a hard position to be in." What would she have done if Mel hadn't wanted kids?

"It was hard for both of us. She didn't want to be the reason I gave up that dream."

"So what happened?"

Quinn shrugged. "The more I thought about driving that decision, the less appealing it became. Lesedi would have done her part, but I don't know. I think I would have felt guilty every time it got hard."

The answer seemed genuine and not tinged with regret. "I respect that. A lot, actually. I think when lesbians started getting married, the assumption of kids came with it. Not quite as bad as straight couples, but kind of."

Quinn's hands came up like she was having an aha moment. "You're so right. I'd never thought of it that way."

"I blame the patriarchy."

"Damned patriarchy."

Amanda moved the vase of flowers from the sink to the island. "I didn't mean to take us on such a personal tangent."

"Yeah. At least let a woman buy you dinner first."

Amanda smiled. "Maybe you should let me buy you dinner in exchange for the third degree."

"Nope." Quinn shook her head. "You've already cooked me dinner. And since I can say with some certainty I'll never cook you dinner, you have to let me compensate."

The comment seemed to have nothing to do with the likelihood of another date and everything to do with Quinn's skills in the kitchen. "You don't cook?"

Quinn cleared her throat. "Maybe we could eat before we have this conversation."

"All right. I'm not going to forget, though." She wanted to know whether Quinn didn't like to cook or if she couldn't. An important distinction in her book, even if neither was technically a dealbreaker.

"Sure, sure. Not like meetings."

The comment, delivered with a straight face, took a second to register. Teasing more than a jab. Another important distinction. "I'm not going to live that down, am I?"

She expected Quinn to let her off the hook, perhaps with a friendly shrug and a smile. Instead, she responded with, "Not any time soon."

Amanda decided to try a little teasing of her own. "I'm good at making things up to people, though."

Okay, maybe not the best double entendre, but she was trying. And Quinn seemed to like it. "I'll keep that in mind."

Since they were so close to Trumansburg, Quinn settled on Fig for dinner. Hell, even without starting in Trumansburg, it was one of her go-to spots for a date. And it would be nice to share a meal there with someone she genuinely wanted to spend time with.

When they stepped inside, Amanda glanced over at the bar and, for the briefest of moments, paused. Quinn flashed back to seeing her there. She'd been at the bar alone and hadn't stayed long. Had she been stood up that night? By whom? Not that it was any of her business, but she had a pang of regret for possibly stirring it up. "You okay?"

Amanda's face went from something resembling irritation to realization she'd been caught to bright smile in about half a second. "Of course."

Quinn respected her ability to do so but wished there wasn't a need. Whether it had to do with wishing away the bad memory or wishing Amanda was more relaxed with her, she couldn't be sure. Either way, it wasn't her place to pry. At least not yet. "All right."

She gave her name to the hostess and they were seated. Fortunately, it wasn't the same table she'd shared with…with? Lisa. It had to be a bad sign she couldn't even remember all their names at this point.

They settled on a bottle of wine and a couple of plates to share. As always, the service was efficient and unobtrusive. The food—an arugula salad with strawberries and bleu cheese, a zucchini and pine nut flatbread, and gnocchi with garlic scape pesto—was outstanding. Drew Davis, the chef, made a round of the dining room and stopped by their table. It was the kind of personal touch she appreciated.

It all paled in comparison to the conversation, though. Amanda was smart and funny and almost ridiculously easy to talk to. She didn't expect any different based on her time with Amanda thus far, but she'd developed such a reticence about dating, she half expected things to turn awkward before dessert.

They didn't, and although Amanda resisted at first, Quinn talked her into sharing dessert. "I know you're a snob when it comes to dessert, so thank you for making an exception."

"I am, but the pastry chef here never disappoints."

"Ah, so you were resisting on principle." It felt like perhaps they were talking about more than dessert.

"Maybe."

"I respect that." She did, too. "But I'd be lying if I said I wasn't glad you can be persuaded sometimes."

Amanda's smile was slow. "Sometimes."

On the walk from the restaurant to her car, she gave in to the urge to take Amanda's hand. Not too forward. Familiar. And it was nice to have the urge again. Just like the urge to kiss her.

From the moment she opened the passenger door for Amanda to the moment she pulled into Amanda's driveway, all Quinn could think about was kissing her. Not whether or not she wanted to. No, the want was coming in pretty loud and clear. The problem was, for as many dates as she'd been on in the last year, she was rusty at this part. She wasn't the most take-charge person to begin with. Not that she couldn't take charge when the moment called for it. She just preferred being cautious to screwing up.

But sometimes being too cautious was the screw-up.

"I had a nice time." Amanda tucked a piece of hair behind her ear.

"I did, too." Quinn stood there, feeling as nervous as a teenager and hoping to God it wasn't evident on her face.

"Does this mean I get to make you dinner again?"

The tiny gift of encouragement did wonders to calm Quinn's racing mind. Her pulse was another matter, but that wasn't necessarily a bad thing. "I don't think I'll ever say no to a meal with you. You cooking it would be an extra layer of awesome."

Extra layer of awesome? Where the hell did that come from?

Amanda smirked slightly but didn't seem put off by the cheesiness of the line. "Something tells me you're easy to impress."

"Nah. I just know what I like." Not the best line, but it made up for "extra layer of awesome." At least a little.

"Good to know." She nodded. "So…" She trailed off but didn't make any move to go inside or even unlock the door. Funny how so much could be conveyed with so little sometimes. It provided the exact right amount of encouragement.

She looked from Amanda's eyes, down to her mouth, and back. Her own version of saying so much with so little. The smirk vanished and Amanda's lips parted slightly. If the "so" was encouragement, that definitely counted as invitation.

Quinn leaned in, pausing just long enough to give Amanda an out if she wanted it. Instead of backing away, she mirrored the gesture, making the distance between them even smaller. Barely an inch separated their mouths now. The smell of Amanda's perfume invaded her senses and addled her brain. But even through the haze, the wanting remained. So different from the haphazard brush of lips the last time.

It would be silly to say she'd forgotten what it felt like, but in a way she had. To be reminded, to remember, standing in the porch light with this beautiful and interesting woman, felt a bit like magic.

She pressed her lips to Amanda's. Softly at first, gently. She wanted to give herself a moment to acclimate as much as she wanted to give that to Amanda. But then Amanda sighed, a sound so soft and so feminine, it sent Quinn's already racing pulse skittering. And she was done.

She brought a hand to Amanda's neck, let her fingers slide into Amanda's hair. It was thick and soft and made her want to wrap herself up in it. Amanda grasped Quinn's arm, her grip stronger than Quinn would have guessed. The idea of Amanda being stronger than she looked made her smile.

She slid her other hand to the small of Amanda's back and pulled her closer. Not that there was much space left between them. But the shift brought their entire bodies together. Amanda's breasts pressing into her made her entire body hum. For someone on the fence about going in for a kiss, she was awfully close to asking for a whole lot more. The realization pierced through the haze in her mind and made her pull back.

Amanda's eyes fluttered open. "I think we should do that again."

Quinn merely nodded. The kiss was more purposeful this time, less of a question. And hotter. The slide of Amanda's tongue against hers cranked up the heat factor tenfold.

It went on and on, making Quinn think vaguely she could—would—happily kiss Amanda for hours. With or without something more. Not that she wasn't already thinking about more. When they finally stopped, she felt lightheaded and out of breath. She hoped it wasn't just her. Amanda didn't let go of her arm—definitely a good sign. She tried to fill her lungs with oxygen, to steady herself. "Wow."

Amanda smiled. "Yeah."

"I really hope we can do this again."

Amanda's eyes, already dark with desire, danced with humor. "Dinner or making out on my front porch?"

"Both?"

"The best answer."

"Name the day."

"Pretty much any day but Saturday." She shrugged. "Wedding cakes."

"Right, right." In her book, the sooner she got to see Amanda again, the better. "How's Tuesday? We could do early dinner and maybe a movie?"

"Perfect."

It was her place to leave at this point, but difficult to tear herself away. "I'll be looking forward to it."

"Same." Amanda seemed like she might be on the verge of inviting her in.

Quinn cleared her throat. If Amanda did, she wouldn't be able to refuse. And as much as she might want it, first date sex was not even remotely her style. "Okay. So, good night."

She was pretty sure her delivery gave away where her thoughts had been, but that was okay.

Amanda fished keys out of her purse and unlocked her door. "Good night."

Quinn started toward her car. At the sidewalk, she turned. Just like the first night she'd been there, Amanda hovered in the doorway and offered a parting wave. Quinn returned it and continued on her way, happy Tuesday wasn't all that far away.

Chapter Fourteen

"You okay?"

Quinn jumped. Arti hovered in her doorway. "Never better. What's up?"

Arti folded her arms. "I was standing there for like five minutes and not only did you not notice me, you didn't even move."

She chuckled. "Daydreaming. You caught me."

"Something good I hope."

"Yes, but not work related." She didn't want to be asked what brilliance she'd come up with when the entirety of her thoughts involved kissing Amanda.

Arti shifted, lifting both hands defensively. "Hey, I'm not judging. Just checking on you."

When she and Lesedi broke up, Arti was beyond understanding of Quinn's sad and distracted state. She hadn't dropped the ball on anything, but also hadn't brought her A-game for months. She'd promised herself she wouldn't ever let that happen again. "All good. Promise."

"Things with Amanda?"

"Yeah." She'd talked with Arti about seeing Amanda before their first official date. It was a gray area, working with clients on contract. But since the design work was complete and the remaining work consultative, Arti agreed it wouldn't be a conflict of interest. Well, agreed might be an understatement. There might have been a bit of cheering over Quinn finally wanting to go on a date.

Arti came the rest of the way into her office and plopped in the chair across from her. "Do I get to ask about it?"

The questions made Quinn oddly self-conscious. She and Arti were friends, for sure, but they still worked together. "There's not much to tell, at least not yet. We went out once and have plans to go out again."

"But you've already had dinner at her house. And you went antiquing."

She flipped her hand back and forth. "Yes, but dinner was more apology than date. She felt bad about forgetting our appointment."

Arti shook her head. "She might have felt bad, but women don't invite you over for dinner if they don't like you. And they certainly don't go antiquing."

She hadn't allowed herself to believe it at the time, but it didn't seem so far-fetched now. "Either way, it set the stage for the real date so I'm not about to complain."

"Of course, of course. But you still haven't told me about the date itself."

When push came to shove, Arti proved an easier audience than her sisters. Probably better to practice talking about it before swimming with the sharks.

"What's wrong? I thought you said it was all good?"

Quinn smiled. "Sorry. I was thinking about the third degree I'm going to get from Kiera about this."

Arti, who knew both of Quinn's sisters, laughed. "See? I'm easy."

"Easy is relative, my friend. All relative."

Arti waited a beat, then said, "Easy but not letting you off the hook."

If she asked for privacy, or hinted she genuinely didn't want to talk about it, Arti would drop it without a second thought or another word. Somehow, that made it easier to confide. "I like her. Like, a lot. And I feel stupid because we've only gone on one date, but I swear there's more chemistry with her than with all the women I've been fixed up with, combined."

Arti offered a shrug and a knowing smile. "That's the thing with chemistry."

She seemed to mean it, rather than put it out there like so many throwaway phrases about the slings and arrows of dating. "What? What is the thing, exactly?"

"It's a beast unto itself. There's compatibility, how things look on paper. Don't get me wrong, those things are important. But either there's spark or there isn't. Everything else in the universe be damned."

Quinn didn't find that reassuring. Quite the opposite, actually. She wanted there to be a certain science to it, a predictability. At the very least, she wanted some sort of insurance policy she wouldn't finally screw up the courage to put herself out there, only to fall in love with someone she had absolutely nothing in common with.

"You don't agree?"

"I don't disagree." Her date with Lisa had sort of proved it—being perfectly compatible on paper didn't count for anything in the romance department.

"But? And don't say there isn't one. I can see your wheels turning."

"It all feels a little, I don't know"—she searched for the right word—"haphazard."

Arti grinned. "That's what makes it so magical."

Quinn rolled her eyes. "Says the woman who's been happily married for a dozen years."

Arti let out a sigh and drummed her fingers on the arm of the chair. "Can I tell you something?"

A knot formed below her ribs. If Arti's marriage was falling apart, she was seriously going to lose faith in love. "Oh, no. Is something wrong?"

"No. The opposite. But it's not something everyone takes well."

For the life of her, she had no idea where Arti was going. "Okay."

"About four years ago, Marguerite and I decided to open our marriage."

"You did?" Her voice squeaked with surprise and she wanted to kick herself. "Sorry. I mean, you did?"

Rather than looking offended, Arti laughed. "We did. We'd fallen into a rut and, as much as I didn't want to talk about it, we did. And we decided we wanted to stay together but didn't want to give up that excitement."

She could appreciate that. "I give you credit for not ignoring that or, you know, having an affair."

Arti offered a sympathetic smile. "Yeah."

"So, you see other people?"

"Sort of. We did a lot of reading because we're nerds."

"Of course you did." It was so Arti and completely endearing. And it wasn't like she'd never heard of polyamory. She just didn't know anyone personally who did it. Correction: she didn't think she knew anyone who did it.

"Yeah, so anyway. We liked what we read and we gave it a try and it's been awesome. A lot of work, and a whole lot of talking. But awesome."

She loved that they were having a moment, but the fact that it needed to be a moment made her sad. "I'm happy for you. And sorry it's not something you feel you can be open about."

Arti waved her off. "Don't apologize. It's not very different from you not wanting to talk about your love life."

Quinn laughed. "Touché."

"Yeah, and don't think I didn't notice how you changed the subject. I still want your scoop."

Unlike with her sisters, she really hadn't been trying to change the subject. "This is way more interesting than anything I have going on."

"You know, we should grab a drink sometime."

It was a line they hadn't crossed. Not the having a drink together part, but doing so as friends, with the clear intention of sharing and bonding. "I'd like that."

Arti stood. "How about after your next date? Then hopefully we'll both have something juicy to dish."

She smiled. "Deal."

"In the meantime, don't overthink it. If there's a spark, enjoy it."

Was it really that simple? "I'll keep that in mind."

Arti turned to leave. She made it almost to the door before Quinn called her back. "Yeah?"

"You came in here for something and I don't think we ever got to it." The least she could do after being caught daydreaming was take care of whatever Arti wanted in the first place.

"Nah. I saw you staring into space and wanted to give you a hard time."

Quinn chuckled. "I appreciate your honesty."

"That's what friends are for, right?"

She wasn't sure how she'd gotten so lucky in the coworker department. Or the friend department, for that matter. "Agreed."

Amanda drummed her fingers on the table. She didn't need their permission, but she also didn't like keeping secrets from her kids. Unlike Mel, this didn't have the weird, terrible idea factor. Also unlike her fling with Mel, things with Quinn seemed like maybe they had the chance to go somewhere. If they did, she didn't want Cal and Daniella feeling blindsided.

"I want to talk to you two about something."

Daniella frowned. "What's wrong?"

Cal looked at her with confusion. "How do you know something's wrong?"

Poor Daniella. She'd inherited her mother's propensity to worry. "Nothing is wrong."

Cal seemed relieved, but Daniella wasn't so readily appeased. "Okay. What is it, then?"

She took a deep breath. "I want to know how you'd feel if I was seeing someone."

Daniella continued to frown. "Like, a girlfriend?"

"Well, she's not going to get a boyfriend. Wait." Cal turned to Amanda. "Do you want a boyfriend? Or have one? Because that would be fine."

Amanda couldn't help but chuckle. She'd raised her kids to be accepting of everyone. It was endearing to see the principle applied to her own preferences. "No boyfriend. Promise."

"But a girlfriend." Daniella looked more suspicious than worried.

"Maybe. I wouldn't use that word yet, but I wanted to see how you'd feel about it."

"You dated when we were younger, after the divorce," Cal said.

It should make her feel better that her kids talked about the divorce so casually, but even now, it never failed to give a pang of regret. "Yes, but it was years ago, and nothing ever serious."

"Is this serious?" Daniella asked.

Why did this conversation make her more uncomfortable than the sex talk? "Not yet."

"But it might be." Daniella nodded knowingly. "Are you sleeping together?"

"Daniella." Cal looked at his sister in horror.

She glared at him. "Don't be a prude."

"I'm…" he hesitated, like the word didn't compute, then settled on, "not."

"You are being such a cis straight guy right now. Women of all ages and orientations have sexual desire and agency, Cal." Even if Daniella didn't like the idea, she couldn't keep her feminist sensibilities from kicking in. It made Amanda smile.

Cal looked at Daniella as though she was speaking a language other than English. "What?"

He was more open-minded than the average eighteen-year-old boy, but even he had his limits. "Your sister is saying it's cool for me to have a girlfriend, or a boyfriend should I decide I wanted to lean that way."

"Exactly." Daniella's tone was smug.

Cal lifted his chin. "Or gender non-conforming friend should she want to date someone who exists outside the binary."

Amanda bit her lip. Only her kids would turn the issue of her dating into a competition of who could be more progressive. "Does this mean you're both comfortable with it?"

"When do we get to meet her?" Daniella asked instead of answering.

Cal frowned again. "Wait. Is there someone specific? Not just a hypothetical?"

Daniella sighed. "She said it wasn't serious yet. That means there's someone she might be getting serious with. Keep up."

"Right. So, yeah, when do we get to meet her?" He shot Daniella a look. "Or them."

She blew out a breath. Most days, she loved that her kids had the confidence and the intellect to go a mile a minute. Today, it left her dizzy. "We've only been on one date, so probably not for a bit."

"But you like her, right? You wouldn't be having this conversation with us if you didn't like her." Daniella folded her arms like she was the mother in this situation. Amanda hoped it was genuine interest and not just a need to be superior to her brother.

"Who is she?" Cal asked before Amanda had the chance to respond.

It felt strange to be sharing details about Quinn, but she'd started the conversation, after all. "It's the architect I hired for the bakery project."

"Ooh. Ooh." Cal waved his hands back and forth. "She's the one who was here. The one I said you should date."

Daniella went back to frowning. "Should you be dating someone who works for you? Isn't that sexual harassment?"

Cal tapped a finger on the island. "She's not an employee. Besides, is it sexual harassment if both people are into it?"

"There's a power dynamic. That's what makes it harassment. Or against the rules at least." Daniella looked to her for validation.

Amanda pinched the bridge of her nose. Why had she decided to do this again? "Technically, I paid her for a service. She's not an employee."

"Yeah, that." Cal looked vindicated.

"I guess it's okay." Daniella conceded the point grudgingly.

"Again, we've only been on one date." She didn't like the defensive edge in her voice, but it was too late now. She cleared her throat. "Besides, her role in the renovation is almost done."

Cal nodded, clearly appeased. "I think it's cool."

"Thank you."

"You should get to have fun." Daniella's scowl didn't match her words.

"And if it gets serious, you'll let us meet her, right? I mean, I technically met her, but you know, spend time together." Whether he didn't pick up on Daniella's reticence or didn't care, Amanda couldn't tell.

"If we get there, yes. Of course."

Of the handful of people she dated after the divorce, she'd only ever introduced one to her kids. She and Bryonny had dated a couple of months before Amanda had brought her home. Shortly after, Bryonny made it clear she wanted to have kids of her own, which was fine for her but a deal breaker for Amanda. Cal and Daniella, barely teenagers at the time, liked her and took it hard when she stopped coming around. The ordeal marked the end of her forays into dating, not just her bringing a woman home to meet her children.

Cal and Daniella were older now. She wouldn't ignore their feelings on the subject, but considering both of them would be out of the house in the next few months, their lives would hardly be impacted. Working through that in her mind reassured her she was doing the right thing. Which was good. Because whether it was Quinn or the whole fiasco with Mel, something in her had shifted. Well, maybe less of a shift and more the realization she was on the cusp of being an empty nester who had very little in the way of a life outside of the bakery.

CHAPTER FIFTEEN

Amanda met Quinn at a tapas place, where they shared a few plates and a bottle of Fairmount Ridge rosé. After, they settled on a Frieda Kahlo documentary at Cinemapolis. She teased Quinn for insisting on a box of Junior Mints, but wound up eating her fair share. Quinn's hand found hers and they held hands until the credits rolled. They walked out, fingers still entwined. Nothing remarkable really, but hands down the best date she'd been on in over a decade.

"At the risk of sounding cheesy, I'm going to put out there that I'm not ready for this date to be over," Quinn said.

Cheesy or not, she was one hundred percent on the same page. "Is it cheesy if I agree?"

Quinn shook her head slowly. "I'm going to go with no. Do you want to get a nightcap somewhere?"

Was Quinn being intentionally vague? And if so, was it hesitation or deference? Her instinct was to defer in return. But she liked Quinn and, for the first time in a long time, she was feeling... what? Sassy? Brazen? Whatever it was, it nudged her to take a chance. "I'd love that. The Watershed is nearby. Or we could go back to your place."

Surprise flashed through Quinn's eyes, but it seemed like the good kind. She ran her hand up the back of her neck, making Amanda's fingers itch to do the same. "I do make a mean old-fashioned."

Amanda angled her head slightly. "That's convenient because I love an old-fashioned."

Quinn frowned. "I'm disappointed we have two cars."

"It's okay. I'll follow you." She certainly didn't want Quinn feeling obligated to bring her back to her car after. Whether that was after a drink or in the morning. As they walked to their cars, she stole a glance at Quinn and wondered if she was thinking the same thing. She'd find out soon enough.

Quinn texted her address, but Amanda had no trouble following her Subaru up 96 a few miles towards Trumansburg. The apartment complex Quinn pulled into was small, maybe a half dozen two-story buildings.

Quinn led her up a short walk and a flight of stairs. Inside, she flipped on a few lights. "It's rather generic." Quinn sounded apologetic. "It's a temporary arrangement I've let become less temporary than I intended."

"I was lucky after my divorce. Since the kids were going to be with me most of the time, I kept the house."

"That makes sense. And it is a great house."

She shrugged. "It is. The problem is it feels strange to think about selling it, even if I'm not sure I want to spend the rest of my life there."

Quinn shook her head. "Not strange at all, especially once the kids are moved out. It's the perfect time to consider your options."

"Is it wrong to say I want only two bedrooms but twice as much kitchen?"

Quinn didn't hesitate. "Nope."

"Thank you. Even if you're just saying that to be nice."

"Home is about having the space you want and need. I'm not saying you're going to have an easy time finding it, but that doesn't mean you shouldn't have it."

She smiled. "You have a gift for saying the right thing."

"Can I quote you on that? My sisters are convinced I have an uncanny gift for putting my foot in my mouth."

Her smile gave way to a snicker. "Do you?"

Quinn blew out a breath and looked at the ceiling. "I have my moments."

"Don't we all?" She certainly said her share of things she wished she could take back.

"We should drink to that, but I've invited you in and neglected to fix you a drink."

She tipped her head. "I'm in no rush."

"Still, I can't have you thinking I'm a lousy host." She gestured to the couch. "Make yourself comfortable."

"Sure there's nothing I can do to help?"

"I'm a terrible cook, but I can handle a cocktail. I'll be right back." Quinn retreated to the small galley kitchen that more than sufficed for her minimalist culinary endeavors. She pulled down a pair of highball glasses and got to work muddling the sugar and bitters with slices of orange. The methodical process calmed her as much as the promise of liquid courage did. "I forgot to ask if you prefer bourbon or rye."

"Will you think less of me if I don't have a preference?"

She poked her head through the doorway. "If you could see the things that pass for dinner around here, you'd know I'm the last person to judge anyone's tastes."

Amanda laughed. God, she had a sexy laugh. "I'll have what you're having."

Quinn finished the drinks with a splash of water and a pair of oversize ice cubes. She joined Amanda on the sofa and handed her one. "Cheers."

"Cheers."

They sipped. They talked about progress at the bakery and some of Quinn's other projects. She'd worried they might run out of things to talk about, but they didn't. At some point, Amanda put her hand on Quinn's knee. Quinn set down her glass and used the opportunity to get closer. She was totally paying attention to the conversation, but she also couldn't tear her eyes away from Amanda's mouth. When Amanda finished her drink and licked her bottom lip, the temptation proved too strong.

Quinn meant to kiss her lightly. But Amanda's lips were impossibly soft and she tasted of bourbon and orange. It took every ounce of restraint to pull back and search Amanda's eyes. What she saw in them—arousal and longing and maybe a trace of challenge—sent her pulse racing. The pounding in her chest had nothing on the throb between her legs. "I'm not sure one kiss should test the limits of my self-control."

"I think you should worry less about your self-control and more about kissing me again."

Short of taking off her clothes, there wasn't a single thing sexier Amanda could have done. The encouragement was exactly what she needed, even as it threatened to short-circuit her brain. She took the glass from Amanda's hand and set it on the coffee table. And kissed her again.

The slow slide of lips became urgent. A tease of tongues became a fervent exploration. Amanda opened for her, welcomed her in. Quinn wanted to steep herself in Amanda, her taste, her textures.

She didn't recall doing it, but they somehow slid down on the sofa. Amanda's hands roamed over her, restless and seeking. Quinn braced herself with one arm, allowing her free hand to creep under the hem of Amanda's shirt.

It was fun. It was playful. It was really fucking hot.

When Amanda's fingernails scratched lightly down the skin of her back, she realized how close they were to having sex right there on the couch. She eased away and ran a hand through her hair. "It seems silly to be confessing this, but I feel a bit like a teenager right now."

"It's not silly. It's cute." Amanda sat up and ran a hand through her own disheveled locks. "You know what would make you feel a lot less like a teenager?"

Quinn sat back and tried to slow her skittering pulse. It was a good thing Amanda couldn't see the hormones and adrenaline coursing through her. If she could, chances were good she'd never take her seriously again. "What's that?"

"Asking me to stay the night."

Her heart went from racing to stopped dead in about two seconds flat. A thousand questions flashed through her mind. Was Amanda serious? Was staying over code for having sex? Was her mouth hanging open and, if so, did it make her look like a complete idiot? None of those were the one Amanda had put out there. Even if everything about this had her tied in knots and practically tripping over herself, she knew enough to ask the question Amanda had essentially requested. "Do you need to go?"

Amanda shook her head.

"I'd love it if you didn't."

"I would, too."

Technically, that could have settled the matter, but she owed it to Amanda, to herself, to make the invitation clear. "Will you stay the night?"

Amanda smiled, and for all her boldness only a moment before, blushed. She nodded.

"Would you, um, like another drink?"

She shook her head.

Even as a ball of anticipation lodged in her chest, she knew it was her turn to take the lead. "Would you like to move to the bedroom instead of making out on the couch like a pair of horny teenagers?"

"That sounds like a fantastic idea."

That, too, should have settled it. But she couldn't shake the cloud of nerves that felt almost as big as her desire. "I don't mean to ruin the moment, but…"

When she didn't finish, Amanda looked into her eyes. "What is it? Talk to me."

She frowned. "It's just, well, it's been a while."

Amanda's worried look turned quizzical. "A while since what?"

Oh, God. Maybe she shouldn't have said anything. Floundering would be better than talking about it. "Since I…you know."

"Had sex?"

Yep. Definitely would have been better if she hadn't said anything. "Yes."

"But haven't you been dating constantly for the last year?"

Quinn closed her eyes. "Dating. Fix-ups. Not relationships."

"Oh." Amanda let the word drag out. Understanding, yes, but Quinn couldn't tell if there was sympathy or judgment or something else there with it.

"I don't know. I wasn't ready, I guess? Or there was no spark? Or maybe both?" Stop rambling. It's only getting worse.

"But you feel a spark with me?"

Air rushed out of Quinn's lungs. "Have I not made that obvious?"

Amanda's eyes danced. "I'd say you have. And do you want to be here, with me, right now?"

"I do." She couldn't remember the last time she'd wanted something so badly.

"Okay. See, that wasn't so hard."

Ha.

"Do you want to take me to bed?"

"If you're not completely turned off by how badly I'm fumbling this, yes."

Amanda's smile was slow. In it, desire and invitation and reassurance. "Then that's what I think you should do."

Was it as simple as that? Obviously, it was. It could be. Should be. She was just so fucking out of practice. "Okay."

She took Amanda's hand and stood. The bedroom wasn't far, so she held on for the short distance. She'd left the lamp in the corner on, just in case. It cast a soft glow over the room. A compromise really, since candles felt presumptuous.

"Quinn?"

The way Amanda said her name sent a tingle up her spine. "Yes?"

"If you're not ready, or at any point change your mind, it's okay. I get that it's a big deal because I've been there myself. Recently, as a matter of fact."

Amanda was giving her an out, one she could take and maybe not blow any chance they might have at a next time. The funny thing was, she didn't want an out. Or rather, the funny thing was Amanda's offering it confirmed an out wasn't what she wanted. "I won't change my mind."

"Still, I want you to know you can and I—"

Rather than letting Amanda finish, Quinn pulled her into a kiss. It started gentle but took on all the heat and urgency that had been pumping through her veins a moment before. The desire that had been clanging around inside her for weeks. "I want you. I haven't stopped thinking about you since we met."

"You don't have to say—"

Once again, Quinn silenced her with a kiss. "Let me show you."

Amanda's mouth under hers tethered her to the moment and quieted the voices, the questions, in her mind. Not questions about whether she wanted this, but the ones that needled her about being so out of practice. Amanda's hand slid up her back, her nails scratched lightly at the back of Quinn's neck. Again, just the encouragement she needed.

She threaded her fingers into Amanda's hair and used the gentle grip to angle Amanda's head. She took the kiss deeper, exploring Amanda's mouth with her tongue. Amanda let out this tiny moan, like she knew it was exactly the sort of sound that would drive Quinn crazy. It gave her the confidence to slip her hands under the hem of Amanda's shirt, ease it up and over her head.

The result—Amanda standing in front of her in a lacy bra and with messy hair—was the sexiest thing she'd seen in as long as she could remember. Now being nervous didn't matter. All that mattered was this moment and making Amanda feel half as good as she made Quinn feel, even before having sex.

She trailed a line of kisses down Amanda's neck, across her collar bone, and down to the edge of her bra. She traced the lace with her tongue, letting her hands creep up to cup Amanda's breasts from underneath. She grazed her thumbs over Amanda's nipples. The way they hardened under her touch made her throat go dry.

"So beautiful."

She could sense Amanda's head shake and looked up. Amanda held her gaze for only a second before looking away.

"Surely, you don't think otherwise." She wanted to see the rest of Amanda, touch her everywhere. Show her exactly how beautiful she was. She tugged at the bow holding Amanda's skirt in place and stepped back to watch the fabric slither to the floor. Amanda's panties, a soft green lace, matched her bra. "Not beautiful. Stunning."

Amanda crossed her arms over her stomach. "You're going to make me bashful."

The moment of vulnerability took her by surprise. She wrapped her fingers around Amanda's wrists and gently pulled her arms away from her body. "Stunning."

Before Amanda could protest, Quinn kissed her again. And again after that. Or maybe, technically, she didn't stop kissing her. Still gripping Amanda's wrists, she walked slowly toward the bed. Amanda followed her lead wordlessly. She didn't know exactly what she expected Amanda to be like in bed, but tractable wasn't it. The surprise was as much a turn-on as the idea of being in charge. "Do you want to tell me what you want, what you like?"

Amanda bit her lip and shook her head without breaking eye contact.

"Are you being shy or do you like someone else running the show?"

An extra gleam appeared in her eyes as she nodded.

Just when she thought it impossible to be turned on any more. "Yes? To both?"

Another nod. "I don't have to be, if—"

Quinn pressed a finger to her lips. "I want you to be exactly what you want to be. You just have to tell me if something isn't good, okay?"

This time she smiled. "Okay."

Even though it was their first time, she trusted Amanda to be honest. And being able to do things her way, at her pace, gave her confidence. She eased Amanda onto the bed and joined her. She continued kissing her, taking breaks here and there to explore her neck, the line of her shoulder, the swell of her breasts peeking over the top of her bra. Amanda sighed and made more of those perfect little noises.

Amanda's hands roamed, tugging the hem of Quinn's shirt and fussing over the buttons. "Why are you wearing so many clothes?"

She chuckled and eased just far enough away to shed her shirt.

"More." Amanda pointed to her belt. "Here, I'll help."

"For being compliant, you sure can be bossy."

Amanda laughed. Like, really laughed. But instead of killing the mood, it gave it a playful edge. Since she had a tendency toward the reverent, the lightness was a welcome addition. Amanda pulled at her belt, then her pants. She slid Amanda's panties down her legs, then backtracked to dispense with her bra.

Pressing her body to Amanda's, skin to skin, seemed to calm the fire in her and stoke it at the same time. As she pulled Amanda's taut nipple into her mouth, she forgot about how long it had been or how nervous she'd felt when they started. All that remained was this gorgeous woman and a mountain of shared need.

She trailed her fingers along Amanda's ribs, across the softness of her stomach that she'd tried to hide, and over the tops of her thighs. Amanda shifted, opened for her, in silent invitation. Well, not entirely silent. Without words, she gave Quinn every encouragement she could have asked for. And Quinn couldn't resist.

Quinn slid over her, thinking to start slowly, give them both a chance to get used to the new intimacy. But Amanda was so wet, so slick and soft, she couldn't hold her hand still. Up and down, small circles. The feel of Amanda under her was hypnotic.

And the sounds. Those sweet, sexy, pleading sounds. Did Amanda know how much they drove her crazy?

Amanda's nails grazed Quinn's back lightly as her hands roamed. Like the noises, it sent her senses haywire. It made her want to touch and taste everywhere at once. It made her ache to be inside Amanda, connected to her in the most intimate way possible.

As though reading her thoughts, Amanda opened her eyes and looked into Quinn's. "More."

That one word made Quinn's breath hitch. It ratcheted up her own desire but made her want to give Amanda everything. She eased a finger into her and everything else—the sounds, the sensations, the wants—blurred. Every cell of her being focused on that connection, that perfect feeling so unlike anything else.

"More." Part command, part plea, Amanda's request just about made Quinn come undone.

She added a second finger. Amanda's hips arched to meet her. Amanda's body took her in, molded around her fingers like they were made for each other. They moved together in perfect rhythm, like they'd done this a thousand times before. It was, in short, perfection. Why had she been nervous, again?

Amanda arched and held; she convulsed around Quinn's fingers. Heat poured from her, dripping over Quinn's hand. She had been wrong before. This, this exact moment, was perfection.

She kissed Amanda's forehead, her cheeks, her eyelids. When Amanda's trembling finally stopped, Quinn kissed her mouth. Amanda continued to shudder, and each tremble sent a ripple of pleasure through her. She wouldn't have said Amanda was the woman she'd been waiting for, but she couldn't shake the feeling that it had been worth the wait.

She settled herself next to Amanda, overwhelmingly content. Her own desire, while not sated, became more of a simmer than a rolling boil. A strange sensation, but one she would happily revel in the rest of the night.

Before she could say so, Amanda squirmed away and rolled over. Quinn frowned. "Hey. Where are you going?"

"Don't think you're going to get away with being one-sided." Amanda slinked down Quinn's body.

"I don't want you to feel—"

She finished neither the sentence nor the thought. Without any hesitation or buildup or anything else, Amanda's mouth closed around her. Quinn bucked, the sheer intensity of it lifting her off the bed.

Amanda softened her movements, but she didn't stop. Quinn's body responded, following her lead and settling into a hypnotic rhythm. Quinn fisted her hands in the sheets, grasping for purchase against the torrent of sensation. It was as though Amanda knew her body, knew what to do and exactly how to do it.

The orgasm cascaded over her like rain, effortless but leaving her drenched. Amanda let out a contented hum and she came again, the second orgasm spilling into the first.

As her body continued to quake, Amanda crawled up the bed, kissing a line all the way up her torso to her mouth. Quinn blinked a few times, trying to get her eyes to focus. She wanted to say something of significance, but when she opened her mouth, all that came out was, "Wow."

Amanda smiled. "I was thinking the same thing."

"You're amazing. And I'm pretty sure it isn't just because I haven't had sex in a really long time."

She smirked. "Maybe a little of both."

"No, no. I remember how it goes and that was spectacular."

"I guess I can't argue since I agree."

Something about the comment made her chuckle. "Good."

They stayed like that for a long while—Amanda stroking between her breasts and her fingers sliding lazily through Amanda's hair. "Are you good? Do you need anything?"

Amanda patted her chest and offered her a sleepy smile. "So good. Thanks for inviting me over."

She reached over and shut off the light. Amanda settled right back against her. If more than half her brain cells had been working, it might have freaked her out how perfectly they fit together. But at this point, she could barely keep her eyes open and couldn't remember the last time she'd felt this content. "If you need something in the night, wake me up, okay?"

Another pat. "I won't, but okay."

Before she could argue, Amanda's breathing evened out with the transition to sleep. Quinn, for all her tendencies to think and wonder and worry, wasn't far behind.

CHAPTER SIXTEEN

A manda walked into the house to the sound of laughter and the smell of cinnamon. Neither seemed par for the course for her kids at nine in morning. "Hello?"

"In here, Mom." Cal's voice came from the kitchen.

Daniella and Cal sat at the island, unusual only because of the time. But when she stepped the rest of the way into the kitchen, she stopped dead in her tracks. Standing at the oven—in boxers, a Cornell shirt, and a pair of oven mitts—was Mel.

"Uh."

"Good morning." Mel turned to her with a big smile and pan of what appeared to be cinnamon rolls, like it was the most common thing in the world.

"M came over last night to watch a movie and decided to stay over," Daniella said.

Mel set the pan down on the stove. "In the guest room, I promise."

She nodded slowly. "Okay."

"I hope you don't mind." Mel gave her best innocent puppy face. "I was texting with Daniella and she mentioned you were out and asked if I wanted to do movie night like old times."

"Oh." She'd never begrudge Mel and the kids a night of hanging out. And, honestly, she didn't mind that it was at her house. But it meant Mel knew she'd spent the night elsewhere. Her kids were one thing, but she certainly didn't owe her ex an explanation.

"How was the date?" Mel asked.

Fuck. There went that. "It was good, thanks."

She expected a jab or maybe a suggestive look, but Mel offered neither. "Coffee?"

"Sure." She'd had a cup with Quinn, but perhaps another shot of caffeine would make this whole situation a little less bizarro.

"I got it." Cal hopped down from his stool and went to the coffee pot.

Mel opened the packets of frosting and started squeezing them over the rolls. "None of us had anywhere to be first thing, so I popped out for breakfast. They're nothing compared to yours, of course, but us mere mortals have to make do the best we can."

Cal handed her the coffee. "I said we could do cereal, but M said we should at least aim for the middle."

"Good life lesson, right?" Mel bumped her hip lightly to Amanda's as she passed with the pan of now-frosted rolls.

Amanda chuckled in spite of herself. "In some instances."

"Will you join us?" Mel asked.

"Yeah, Mom. Join us." Daniella, who'd been mostly quiet, got up from the island. "We can sit at the table even."

Part of her wanted to start laundry and do yoga so she could drive out to the bakery before lunch. It was such a small ask, though. And it might help things with Mel get back on an even keel. She didn't want hard feelings, but even more, she didn't want Cal and Daniella to pick up on any weird energy between them.

She agreed and moved to grab plates, but Mel waved her away. Daniella got napkins and Cal snagged utensils from the drawer. In under a minute, they sat around the table with coffee and breakfast and she'd not lifted a finger. That might be as strange as all of them having breakfast together in the first place.

"They really aren't as good as yours." Mel licked her fingers and offered Amanda a wink.

"They're not bad, though," Cal said.

Daniella rolled her eyes. "That's because you'd eat anything."

"True." Cal nodded affably. He turned to Amanda. "How was last night? We were all talking about how crazy it was for you to stay over somewhere."

There was a thump under the table and Cal let out an "ow." Amanda lifted an eyebrow at Daniella, who'd clearly been the instigator. "It was nice. And I'm going to leave it at that."

Daniella let out an exasperated sigh, but Cal grinned. "You know this means you're not going to be able to say, 'Don't do anything I wouldn't do' anymore when it comes to girls."

Despite sitting at the kitchen table, surrounded by her kids and her ex-wife, her mind flashed to the night before. She'd seen a different side of Quinn and the truth of the matter was, the more she saw, the more she liked. "How about, when you're my age, you can do whatever you want."

Cal laughed, but Daniella scowled. The latter gave her pause. Daniella had seemed okay with, if not keen on, the idea of her dating. But something had changed. She didn't know if it had to do with Quinn specifically, but she clearly wasn't happy. Amanda filed the detail away. No way in hell was she having that conversation in front of Mel.

Before they finished eating, Cal put in a request for real cinnamon rolls before he left for college. Daniella concurred and invited Mel to join them. Mel offered a playful shrug and, when Amanda didn't protest, accepted. The whole thing gave Amanda a sense of unease. Less the invitation itself and more because Daniella seemed so pleased by it. She'd have to do some digging the next time they were one-on-one.

But today was not that day. With breakfast done and everyone sufficiently amped up on sugar and caffeine, the day ahead took on a new level of urgency. Despite her reflexive tendency to join the bustle, if not direct it, she remained seated. Dishes were loaded into the dishwasher, the last of the coffee found its way into travel mugs, and everyone scattered to work or shower or whatever else beckoned.

Once she was alone, she contemplated the laundry and the yoga and all the other chores she generally busied herself with. But still, she didn't get up. Instead, she sipped her coffee and shut off the worry about Daniella's weird behavior and Mel standing at the oven in her pajamas and how she probably needed to do something about both those things. And she thought about Quinn and the way Quinn made love to her and how soon they might be able to do it again.

❖

"Second date, huh?" Kiera gave Quinn a look of suspicion over the rim of her coffee cup.

"There's no reason to sound so surprised." Aside from the fact she'd only managed a couple of second dates after a couple dozen fix-ups. Zero third dates. And not a single hookup to speak of.

Kiera smacked her lips together, clearly dismissing the assertion. "So, what, ten more and maybe you'll think about sleeping together?"

She pressed her own lips together, but silently. Her way of saying nothing and everything at the same time.

"You didn't."

She angled her head.

"Oh, my God. You did."

She sipped her coffee, enjoying the emotions play so clearly across her sister's face. "Again, there's no reason to sound so surprised."

Kiera folded her arms and leaned forward on the table. "I beg to differ."

"Okay. I'll give you that one." As much as she didn't relish discussing her sex life with her sisters, they knew she'd been celibate for the last two years. Kiera harassed her about it, Alana respected it, but both of them had started to worry about it.

"Tell me everything."

"I will not."

Kiera frowned. "Come on. Not the X-rated version or anything, but something. Even Alana won't let you get away with complete silence."

She could be vague, or coy, but she decided to be honest. "It was worth the wait."

"Worth it as in the sex was good or as in you're falling for this woman?"

A loaded question to be sure. One she wasn't ready to answer, even to herself. "I'm going to say the former, but that still doesn't mean I'm giving you the details."

Kiera's gaze narrowed. "You say that, but there's something in your eyes that has nothing to do with being a prude. You've got feelings."

She shook her head, as though doing so would somehow prevent it from being too real. "I think that's a bit premature."

"Maybe, but it doesn't make it not true." Kiera twisted a piece of hair around her finger, her signature fidget when she was worried about something. "How far gone are you?" Kiera's reaction did more to stress her out than her feelings. Well, maybe not more, but as much as, at least.

"Not that far."

"We need to meet her. Stat."

Quinn lifted her hands, as though the gesture might defend her against the demand. "Whoa, whoa, whoa. We are not there yet. Two dates, remember?"

"But pseudo dates before. You said as much. And you slept together. You don't do that lightly."

She could pretend or say otherwise, but it would be a lie. "I like her. We click better than I've clicked with anyone in a long time. It doesn't mean we're in serious relationship territory."

"You don't have to be engaged to let your sisters meet the woman."

Quinn raised a brow.

"What? We wouldn't give her the third degree."

"No. We wouldn't." Quinn put extra emphasis on the "we" because it wasn't Alana she worried about. Or Xinxin or Gary, for that matter.

Kiera frowned. "I see what you're doing there."

"I wasn't trying to be subtle."

"Do you really not want us to meet her?"

She'd been mostly teasing, so the look of genuine concern on Kiera's face gave her pause. "I'm sure you'd be gracious and lovely. If things keep going well, then soon. I promise."

Like a switch being flipped, Kiera's demeanor changed. Worried to victorious in exactly two seconds. "Fantastic. You name the day. I'll host. Ooh, or better. We can get a babysitter and do a triple date."

Quinn shook her head. Kiera shouldn't be able to play her so easily at this point. Yet here they were. "One day, I'm not going to fall for it, you know."

"Fall for what?" Her smile was all innocence.

"Don't you need to get to work or something?"

"No, I'm killing time until the Chamber lunch at twelve."

Quinn drained the rest of her coffee. She should start going to those again. They were good for networking, which she didn't mind when networking wasn't code for speed dating. "Well, I should probably get to work."

Kiera smirked. "That's what she said."

Quinn groaned on principle. "You're impossible."

"Give me a break. I spend most of my days tailoring my sense of humor to the under ten crowd."

"Fair enough. I should get to the office, though. We're pitching for the new Planned Parenthood annex."

Her eyes lit up. "You are?"

"They're far enough along in the capital campaign to take bids. It'll be a while, but they're getting there."

"Day made. It almost makes up for you holding out on me."

Quinn stood and slung her messenger bag over her shoulder. "I'm not holding out."

"I'll concede the point when I meet her. What's her name again?"

"Amanda."

"And she's divorced? With kids?"

She could literally see Kiera filing away the details. "Yes, on both counts. College age, though, or one in and one starting."

Kiera nodded slowly. "I like it."

Quinn chuckled in spite of herself. "I'm so glad you approve."

"Don't be a jerk." Even as she said it, she stood to give Quinn a hug. "Love you."

"Love you back."

"See you Sunday?"

"Yes. Solo, but yes."

Kiera sighed. "Baby steps."

Quinn left the café and headed to her office. It wasn't hard to imagine Amanda at one of their big family dinners. Maybe after her parents were back from their trip. Ironically, more people seemed to make for less pressure or, at least, less chance too much attention would end up focused on her.

Just as easily as she could imagine it, it struck her that she knew virtually nothing about Amanda's extended family. And hardly anything about her kids. Really, she and Amanda hadn't spent all that much time together. Maybe it was a sign she should slow down. Well, if not her moves, then her imagination. Because no matter how timid she might still be in the moves department, it wouldn't take much for her imagination to get the better of her.

Chapter Seventeen

Amanda opened the back door of the bakery and found herself face-to-face with a giant curtain of plastic sheeting. The banging she'd heard from the parking lot was even more pronounced inside. The whine of a saw—it was a saw, right?—joined in. "Hello?"

No response. Not that she expected one. She didn't know how anyone could hear anything over the racket.

She parted the curtain and stepped through. White dust filled the air like a fog, giving her new appreciation for why half her bakery was draped in plastic. A couple of guys she didn't recognize moved around the space, clearly the ones responsible for the sawing and banging. One of them looked her way.

"Are Quinn and Joss here?" she asked.

He angled his head toward the front of the bakery. "That way."

"Thanks."

He offered her a nod and resumed his work. Efficient. She liked it.

Even though it felt silly, she plopped the hard hat on her head and tiptoed her way through the construction, thinking maybe it would have been better to go back the way she'd come and around to the front of the building. Too late now.

It took her a minute to find the opening in the plastic this time. She felt around like a slapstick comedian who couldn't make it through a stage curtain. Unlike a comedian, she resisted the urge to flail her arms.

She found Quinn and Joss poring over blueprints spread out on a makeshift table made from sawhorses. "The brain trust is hard at work early, it seems."

Both women looked her way and smiled. She'd already developed a soft spot for Joss. Between her butch contractor aesthetic and her keen attention to detail, it would be hard not to. Truth be told, though, she had eyes only for Quinn. She was dressed like a contractor today—work pants and a plaid button-down over a navy T-shirt. And boots. Who knew she had a thing for women in work boots?

"Good morning," they said in unison. It was kind of adorable, really.

"I thought I'd check on the progress." She crossed the room to where they stood. "I might have also brought breakfast for the crew. You know, to stay in their good graces."

Joss folded her arms. "Are you implying my crew needs to be bribed?"

Her tone was teasing, but Amanda wanted to stay in her good graces, too. "Not bribed. Appreciated."

"Oh, well, then. Appreciate away."

"It's all out in my car."

"Would you like a tour first?" Quinn asked.

"Yes. Yes, I would." Quinn probably wouldn't kiss her in front of Joss, but a tiny part of her wanted her to.

"Excellent. Joss, would you like to do the honors?"

"It would be my pleasure." Joss bowed, but when she stood, she winked at Amanda. "Especially if there's breakfast to be had."

"I promise I'll make it worth your while."

They started with the blueprints. Amanda had seen them at least a dozen times before, but not like this, where Joss could point to a line on the page and indicate exactly where and how that line translated to her space. Next came the good part—large openings in the walls. Joss gestured for her to walk through, so she did. Then back. And back again.

A decidedly unprofessional giggle escaped. "Sorry."

"You should never apologize for joy," Joss said without missing a beat.

"What she said, one hundred percent." Quinn hooked a thumb at Joss.

"Thanks for that. I don't want to say I can't believe it's happening because you're both professionals and I trust you. But a little part of me can't believe this is happening."

"Totally allowed," Quinn said.

Joss nodded. "We've got all the old paneling out and are cleaning up the electric on this side."

"Already?"

Joss led the way around the room, pointing out where new outlets would be. "As soon as we get the insulation in and the new wall framed, the drywall and wainscoting can go up."

"And you do that before floors, right?"

"Yes, but the flooring arrived yesterday. We've got it up front where the new counter will be."

"Oh, that's exciting." She'd been disappointed the original floors couldn't be salvaged, but then Joss had introduced her to the world of ceramic tile crafted to look like wood. The durability and ease of cleaning won her over in about two seconds.

"Would you like to see it?" Quinn looked at her with a smile she couldn't quite read.

"Yes, please."

Instead of going back the way they'd come, they kept going. The wall that would divide the decorating room from the seating area hadn't been framed yet, but Joss indicated where it would go. Amanda paused and turned back, taking a second to appreciate how much room she was going to have. The blueprints hadn't been able to do it justice. She let out a contented sigh and followed Quinn and Joss around to the front of the bakery.

Quinn put a hand under her elbow. "Watch your step right here. The subfloor is uneven."

The casual touch shouldn't have made her heart beat faster, but it did. And despite being in the middle of a construction zone and getting her first peek at what her bakery would look like when the work was done, all she could think about was Quinn putting her hands in all sorts of other places.

"Is everything okay? I know it can be hard to imagine the finished product when everything is such a mess."

Amanda shook her head, wanting to dispel the concern in Quinn's eyes. "No, no. It's perfect. I got a little distracted is all."

Joss offered an encouraging smile. "It can feel like sensory overload at times."

It was sensory overload all right, but not the kind Joss had in mind. She laughed. "That must be it."

Quinn took a few steps and turned around, expanding her arms wide. "So, this is where your display counter and register was." She shuffled ninety degrees. "And this is where they will be."

She enjoyed Quinn's gesture as much as she did imagining how it would look. "It's going to be perfect."

Quinn tipped her head and lifted a shoulder. "I'm not sure about perfect, but I think it's going to work."

Joss lifted her chin. "Hey, speak for yourself. I'm aiming for perfection."

"I only mean perfection is a problematic term when it comes to old buildings."

Watching the two of them debate the semantics of perfection was beyond cute. "How about perfectly imperfect? Can we agree on that?"

Both Quinn and Joss seemed willing to concede the point. They finished the tour and Quinn helped Amanda bring in the treats she'd brought for the crew. As much as she wanted to linger, she didn't want to be in the way. Or impede progress. She thanked Joss and said her good-byes, but Quinn offered to walk her out.

"I didn't expect to see you this morning. It was a pleasant surprise," Quinn said once they were out in the parking lot.

"Likewise."

"Are we still on for dinner tonight?" Quinn looked at her hopefully.

"Absolutely."

"Are you sure there's nothing I can bring?"

She contemplated answers for a moment, then decided why the hell not. She looked down for a second, then into Quinn's eyes. "You could bring a bag."

Any worry or hesitation she had over being so forward evaporated as she watched confusion, understanding, and arousal play across Quinn's face in rapid succession. Quinn swallowed, but didn't speak.

"No pressure, of course. But we'll have the house to ourselves and it might be nice not to think about driving home."

Quinn nodded slowly. "Very practical."

She smirked. "That's me."

"I like that about you." The comment was innocent, but Quinn stared at Amanda's mouth as she said it.

"So, I'll see you around six?"

"You most certainly will." Amanda made to open her car door, but Quinn took her hand. She glanced briefly at the building, then back at Amanda. "How would you feel about me kissing you in your parking lot in broad daylight?"

She appreciated that Quinn asked, but appreciated even more that Quinn wanted to. "I feel very positively about it."

"Oh, good." Quinn closed the distance between them and slid her mouth over Amanda's.

Her eyes closed instinctively, but sunlight caressed her eyelids. The breeze teased the hair at the base of her neck. Quinn's hand cupped her cheek in a way that was familiar at this point, but there was a novelty in the combination of sensations. Something that managed to be innocent and suggestive, like the way Quinn had looked at her a moment before.

When Quinn eased away, she almost whimpered. She settled for a blissful sigh.

Quinn grinned. "I'm going to have to do that again. Is that okay?"

"Yes, please."

The second kiss had more heat than the first and left her tempted to pull Quinn inside. Too bad there wasn't a square foot of privacy to be had in the bakery at the moment. The thought made her giddy. She'd never had sex in the bakery. Would Quinn indulge her? Not today, obviously, but maybe before she reopened.

"What? What are you thinking right now?"

She shook her head, suddenly embarrassed. "Only that I should let you get back to work and I don't really want to."

Not untrue, and it made Quinn smile. "I'll see you soon."

"Can't wait." Especially now that they'd established Quinn would spend the night.

Quinn returned to the bakery, whistling. Work had stopped. Some of the guys huddled around the boxes Amanda had brought; others stood around with cups of coffee and what appeared to be muffins. Joss stood off to the side on her phone, so she helped herself to a cup of coffee and a muffin. Sure, she'd eaten breakfast only a couple of hours prior, but these were Amanda's muffins.

She took a bite and suppressed a moan, if only because she was surrounded by construction workers. It had all the elements of coffee cake—a cinnamon swirl through the middle and crumb topping. She sipped her coffee and let out a contented sigh. She'd never had a baker for a girlfriend before. Not that they were officially in girlfriend territory, but she liked the idea of moving in that direction.

When her phone buzzed, she set down the coffee and pulled it from her pocket. Seeing Amanda's name made her smile. She swiped her thumb across the screen to read the message. *There was something I wanted to ask you earlier, but I chickened out.*

Considering Amanda had asked her to spend the night, her curiosity piqued. *What's that?*

Um.

What could she possibly be shy about now? *Go on. TBH, I can't imagine saying no.*

She hit send, then realized maybe the question wasn't a request. Maybe Amanda wanted to know her sexual history. Or maybe it was something about the bakery. Maybe she was unhappy with something and felt uncomfortable bringing it up. Maybe—

I wanted to make a request for your overnight bag.

Pajama preferences? Maybe Amanda didn't like her cologne. Or maybe she—

I was hoping you'd pack.

It took her a second, but only a second. And then her throat went dry and other parts of her did the opposite. The thought of strapping on with Amanda was ridiculously sexy. Having Amanda bring it up, ask for it? Well, that was next level.

If that's not your thing, it's okay.

Crap. She'd been so busy getting turned on, she'd not answered fast enough. Before she could make her fingers work, another message came through.

But I'm trying to be bold. And then, *So I thought I'd ask.*

In another time and place, maybe she'd be eloquent. This was neither that time, nor that place. *Sorry, you melted my brain a little and I couldn't type.*

Amanda replied with a smiley face.

Yes. So many times yes.

It took a second for Amanda to reply this time, although when it came through, it was a single word. *Phew.*

Her brain had yet to resume normal functioning, but Amanda needed to understand exactly how welcome her invitation was. *Can't tell you how sexy it is that you asked.*

Amanda's answer to that was the smirking emoji.

A member of the crew brushed past, reminding her where she was. Something about being in Amanda's space, even under construction, made the whole exchange even hotter. She moved to a quieter corner and considered what to say back.

Requests? Preferences? Things I should know? It was at least sort of a sexy reply. It also saved some of the negotiation that could be hot in the moment but just as easily could be awkward as hell.

I'm not overly picky. But I'm also not delicate.

Quinn's already active imagination kicked into overdrive. Not that she kept an arsenal of toys, but the description gave her everything she needed to know. *Perfect.* She hesitated for a moment, then sent a follow up. *Just like you, I think.*

Amanda's reply was a blush and *Can't wait to see you later. Ditto.*

"What are you grinning at?"

She looked up to find Joss studying her with amusement. "Nothing."

Joss lifted a brow. "I thought we were better friends than that."

They were. They'd known each other for close to ten years. "Sorry. It's my own sheepishness, not anything to do with you."

"What's got you so sheepish? Or maybe I should be asking who?"

Joss so had her number. More than Arti, and so differently than her sisters. Like kindred spirits or something. Even if they didn't spend loads of time together off the clock, Joss got her. And she liked to think the feeling was mutual. "Or maybe you already know and don't even need to ask."

That earned her a smile. "Fair enough. Do I get to ask about the specifics?"

"I'm seeing Amanda tonight."

"Definitely worth smiling over. Why sheepish, then?"

Quinn blew out a breath. "She asked me to pack a bag."

"Ah." Joss nodded. "Nice."

She could leave it at that, but they were sort of having a moment. And this wasn't the kind of thing she could say to anyone else. "And to pack."

"Oh." Joss let the word drag out. "Very nice."

"I'm going to try not to think about how long it's been." She could have said the same thing about sex in general last week and that had turned out all right. Okay, way better than all right.

Joss clamped a hand on her shoulder. "Like riding a bicycle."

That's what she was afraid of. "Have you ridden a bike lately?"

Joss laughed. "As a matter of fact, I have."

"Wait, are we talking about metaphorical bikes or literal ones?"

"Who says it can't be both?"

It was Quinn's turn to laugh, then. "I needed that. Thank you."

"Any time, my friend. Any time."

She was tempted to linger, but Joss had work and so did she. "Text me if you need anything. Otherwise I'll stop back in a couple of days."

"Will do."

Quinn turned to leave but Joss called her name. "Yeah?"

"I don't expect you to kiss and tell, but have fun tonight."

She offered a nod. "Thanks."

Work was the last thing on her mind at this moment, but she had two projects waiting on her desk. She also had several hours to fill before she'd see Amanda. And as much as she didn't like to think of herself as the impatient sort, keeping busy would help them go by faster.

Chapter Eighteen

Quinn let out a contented sigh. She could get used to having a girlfriend who liked to cook.

"So, Joss thinks things are moving along on schedule?"

She contemplated a second helping of potatoes but thought better of it. "From what I can tell, yes. Demo is completely done, framing is underway, and materials are arriving on schedule."

Amanda raised a hand. "Not that I was doubting, based on what I saw today, but I'm glad."

"The thing with renovations like this is the parts you see take the least amount of time. Does that make sense?"

"That's usually the way with cakes, too." She tipped her head slightly. "Usually."

"There are cakes that take longer to decorate than bake? I mean, I know those crazy ones on TV, but ones for real people?"

Amanda sniffed, making her worry maybe she'd accidentally said something offensive. "Sometimes real people want those crazy designs."

It hit her that she'd sampled plenty of Amanda's work, but she'd not seen much of her decorating. "Do you like doing that? The elaborate decorations?"

"It has its moments. I like the creativity of it, doing something I've never done before. But it's always the inside that counts."

They were talking about cakes, but she got the feeling the philosophy extended to all aspects of Amanda's life. Reassuring in a way. Not that she thought Amanda might be superficial, but it seemed like her ex had one of those big, flashy personalities. The kind of personality she couldn't even pretend to compete with. It made her feel better to think Amanda didn't put a lot of stock in—or perhaps more importantly, have an inherent attraction to—that sort of person.

"What? Why do you look so concerned?"

She didn't want to bog down their evening with the trajectory of her thoughts. "I'm imagining you on one of those shows, disheveled and frantic, climbing a ladder to decorate a cake as the clock winds down."

Amanda shuddered. An honest to God shudder. "It wasn't a huge production, but you've already seen me frantic."

She smiled at the memory, and everything that had unfolded since. "You were adorable."

"You are way too kind."

"Not at all. We all have those moments. At first, I was afraid I'd made so little impression you found me forgettable."

Amanda's smile managed to be both sensual and playful. "Absolutely nothing about you is forgettable."

She didn't want to read too much into the compliment, but it was hard not to. For someone with a track record of being overshadowed, Amanda finding her memorable went a long way in boosting her confidence. Paired with the text exchange from earlier, it was enough to give her some swagger. Okay, maybe not quite swagger, but closer to it than she'd been in a while.

"What? You seem incredulous."

Not the time to own the extent of her slump. Especially since she'd sort of done that the last time. "I was calculating out how to return the compliment without being corny."

Amanda raised a brow.

"See, now that ship has sailed. Such a shame."

"Maybe I like corny."

It was a game now, not some self-deprecating move she'd kick herself for later. "No, no. Don't try to make me feel better now. The next thing I know, you're going to be calling me nice."

Amanda took a sip of her wine, studying Quinn over the rim of her glass. "You are nice."

She shook her head. "You can't tell a woman she's nice, then ask her to strap on."

Amanda set the glass down. She leaned back in her chair and folded her arms. "Well, that's just silly."

"I have it on pretty good authority the two are mutually exclusive." Part of her problem of late, landing in the you're too nice category.

"I reject this hypothesis." The comeback—instant and adamant—made Quinn smile.

"Do you, now?"

"I do. And I'm going to prove it."

She had no idea how Amanda would go about such a thing, but she was having fun. "How do you propose to do that?"

"Well, we've already established you're nice."

Quinn let out a sign. "We have. Kiss of death, really."

"But you came prepared to…" Her gaze flashed to Quinn's crotch. "You know."

Oh, this was fun. "I did."

"And if I asked you to take me to bed right this instant, surely you wouldn't want to disappoint me."

"I don't think I could deny you a thing you asked for." Even if the full truth of that gave her a hitch of anxiety.

"Quinn?"

"Yeah?" Even knowing where the conversation was headed, getting Amanda to say the words was a total turn-on.

"Take me to bed."

She got up from the table. "Do you want to clean up first? I'm more than happy to do dishes when a beautiful woman cooks for me."

Amanda shook her head.

Quinn extended her hand. "Well, then. Lead the way."

❖

Amanda blew out a breath. She sat on the edge of the bed, one leg crossed over the other. Her foot bounced. She forced it to stop. Why was she nervous?

Because she'd gone back and forth about fifty times before asking Quinn if she liked to strap on. Because a tiny part of her still worried Quinn's reply, while enthusiastic, was more about pleasing Amanda than herself. Because it had been more than ten years since she had done it with anyone and that alone was scary as hell. What if her body didn't work the same way? What if she'd put it out there but couldn't actually do it? What if—

Quinn emerged from the bathroom in a pair of loose fitting boxers and a black T-shirt. Amanda couldn't stop her gaze from going right to the bulge in the fabric. Even as her mouth went dry, wetness gathered between her thighs. Nerves or not, she wanted this.

Quinn crossed the room slowly, like she was giving Amanda time to get used to the idea. Or maybe she was psyching herself up. Her gaze moved up and down Amanda's body. "I feel underdressed."

Amanda stood, the black silk of the slip slinking over her body. She'd hesitated about putting it on, but was glad she did. "You're dressed perfectly."

Quinn lifted a brow.

"Well, maybe with one or two exceptions." She grasped the hem of Quinn's shirt, lifted it up and over her head. She smiled at Quinn's bare breasts, several shades paler than her suntanned arms and shoulders. "Much better."

Quinn's hands went to her waist, sliding up to her breasts, then down to her hips. "I'm torn between wanting to take this off and wanting you to keep it on. You are absolutely stunning."

"It'll come off eventually." The compliment fueled her courage. She cupped the cock in her right hand. Even through the cotton, the firmness and the weight of it ratcheted her arousal up a few notches. "Although I think your shorts should come off now."

"I'm pretty sure your wish is my command."

"Allow me." She slid her hands into the waistband. The leather of the harness was smooth and warm under her fingers, the tautness a delicious contrast to the softness of Quinn's skin. She swallowed.

"If you're having second thoughts, it's okay. I never want you to feel pressured."

"Oh, no. That's not why I hesitated." She looked into Quinn's eyes. "I was savoring."

"Ah. Well, in that case, take your time."

She slid the shorts over Quinn's hips and they fell to the floor. The dildo sprang to attention. She took it in her hand. Like the harness, it had warmed from the heat of Quinn's body. "Definitely savoring."

Quinn threaded her fingers into her hair and pulled their mouths together. Amanda sank into the kiss, happy to let Quinn take the lead. At least for now. When they tumbled onto the bed, the cock pressed against her, making the material of her lingerie pull tight. The constriction managed to turn her on and frustrate her at the same time.

Her body hummed with increasing urgency, but Quinn seemed in no hurry. She moved against Amanda slowly, kissing and caressing like it was all she wanted to do. There was almost a reverence to it, and it made Amanda's heart flip uncomfortably in her chest.

She kissed Quinn's shoulders, her collarbones, her neck. Basically anything she could get her lips on with Quinn's body pinning hers to the bed. She was torn between impatience and longing for this exact moment to never end.

Quinn shifted slightly. Her fingers grazed down Amanda's thigh and back up. When they slid over her and dipped inside, Amanda arched off the bed. "Oh. Yes."

Quinn stroked her languidly, again as though they had all the time in the world. "You feel so good."

Amanda shook her head. Not to disagree, but to indicate that was supposed to be her line. Only her brain had lost the ability to form sentences.

"No?" Quinn looked in her eyes but didn't stop.

"I mean yes." She switched to a nod. "I mean, you, too."

Quinn smiled, a trace of smugness in her eyes. Maybe it shouldn't have been, but it was really, really hot. "Good."

Amanda continued to nod and Quinn continued to stroke. Until the strokes turned into thrusts and Amanda's eyes rolled back and closed of their own volition. She so wanted to come, but she didn't.

As if sensing her indecision, Quinn eased her hand away and knelt between her thighs. She slid the head of the cock up and down with excruciating precision. "You're really wet, but I think a little lube never hurt anything."

Amanda, suddenly at a complete loss for words, nodded.

Quinn picked up a small bottle and squirted some onto the dildo and her hand. She tossed the bottle aside and slid her fingers over Amanda. The sensation, hot and slick and featherlight, made her gasp. "You're so perfect."

Again, all she could do was nod.

"You'll talk to me, right? Tell me if you want more or less or if something doesn't feel good?"

She managed a breathy, "Yes."

"You don't mind if I touch you first, do you? You feel so amazing."

As Quinn spoke, she slid her thumb across Amanda's clit, then traced slow circles over it. "Uh-huh."

"Ms. Russo, are you at a loss for words?"

The comment, playful but confident, made her laugh. "Something like that."

"Let's see what we can do about that." Without stopping the movement of her thumb, she eased two fingers into Amanda, all the way to the knuckle. Amanda gasped. "You seem ready."

"So ready." Any nerves about being out of practice evaporated. "So very ready."

Quinn eased her fingers away and positioned the head of the cock. "I'll go slow."

She was about to say there was no need, but Quinn eased inside of her and even the most basic of words vanished. A moan of pure, raw pleasure escaped. It had been too long. Way, way too long. And yet, she couldn't imagine doing this with anyone but Quinn.

"Are you okay?"

At the genuine concern in Quinn's voice, she opened her eyes. She must have conveyed sufficient meaning with her look because Quinn smiled. And then she began to move. As promised, she started slow. With each languid stroke, her body welcomed Quinn in, molded around her. Like their bodies were made to fit together.

Quinn shifted forward, taking one of Amanda's nipples into her mouth. The added sensation, paired with the change of angle, sent her tumbling into orgasm. It caught her by surprise and left her body quaking. Quinn stilled.

"Sorry. That sneaked up on me."

Quinn grinned, this ridiculously sexy and self-satisfied grin. "Don't apologize. Unless, maybe, you're asking me to stop."

Amanda shook her head. "Please don't stop."

Quinn kissed her again and resumed fucking her. Amanda wound her arms around Quinn's neck, her legs around Quinn's waist. She'd never been so glad for dragging herself to yoga two mornings a week.

They moved together, Amanda lifting her hips to meet Quinn each time. The pace quickened, along with the force of each thrust. She felt herself building to another orgasm. She managed to work in a handful of yeses and pleases in between the noises she couldn't seem to contain.

"Amanda."

The way Quinn said her name as she came did her in. Amanda's body tensed, her own orgasm tumbling right after. She clung to Quinn as Quinn continued to move, riding it like a wave with her until they were deposited, breathless and spent, on the shore.

Quinn collapsed on top of her, blanketing Amanda's body and pressing it into the mattress. Amanda kept her arms and legs around her, willing her not to go anywhere.

"I'm crushing you."

She held tighter. "You're not. Don't go. Not yet."

Quinn stilled and they lay like that for a long while. Her breathing steadied and her skin cooled. Still, she wasn't quite ready to let Quinn go. She once again found herself at a loss for words, but it was different. If Quinn had managed to short-circuit her brain before, this overload had more to do with the heart. She might not be ready to own that out loud, but she wasn't the kind of woman to deny it.

"Are you sure I'm not crushing you?"

She took a deep breath and let it out slowly. "No, but you're probably not comfortable like that."

"Maybe. But it sure as hell has its perks." Quinn pulled just far enough away to slip off the harness. When she came back, she opened her arms and Amanda settled in. As amazing as the sex was, the ease of how well they fit together had to be a close second. She'd never wanted to admit how much she'd missed this kind of intimacy in all her years of being single.

Quinn, who'd been tracing circles on Amanda's shoulder with her finger, paused. "Penny for your thoughts."

"I'm thinking how good you feel. Like, a little bit ago, but now, too."

"I like that." Quinn kissed the top of her head. "And ditto."

"I'm also thinking how long it's been since I've done that, but how perfect it was."

Quinn grinned. "Like riding a bike?"

"Way, way better than riding a bike." And pretty much anything else she could think of.

"Okay, I'll give you that. Absolutely."

She nuzzled in closer. "Thank you for not thinking me too forward earlier."

Quinn's expression turned serious. "About that."

Despite her generally blissed out state, Amanda's stomach flipped uncomfortably. "Too much?"

The serious morphed into exasperated. "I've already made it clear it was both welcome and incredibly sexy. I was thinking more about myself."

"What about you?"

Quinn took a deep breath, blew it out. "Being with you, is…"

Amanda waited for her to continue, but she didn't. "Is?"

Another deep breath. "It's amazing. Let me lead with that. It's also, I don't know, kind of a wake-up call."

"How so?"

"Like, I haven't been myself lately and you reminded me of who that person is."

Not unlike her feelings about her brief affair with Mel. She could appreciate the sentiment—like, a thousand times over—but the parallel left her uneasy. What if Quinn's wake-up call woke her up to a thousand things that weren't her? "I get that."

"So, like, I'm not going to turn into some super intense alpha butch or anything, but I think I might have come across as more timid than I really am."

Oh. Oh, that was interesting. "Is that an apology or a warning?" She bit her lip and let her gaze linger on Quinn's mouth. "Or a promise?"

"At the risk of sounding wishy-washy, may I ask if you have a strong preference one way or another?"

She tucked her tongue in her cheek, trying decide how best to answer.

Quinn didn't give her the chance to. "You know what, never mind. I need to be authentic here. So, it's kind of all three, but mostly the last one. I can keep it in check, to a certain extent. Like I said, I'm not some swaggery alpha and I don't like being the center of attention. But I'm bolder than I've let on so far and I think it's fair for you to know it."

Just when she thought her night couldn't get any better. "Out of curiosity, what exactly might that look like?"

"Well—"

"You could tell me or, if you'd rather, you should show me."

Quinn's gaze raked over her. "I'd very much like to show you."

"Then, by all means."

"Don't mind if I do." She shifted, sliding her arm out from around Amanda. She trailed fingers down Amanda's arms, encircling each of her wrists. She pinned Amanda's hands over her head, gave Amanda a look that threatened to set her insides on fire, and then she proceeded to do exactly that.

CHAPTER NINETEEN

Amanda flipped the switch on the coffee pot and puttered around the kitchen, humming to herself. When Quinn appeared, gorgeous and rumpled in the doorway, she couldn't suppress a smile. "Good morning."

Quinn ran a hand through her hair, only making matters worse. Or, in the context of rumpled and gorgeous, better. "Morning."

"Coffee?"

Quinn nodded. "Oh, yes."

She readied cups, taking pleasure in knowing how Quinn liked her coffee at this point. "It'll just be a minute."

Quinn crossed the room and put her arms around Amanda, pulling her close. "How are you this morning?"

A string of clichés and a few sexually explicit responses danced through her mind, but she settled on, "Really good."

Quinn loosened her grip but didn't let her go. "I swear I'm not the woman who needs a lot of feedback in the sex department, but could you maybe be a tad more specific?"

She laughed, given what had been on the tip of her tongue.

"I said specific." Quinn made small circles with her index finger. "That could be read a lot of different ways."

"It was amazing." She kissed Quinn. "Perfect." She kissed her again. "So exactly what I wanted." Another kiss. "Needed."

"See, that's better. Although I don't want you to think I'm fishing for compliments."

She shook her head. "I don't. And, for the record, the laugh was because I was thinking about a dozen inappropriate comments about how good the sex was and I refrained."

"Inappropriate, huh?"

It was the first time she'd seen Quinn look truly smug and, to be honest, it was a good look for her. "Trust me on this one."

She poured the coffee and handed Quinn a cup. Quinn stared at it for a moment, then leaned in and breathed in the steam wafting from it. "Okay. You hand me coffee and I'll go along with pretty much anything you ask."

"I'll keep that in mind. What can I make you for breakfast?"

Quinn took a sip of coffee and let out a sigh. "You don't have to make me breakfast, you know. I mean, I love your cooking, but that's not what I'm in it for."

"Is that so?" She sipped her own coffee and indulged a passing thought of how easy it would be to get used to mornings like this.

"Uh-huh."

"So, do I get to ask what you are in it for?"

"The sex."

She said it so casually, Amanda couldn't help but snicker. "It's good to know what I bring to the table."

"Don't get me wrong. Your cooking is literally the best I've ever had. Don't tell my mother I said that."

Amanda laughed. "Your secret is safe with me."

"I'm just saying that so you understand exactly how next level the sex is."

She didn't disagree, even if it felt strange to say so out loud. "I'll still make you breakfast."

"A woman of many talents. I love that about you."

Quinn insisted she didn't want Amanda to go to any trouble, so they settled on a vegetable omelet and toast. They sat at the island, side by side, bumping shoulders and playing footsie while they ate. It made her feel goofy and far younger than her forty-nine years.

When the conversation turned to getting together again, she found herself saying, "Would you be interested in coming to dinner if my kids were here?"

Quinn, to her credit, didn't seem taken aback. "Absolutely, but I don't want you to feel obligated."

"I don't feel obligated. But same. If that feels like a big deal and you're not ready to go there, it's totally fine."

Quinn shook her head, but then said, "I'd like that."

"Do I get to ask why you were shaking your head then?" She wanted Quinn to be honest, because as much as she liked the idea, it wasn't some pressing thing. At least not yet.

"Just the fact that my sister was poking at me about when she'd get to meet you."

As much as she liked the prospect of Quinn meeting Cal and Daniella, she liked the idea of Quinn telling her family about her even more. "And what did you tell her?"

"First, I told her she was nosy and pushy, because she is. But then I told her soon, assuming things continue to go well."

Amanda laughed, at both the honesty and the authenticity of the statement. "Fair assessment."

"Right? You'd think it would be less complicated at our age."

"Ha." She had a flash of coming home after their first night together, to Mel making breakfast.

"I'm glad we're on the same page, though."

An excellent point. "So, which should we do first?"

"Your kids. Definitely." She angled her head. "Just don't tell my sister I said so."

Amanda tapped a finger to her lips, then pointed at Quinn. "You realize that's the second secret you've asked me to keep from your family this morning."

She covered her mouth with her hand. "It is, isn't it? That's not good."

"Since I'm pretty sure you're only half serious, it's more cute than concerning."

"Less than half. My mother is lovely and my sisters—well, one in particular—harass me on principle. But we're all very close and the harassment is a sign of affection."

"That's sweet. I always wanted siblings."

Quinn's eyes narrowed. "Wait. You're an only child? But you're Italian."

She shrugged. "I know, right? I thought it was against the rules or something, but here I am."

"Your parents realized they couldn't improve on perfection?"

Amanda laughed. "It was more that my mother didn't want to sacrifice her career. She was too much of a traditionalist not to have any children, but one was enough."

"What did she do?"

"Chemist. She's retired now. My parents moved to South Carolina a couple of years ago."

"Whoa."

"I know, right? She was the only woman in her graduate program and one of only a few in her undergraduate class."

"That's awesome."

"She was horrified when I announced I wanted to go to culinary school." It had been difficult at the time, but now she could smile at the memory.

"Did you ever win her over?"

"It helped when she learned professional baking is a very male-dominated field."

Quinn chuckled. "Of course."

They finished breakfast. They showered. They might have tumbled back into bed for an hour before getting dressed and Quinn reluctantly left for work. Amanda couldn't remember the last time she'd had such an indulgent morning.

She liked that Quinn brought this out in her. The sexual energy, sure, but it was more. Quinn helped her slow down, focus more on the moment than her running to-do list. It helped that she was taking essentially a month-long vacation, obviously, but even then, old Amanda would have found a thousand things to do for the kids or around the house. She thought of the million or so times over the years Mel told her to just fucking relax already. And yet it was Quinn, without commanding it once, who actually got her to do it.

❖

Quinn drove into town and pulled into the small lot next to Ithaca Bakery. Inside, business people and college students and senior citizens milled around, looking at menus and peering to see what bagels were still available. She turned at the sound of her name and found Jacob coming in the other entrance.

She gave him a big hug, convinced he was still growing, despite turning nineteen that spring. "How's summer treating you?"

"Not bad. Working my ass off, but making decent money, so I can't complain."

He'd spent every summer since he was old enough at one of the local nurseries. She knew the owner and, by extension, knew he was worked hard but paid well. "That's the spirit. Gotta do it while you're young."

He rolled his eyes. "You say that like you're ancient."

"It's relative, my man. It's all relative."

"I know Mom's only a few years older than you, but you seem way younger."

"It's the single and childless thing. It fools people."

He laughed. "I'll have to keep that in mind."

She thought about where she'd been a few hours prior. "Relationships have a lot to recommend them. I'd like to go on the record saying that."

He gave her a quizzical look. She hadn't confided the extent of her broken heart and collapsing marriage, but he was old enough—and sensitive enough—to pick up on how bad it had been. "You got a bae, don't you?"

The question, delivered in millennial or Gen Z or whatever he was speak, made her laugh. "How about you let me buy you lunch and maybe we'll talk about it?"

He nodded affably. Like his mother, he was curious but not pushy. They ordered sandwiches and took the number placard to an empty table. Not that she wouldn't talk about Amanda at all, but she was much more interested in what he had going on. "Looking forward to the fall semester or no?"

He shrugged and looked down. "Kinda."

"Not very convincing, there."

He lifted his gaze, eyes full of worry. "I'm just…I think I might change my major."

"Okay?" She let the word dragged to show her confusion. "Is that a bad thing?"

"I don't want you to be mad that I might not stay in architecture. Or disappointed or whatever."

It never occurred to her he'd worry so much about her opinion. It made her smile and gave her a pang all at the same time. "Jake, you should do what makes you happy. Always."

"But I was going to do an internship with you and it was going to be so cool."

They had discussed that possibility, and she relished the prospect of having him work with her. But it was because she loved spending time with him and wanted to help him get a leg up professionally. "You figuring out what you want to do, and doing it, is way more important than an internship with me."

He frowned but looked more relaxed. "Yeah."

"So, any contenders? Or do you just hate architecture?"

"I don't hate it." His tone was equal parts defensive and apologetic. "It's just, like, a lot of math."

"I warned you about that."

"I know, I know. I used to like math?"

That he phrased it as a question made her chuckle. "What happened?"

He blew out a breath. "Calculus."

She could empathize. She'd gotten the grades she'd needed to advance to the upper level courses, but she hadn't hit it out of the park by any means. "No argument there."

"I took this lit class for one of my electives and I really dug it."

"Lit, huh?" She did not see that one coming.

"The professor was amazing. This southern chick. Gorgeous, but that's not why I loved her class. She was so excited about Eudora Welty. She made me want to read all these books and, I don't know, maybe write one."

It was hard to decide what part of this delighted her more—the idea of her nephew becoming a writer or having a pretty good idea who the inspiring professor was. "Dr. Bennett?"

His eyes got huge. "You know her?"

"A little. Her wife is a contractor I work with a lot."

"You can't tell her I said she was gorgeous."

The genuine fear in his voice made her smile. "Your secret is safe with me."

"I signed up for her creative writing seminar in the fall. It's just an intro. You don't have to be good to take it or anything."

She had no intention of telling Olivia, or Joss for that matter, that her nephew had a crush on her. But she would pick Olivia's brain for things she might do to encourage him along the way. Things completely out of her wheelhouse. "Have you told your parents?"

"Yeah, yeah. They're cool. I was more worried about telling you."

"Aw. You know I'll support you no matter what."

"Yeah." He blushed and looked relieved when their food came. "Thanks."

"Always."

He picked up his sandwich and took a huge bite. Mouth full, he lifted his chin at her. "Tell me about your girl."

She laughed, both at his interest in her love life and his use of the word girl, not because he was being condescending but because he was relating to her as a peer. "Well, she's a baker. And she's gorgeous."

He nodded his approval. "That's lit."

Between time with her nieces and nephews and context clues, she was pretty sure lit meant cool and not the kind of lit they'd been discussing a moment before. "It kind of is."

They finished their sandwiches and she bought him a box of cookies to take to work that afternoon. "You going to bring her to a family thing soon?"

"Has Aunt Kiera been feeding you lines?"

"Huh?"

He looked genuinely confused, so she slapped him on the shoulder. "Kidding. She's been needling me about the same thing."

"Oh. Ha ha. Yeah. That sounds like her."

The simplicity of the statement made her laugh. "What about you? Any girls? Boys?"

He lifted a hand. "Pretty sure it's girls, but no."

She hung her head and shook it dramatically. "Not an architect and straight. What am I going to do with you?"

He winced. "You're sure you're not mad about that?"

"No. I'm proud of you for following your heart, on both counts."

"All right."

"I can't wait to hear about your class with Olivia."

It took him a second to realize who she meant. "I can't believe you know her. And that you call her Olivia."

"You should probably still call her Dr. Bennett." She winked at him. "At least for now."

The idea of calling her anything else seemed to mortify him, which she found endearing. They hugged in the parking lot and went their separate ways. Quinn headed to work, thinking a bit about the bank branch plans she had waiting for her, but mostly about Amanda and the prospect of meeting each other's families. She'd expected the prospect to give her pause, but it didn't. Perhaps, when it came down to it, her hesitation to get involved with someone again had less to do with getting involved and more to do with the person in question.

CHAPTER TWENTY

Quinn strode up the walk, telling herself not to be nervous. It didn't do much good, but she told herself anyway. Who would have guessed meeting a girlfriend's kids would prove more daunting than meeting her parents? The adventures of dating in middle age.

Amanda greeted her at the door with an encouraging smile. "Thanks for coming."

She didn't seem nervous, just happy for Quinn to be there. That unspoken energy did more to calm her nerves than any reassurance could have. "I brought ice cream, as instructed."

"Excellent."

Amanda took the bag from her. Quinn leaned in and kissed her cheek. That was okay, right? Based on Amanda's smile, yeah, it was okay.

In the kitchen, Daniella and Cal seemed to be waiting for her. Nope, not nervous at all. "Hi."

"It's nice to meet you." Daniella crossed the room and extended her hand.

Quinn accepted the handshake. "Likewise."

"Good to see you again." Cal mimicked his sister's gesture.

Quinn shook his hand as well, wondering if they'd been coached or raised with such impeccable manners. "You, too."

Amanda went to the oven and peered in. "Should be just a few minutes."

She sniffed the air. "I'm not sure what you're cooking, but it smells amazing."

"You're easy." Amanda offered a wink.

"There's nothing wrong with being easy when it comes to food," Cal said.

"Thank you." She appreciated that he was looking for common ground.

Daniella smirked. It reminded Quinn so very much of Amanda. She refrained from saying so, at least until passing the initial sniff test. "So, you designed the bakery expansion."

It was more statement than question, but Daniella clearly expected a response. What she couldn't tell was if Daniella was trying to make conversation or preparing an offensive. "I did. Even without how nice it's been to get to know your mom, I would have been thrilled to take the job. It's a fantastic space."

The smirk softened into a half smile and she nodded. "I like the new layout you came up with. It's much better than Mom's idea."

"The original idea was nice, just not feasible without a massive cost." She hoped that came out as diplomatically as she intended.

Amanda pulled a bottle of wine from the fridge. "I think we can all agree your design is better no matter what. Wine?"

She'd hesitated to bring a bottle, not wanting to send the wrong message, but she wasn't about to turn down a glass. "Sure."

"Daniella?"

"Yes, please." Daniella turned her attention back to Quinn. "I'm not twenty-one yet, but Mom lets me drink wine at home so I'm less tempted to get hammered at parties."

Given the delivery, she decided to take a chance. "Does it work?"

Daniella straightened her shoulders and lifted her chin. "I haven't gotten hammered yet."

Amanda handed Quinn a glass first, then Daniella. She gave Daniella a kiss on the forehead. "And I appreciate you saying that, even if it's not true."

"Cross my heart." She made the gesture, then shrugged. "Who has time for hangovers?"

Cal opened the fridge and pulled out a Pepsi. "Spoken like a true nerd."

"Yeah, 'cause you're such a party animal."

"I can be. I just don't like wine." He curled his lip.

She took it as a good sign they were antagonizing each other in front of her. It meant they were comfortable. Amanda didn't look quite as amused, but instead of scolding, she made them set the table.

To their credit, they didn't grumble at all. It must be a chore they were used to. Quinn respected that as much as Amanda's take on alcohol consumption.

They stood at the kitchen island around a platter of antipasti and focaccia. She learned about Cal's job at Rustic Refined and his plans to study environmental engineering at Cornell, Daniella's decision to work as a counselor at a music camp for disadvantaged kids instead of trying for a position in a lab or at a hospital. By the time they sat down to chicken parm, Quinn was thoroughly charmed. Even if Daniella still seemed to be reserving judgment.

"Do you have kids?" Cal asked.

The question seemed more casual than a fishing expedition, maybe because it came from Cal. "None of my own. My ex-wife never wanted them. I've got two nephews around your age, though, and a niece who's six."

"Do they live close?" Daniella asked.

"They do. I've been lucky to be part of their lives since they were born."

"Cool." Cal nodded affably.

"Jacob is going to be a sophomore at Cornell, and Adam is going into his senior year."

Cal's eyes lit up at the mention of Cornell. "What's Jacob's major?"

"Well, he started with architecture, but I have a feeling he might change to English."

"Whoa." Cal seemed alarmed by such a dramatic shift.

Amanda didn't miss a beat. "It's okay to change your mind."

A lot of parents would balk at the idea of their kid switching from a professional program to something in the humanities, especially at a school like Cornell. She liked that Amanda wasn't one of those parents.

"If you want, I can give you Jacob's number. I'm sure he'd be happy to share some of the things he wished he'd known."

Cal smiled with genuine enthusiasm. "That would be awesome."

The rest of the meal passed in a blur. Dinner gave way to coffee and dessert—the ice cream she'd brought scooped onto the most amazing berry crumble she'd ever put in her mouth. The hardest part was trying to divide her attention equally between Daniella and Cal, without ignoring Amanda completely. Easier said than done.

Cal seemed to like her. Whether it had more to do with actually liking her or his easygoing personality, she couldn't be sure. But she could easily imagine spending time with him, even without Amanda around. Daniella was a tougher nut. Reserved, but like Cal, it was hard to tell if it was her personality or something specific to Quinn. Or maybe more accurately, Quinn's relationship with her mother. Still, the whole evening went smoothly and even Daniella was thoroughly polite. For a first meeting, she'd take it.

Amanda set the kids to doing dishes and walked Quinn to the door. "Thank you for coming."

"I should be the one thanking you. Dinner was, once again, incredible. And it was great to meet your kids."

Amanda rolled her eyes but smiled. "They can be overwhelming at first. Cal because he's sweet but a chatterbox. Daniella because she's convinced she's an adult who has everyone and everything figured out."

The descriptions were so on point, Quinn couldn't help but laugh. "They clearly adore you. I expected an interrogation, so I was prepared for much worse. They're great."

"Interrogation, huh?" Amanda raised a brow.

"You know what I mean. I hope they weren't just pretending because of good manners. You'll have to tell me if they secretly hated me."

"Stop."

Quinn shrugged. "Kidding. Mostly."

"Not that it was a test, but you did great."

She might say that, but Quinn knew perfectly well it was a test. Amanda was not the kind of woman to keep someone in her life her kids hated. And to be honest, she wouldn't want to date a woman where that sort of tension was constantly there. "I give myself a solid B, but I'm going to keep working for the A."

Amanda folded her arms.

"Again, kidding." She couldn't resist adding a wink this time. "Mostly."

Amanda shook her head. "You're as bad as they are."

"Tonight, I'm going to take that as a compliment."

She laughed. "Text me when you get home?"

"Absolutely." Once again, she kissed Amanda on the cheek, even though she wanted more.

Amanda put a hand on her arm and leaned back in. The second kiss was brief, but having Amanda's lips on hers sent a tingle of pleasure down her spine. She let out a contented sigh.

Amanda opened the front door. "I'll see you soon?"

Quinn stepped onto the front porch but turned back to look at Amanda. "Name the day."

Amanda nodded. "Have a good night."

She offered a parting wave. "You, too."

❖

Amanda waited for Quinn's car to pull out of the driveway before closing the door and returning to the kitchen. She found Daniella wiping the counter and Cal drying the spaghetti pot. She desperately wanted to know their opinions but didn't want them to feel put on the spot.

Fortunately, Cal didn't make her wait. "Quinn seems really cool."

He was, hands down, the absolute sweetest boy. She so loved that about him. "She said the same about you."

Cal grinned, but Daniella rolled her eyes. "I don't know. I thought she was maybe trying a little too hard."

Cal swung his towel at her. "Don't be mean."

"I'm not being mean." Daniella's defensive tone gave her pause.

"Did you not like her?" Amanda asked. No point beating around the bush.

Daniella lifted a shoulder. "No, she was fine. It's just, I don't know, weird."

She might have taken that at face value, but it didn't add up with the conversation they'd had only a couple of weeks before. The one where Daniella seemed to think her mom was overdue for a girlfriend. "Do you want to talk about it?"

Daniella shook her head. "It's cool. I'm going to bed."

Without another word, she picked up her phone and ran up the stairs. Cal plopped onto one of the stools at the island and looked after her, clearly confused. "What was that about?"

"I'm not sure." Maybe the reality of her mom dating was proving less cool than the idea of it. Or maybe she felt bad about being aloof but didn't know how to walk back from it. She might be older than Cal, and more mature on most fronts, but she was still a teenager.

Cal shrugged. "She's so weird sometimes. I liked Quinn a lot and I hope you keep seeing her."

Amanda put her arm around him and rested her cheek on the top of his head. "Thanks, honey."

He stood up and gave her a full hug. "I like seeing you happy."

The comment put a lump in her throat. Not trusting herself to reply, she squeezed him tighter.

When she let go, he stepped back and offered her a bright smile. "I don't have to be at work until noon tomorrow, so I'm going to go play *Fortnight*."

She laughed. He might be a sweet and sensitive kid, capable of saying the exact right thing at the exact right time, but he was still a teenager, too. "All right. Not too late."

He disappeared to the basement and she headed upstairs. She changed into pajamas and washed her face. It might still be early August, but with the windows open, her room was almost chilly. She climbed into bed and pulled the blankets up. She had no use for fall or winter anytime soon, but the burrowing made her happy.

After getting settled, she pulled up her text conversation with Quinn. She'd not responded to Quinn's last message, about liking spending time with her every which way. She spent a minute trying to think of something clever, then settled on one of Quinn's phrases. *Ditto.*

Instead of waiting to see if Quinn saw it or replied, she switched over to her group text with Erin, Jack, and Julia. Over the course of the evening, each of them had sent some sort of inquiry, ranging from a simple *Well?* to a GIF of fingers drumming on a table. As much as she protested their harassment, she was grateful for it. She couldn't even imagine navigating dating without her little group of confidants.

Success. D was a bit cool, but Cal made up for it.

Erin replied first. *She feels obliged because she hates Bella.*

Maybe that was it. Paired with her current phase of being aloof and impossible to impress. *Not full on rude, but I hope she warms up.*

Did Quinn pick up on it?

Amanda sighed. *Yes, but she was beyond gracious.*

Julia chimed in. *And that's why we like her.*

Before Amanda could reply, a text popped up from Quinn. She toggled over. *I hope they liked me enough to want to hang out again before school starts.*

Definitely. Maybe a picnic. She hit send and returned to the group text. Jack had joined in with a *Hooray for successful kid meet* and a string of festive emojis. The group went back and forth for a bit with a mix of teasing and encouragement. Meanwhile, Quinn said she loved the idea of the picnic. The earnestness of the message made her smile and she told her friends as much.

That set off a string of teasing about being smitten. It didn't bother her, but she wasn't sure she wanted the conversation to turn sentimental. *I'm glad she wanted to meet the kids, but I'm mostly thinking about the next time I can get in her pants.*

A microsecond after hitting send, realization hit. She'd not sent that to her closest friends. She'd sent it to Quinn. Oh God, oh God, oh God. Why wasn't there an undo function in texting? She immediately added a *Not for you! Sorry!*

Then she waited. Delivered, but not read. Seriously, why couldn't there be a recall option?

While she stared at the screen, the other conversation carried on. Notifications flitted across the top of her screen, teasing her but also each other. When it became clear Quinn wasn't going to reply right away, she switched back over and read what she'd missed. She sighed. At least she could commiserate in real time. *You'll never guess what I just did.*

She sent a screen shot and got line after line of laughing emojis in return.

Laugh away, but srsly, what do I do?

I think you have to own it. Jack said. Erin and Julia agreed.

Quinn's reply came through before she could. *I hope you mean the message and not wanting to get into someone else's pants.*

Amanda laughed. She could do embarrassed and apologetic like a boss. But what if, this time, she didn't? She bit her bottom lip while she typed, not giving herself the chance to second guess the decision. *Yours are the only pants I want to get in. Promise.*

She held her breath while Quinn typed a reply. Technically, she'd just floated the idea of being exclusive. Quinn could take that seriously or not. Weirdly, she wasn't sure which option made her more nervous.

Same here. Except sometimes you wear skirts and that's nice, too.

She laughed again. *Fair enough.*

She took a screen shot and sent it to her friends. They cheered. She wished them a good night, then did the same to Quinn. She turned off the light and snuggled back under the covers. The whole thing made her feel a bit like a giddy teenager with a crush. Sure, cell phones didn't exist when she was a teenager, but still.

CHAPTER TWENTY-ONE

Quinn left the site survey for the new bank, satisfied they'd break ground in the next week or two. Since she was on the west side of the lake, she decided to swing by the bakery. Joss had mentioned she had a crew working weekends to keep the timeline on track. It wasn't her habit to keep such a close eye on the construction phase, but this wasn't a typical project. Or, perhaps more accurately, it wasn't a typical client.

She arrived, expecting the sound of hammers and saws to greet her. She heard neither. In fact, it was so quiet, she could make out the call of a chickadee chattering in a nearby tree.

Several vehicles sat in the small lot, though, including Joss's truck. A familiar foreboding settled under her ribs. She walked to the back door and found it ajar. There were definitely people inside. No noise from tools, but a pair of frustrated voices and a handful of expletives greeted her. "Hello?"

Whatever conversation was unfolding stopped and Joss called out, "Quinn? Is that you?"

She stepped inside. Gone was the plastic sheeting from the earlier phase of the project. New walls were up, but wiring still protruded from where outlets should be. The flooring looked about half done. "It is. Bad time?"

Joss rounded the corner. "More like a bad day."

Her stomach sank. "What's wrong?"

"Half the flooring we ordered is the wrong thing."

"How could we have ordered half the wrong thing? We're using all the same." Amanda had decided she liked the wood grain tile so much, she wanted it in the kitchen, too.

"We didn't. Half the boxes are the wrong color."

"Oh." That wasn't good.

"I should have opened them all when they arrived, but I checked one and assumed they were all the same."

"Which should have been a reasonable assumption." One she would have made, and readily forgiven. Only it wasn't hers to forgive.

"Maybe, but it's a costly one."

It wasn't the money she worried about. The supplier would correct the mistake without question. It was time. "What are we talking about?"

"Well, two to three days to get the right materials in."

"That's not so bad." They had a target completion date, but it was padded a little.

"But a couple more to tear up what got laid before I caught it."

"Oh." Her mind raced, imagining possible solutions.

"It's my own damn fault. Charlotte was sick yesterday, so I didn't come in. And my guys didn't think twice about it. They just figured it was supposed to be one color in the kitchen and a different color in the dining area."

"Where is the stuff that's wrong?" She didn't want to ask Amanda to change her mind, but it would only be fair to give her options.

"The dining area. We're going to fix it, without question. And if I can talk a few guys into overtime, we might make up at least some of the time."

"All right." This sort of thing happened. She hated it, but she was used to it. But telling a client and telling her girlfriend felt like vastly different propositions.

Joss gave her a knowing look. "I know this is the sort of thing you communicate, but I can."

Quinn shook her head. "No, no. I can do it. I should do it."

"Obviously, I'll absorb the cost of the tile we wasted. And the overtime."

In addition to being good at her job, and a fellow lesbian, Joss had the highest integrity of any contractor she'd ever worked with. "Let me talk with Amanda, see how upset she is."

Joss winced. "I'm really sorry."

Quinn waved her off. "This kind of thing happens, way more often with everyone else I work with than you."

"Still."

She could tell part of Joss's frustration was her own sense of responsibility, but part of it was knowing Quinn's personal connection to Amanda. No way should Joss take on the responsibility for that. "It's fine. I'll see if Amanda is home and swing by to talk in person."

Joss blew out a breath. "Sounds good. Let me know what she says."

"Will do."

Quinn left, sending Amanda a text before heading toward her house. When she arrived, Amanda had scones and fresh coffee waiting, making her feel like a heel. She conveyed the issue, sort of wanting to leave out the part about half of the wrong floor being installed before it was caught. But she didn't. She didn't believe in hiding things from a client. She believed even less in hiding things from a partner.

Partner might be a bit of a stretch, but the principle wasn't.

"It should only push things back by a few days."

Amanda closed her eyes and took a deep breath. Part of her wanted to pull out her stern, this is not acceptable routine. She'd perfected it in the early days of the business, when suppliers and the occasional contractor thought they could push around a newcomer—a woman, no less—when they didn't deliver. But she didn't want to do that. Partly because it was Quinn and she didn't want any hard feelings between them. But more, she trusted it was an honest mistake, and not even the doing of Quinn or Joss. Also, she didn't need to be that woman anymore. She didn't have anything to prove.

"How mad are you?"

She opened her eyes and found Quinn regarding her with concern. "I'm not mad."

"You're saying that in that really ominous way women who are seething do."

The description made her laugh and dispelled any lingering frustration. "I'm not. I promise."

"Joss thinks she'll be able to make up some of the time if she can get a rush delivery of the correct tiles. And she'll absorb the cost."

Amanda shook her head. "I'm really not angry. And I trust her to make whatever call she thinks is best. If that makes sense for her crew, great. If not, I'm okay with a short delay."

Quinn seemed genuinely confused. "You are?"

She tipped her head slightly. "As long as it is, in fact, a short delay."

Quinn's shoulders relaxed. "Okay. That's great. Thank you for being understanding."

She didn't need to ask, but curiosity won out. "Did you expect me to flip out?"

"No, but I did expect you to be disappointed. I worried you might think I was counting on you being okay with it because of our personal relationship."

That hadn't occurred to her. "Were you?"

"No." The declaration came out with more vehemence than she'd ever seen in Quinn. "I was worried that's what you'd think."

"I don't expect special treatment or lousy treatment."

Quinn laughed. "Right. That's fair. I promise you're not getting either. Well, maybe a little special treatment."

She smiled. "I can live with that."

"Not that I think sex and romance can make up for work delays, or that one should have anything to do with the other, but maybe I could try to make it up to you later?"

The question was playful, but she liked the forwardness of it. Quinn seemed to be coming out of her shell. Into her own. She appreciated the general sentiment, but also what it meant for her. "In that case, I'm very, very upset."

Quinn shook her head, expression grave. "We can't have that."

Amanda folded her arms and resisted smiling. "What are you proposing to do about it?"

"Dinner, for sure. Maybe a massage. Your wish will be my command."

She didn't need that, but she was enjoying the game. More than she would have expected, to be honest. Perhaps because it was a game. Such an unexpected surprise. "Pick me up at six?"

Quinn grinned. "Done."

Quinn tiptoed from the bedroom to the kitchen. She wouldn't go so far as to say the construction snag was a good thing, but she had no complaints about the evening that unfolded as a result. She puttered around the kitchen, wishing she had the skills to make Amanda a fancy breakfast. She flipped on the coffee pot and turned. Amanda stood in the doorway, looking sex tossed and beautiful. "I would have brought you coffee in bed."

"That's not necessary."

She glanced at the pot to make sure it was going, then gave Amanda a kiss. "That's what makes it fun."

"You're going to spoil me and make me lazy."

"A little spoiling won't make you lazy, I promise." She kissed her again. "You should let me spoil you so I can prove my point."

Amanda wrinkled her nose. "Maybe."

"I should warn you that spoiling will not extend to homemade breakfast. But I did pick up bagels yesterday."

"Bagels definitely count as spoiling, but I think I'll start with coffee."

She gestured to the small eating area in the corner. "Make yourself comfortable."

To her credit, Amanda didn't argue. She pulled out a chair and sat, tucking one foot under her. Everything about it—from having Amanda there in the first place to how adorable she looked with her elbows propped on the IKEA table Quinn bought to fit in the tiny space—made her feel about twenty years old. She grabbed a pair of mugs from the cupboard and poured coffee.

Amanda accepted, taking the cup in both hands and breathing in the steam that wafted up. "Thank you."

Quinn smiled. It was her turn to say, "You're easy."

She lifted a shoulder. "Maybe."

She sat with her own cup and mimicked the gesture. She couldn't deny the magic of the first cup of the day. After taking a sip, she set it down and leaned forward, resting an elbow on the table. "So, I was thinking."

Amanda regarded her with alarm. "What?"

"Why do you look so freaked out?"

"Nothing. Sorry. What were you thinking?"

Quinn shook her head. "No, you can't look at me like I just suggested we rob a bank, then pretend you didn't."

Amanda laughed. "Too many years of teenage children."

Oh. That made sense. And far more harmless than the dozen or so directions her thoughts had taken. "See, I'll give you that one."

Amanda lifted her cup. "Thank you."

"Did you think I was going to suggest we rob a bank?"

"No, my kids weren't that kind of trouble. More the bring home the class iguana for summer vacation without telling me type."

It was her turn to laugh. "Cal?"

Amanda shook her head. "You'd think."

She had this vivid image of Daniella with her hair in braids and a cheerful grin on her face, holding an iguana the size of her arm. "Is it okay to say I'm sorry I wasn't around for that?"

"As long as that's not what you're suggesting we do now."

She looked up at the ceiling. "Well, now that you mention it."

Amanda lifted a finger. "Don't even think about it."

"I was thinking more along the lines of getting out in nature, not the other way around."

She set down her coffee. "Go on."

"I have a cabin up in the Adirondacks. It's rustic, but the spot is beautiful. There's a lake and a fireplace and it's off grid."

Amanda closed one eye. "What do you mean by 'off grid,' exactly?"

"Running water, but no electricity or cell service."

"Huh."

"Too rustic?"

"It's not the rustic so much as the off-grid part."

She'd been worried about the lack of electricity, not the being online part. "Really?"

"It's the mom thing. It's hard for me to be unreachable." She lifted both hands. "I know, I know. It's silly given they're practically adults."

"It's not silly." She just hadn't thought about it. "It's not something on my radar, you know?"

"I'm not saying no, it's just, um, out of my comfort zone."

Quinn took her hand. Even if part of her hated the idea of never being able to unplug completely, she didn't want Amanda to feel pressured to do it to make her happy. "It's okay. I understand."

She thought that might be the end of it, but Amanda shook her head. "No."

"No?"

Amanda sat up straight and got this serious look on her face. Paired with her messy hair and the rumpled T-shirt, it made Quinn's heart flip uncomfortably in her chest. "I want to go."

"You really don't have to—"

"I want to go. I mean it. The whole point of this is putting myself first."

The prospect of having Amanda all to herself for a couple of days was thrilling. "You're sure?"

"Absolutely sure."

"We can wait until the kids go back to school, but I thought you might prefer to get away while the bakery is still closed." She offered a half smile. "And the weather is still nice and warm."

"You're right. Sooner is better. And Cal and Daniella are perfectly capable of fending for themselves. I worry too much."

Quinn tipped her head to one side. "I know better than to have an opinion on that."

"Oh, really?" Amanda folded her arms, but the look on her face was playful.

"A woman's worry is her own prerogative, one hundred percent."

"I wouldn't mind you telling me to worry a little less now and again."

"Wouldn't mind or would like?" She could appreciate needing a nudge. And as much as she wanted to stay in her lane at this point in their relationship, she also wanted to be what Amanda needed.

Amanda took a deep breath and blew it out. "Would like. My ex was one for telling me to chill out, but she had this way of putting more on my plate rather than less. You're different."

She wasn't in the business of wanting to be compared, but the compliment went a long way. "I'd rather help you relax than tell you to."

Amanda's face softened and she smiled. "You're pretty good at that already."

She might be pressing her luck, but she'd gotten Amanda to agree to go away with her, so it felt like she was on a roll. "And if I said I was just getting started?"

"I'd say show me what you've got."

She stood. On a roll, indeed. "How about we start with a shower?"

Amanda lifted a brow. "Together?"

She took Amanda's hand and led her to the bathroom. The small and uninspired space made her think again it was time to give up apartment living and put herself in the market for a house. But, for the moment, she had more pressing matters to attend to. Like slipping off Amanda's clothes and pulling her in for a kiss. Like turning on the water and getting the temperature just right. Like reminding Amanda of all the reasons showering with company was an excellent idea.

Chapter Twenty-two

Getting Amanda to agree to a weekend away was a big deal. Making it happen in a matter of days, rather than weeks or months? Well, that was the magic of the bakery being closed. Not that she'd wish for more delays, but it was almost enough to make her wish for more delays.

Despite Amanda's initial hesitation about being off grid, she seemed to have settled into the idea nicely by the time Quinn picked her up. On the drive, they alternated between talking and each other's favorite podcasts. When they lost service with about twenty minutes to go, she flipped on the radio. With each mile they got closer, she felt herself relax. She hoped Amanda felt the same.

When they pulled in and up the long and winding gravel driveway, Amanda exclaimed at how beautifully wooded it was. "I know we're not that far from the Finger Lakes, but it feels so different."

"Right? That's one of my favorite things about it."

Quinn grabbed her duffel bag and Amanda's while Amanda hefted the bags of food she'd insisted on preparing. And the wine to go with it, of course. She unlocked the door, then stepped back so Amanda could go in first.

"Wow. It's, um, nice."

Quinn set down their bags and suppressed a chuckle. "Why do I get the feeling that isn't the word you really want to use?"

"No, it totally is." She nodded with enthusiasm.

"It's rustic. You can say it. I know I told you, but thinking it and seeing it for yourself aren't the same thing."

Amanda frowned. "I just don't have a lot of experience. I'm not delicate, or changing my mind, or anything like that."

"I wasn't worried."

"Really?"

"You seem surprised that I have faith in you." Funny, given how self-assured Amanda was about most things.

Amanda ran a hand through her hair, then placed her hands on her hips. "Huh. Maybe I am."

"You're more adventurous than you give yourself credit for."

"Yeah." She nodded slowly, then with more vigor. "Yeah."

Quinn's heart did that thing it had started doing every time Amanda said or did something perfect. Which was kind of all the time. She was going to have to think about what that meant soon, but not today. "I'm glad you're letting me drag you on adventures."

Amanda took her hands from her hips and threaded them around Quinn. "I like adventuring with you."

If her heart had stopped doing that thing, it would have started up again. "I do, too."

Amanda smiled, then pressed her lips to Quinn's. The kiss lingered and Amanda's hands crept under the hem of Quinn's shirt. "Do all of our adventures need to be outdoors?"

"No, no they do not."

"Good." Without further discussion or fanfare, Amanda pulled the shirt over Quinn's head. Her bra quickly followed, and Amanda began a trail of kisses down her torso.

"Oh, this feels very adventurous."

Amanda paused and looked up. "Don't make fun."

"I'm not. I swear." She might have been the one to get Amanda hiking and camping, but it was Amanda who'd reminded her what sexual chemistry was, who'd awakened desire that had been dormant for far too long.

"Good. Otherwise, I'd have to get very stern with you."

They'd settled into a dynamic where she was the top. It was definitely her preference, but that didn't mean they couldn't play with it. "Maybe you should."

"Oh, really?" Amanda's fingers encircled Quinn's wrists.

"I mean, I'll turn the tables eventually." Quinn smirked. "But you should totally try."

Amanda glanced around the room, her eyes settling on the bed in the corner. She nudged Quinn and started inching in that direction. Quinn allowed herself to be led, enjoying where this was going. When they got there—not like it was very far—Amanda gave her a push. Quinn flopped onto the bed and spread her arms. "I think I like you like this," Amanda said.

"Just don't get too used to it."

"No?" Amanda joined her on the bed, straddling Quinn's hips.

Despite preferring to be the top, the position might be Quinn's favorite. "Well, maybe if you keep doing that."

"I thought so." Amanda moved against her.

"You should be naked, though. Really show me who's running this show."

"Yeah? You think so?"

Without stopping the movement of her hips, Amanda pulled the V-neck tee over her head. Despite the promise of rustic conditions, she wore a sexy bra. Quinn sighed her appreciation. "Better."

"Oh, no. I strive to be the best." She tossed her bra aside and leaned forward, brushing her nipples against Quinn's.

Quinn sucked in a breath. She angled her head to try to pull one into her mouth, but Amanda pressed a finger to her chest. "Ah, ah. Not yet."

She dropped her head to the pillow and heaved out a sigh of mock frustration. Well, mostly mock. Amanda was torturing her for sure. She just couldn't bring herself to mind.

She tried using her hands instead, but no sooner had she cupped Amanda's breasts than Amanda's fingers once again wound around her wrists. Amanda pinned them over her head. "Not yet."

Truth be told, she was stronger than Amanda and could have turned the tables. But she didn't want to. She wanted to let Amanda have her fun and to see where things went. She let her arms go limp and let out another sigh. "Fine."

"Good answer."

Amanda spent a few minutes sliding over Quinn's body, kissing and teasing as she went. She sucked Quinn's nipples; she nipped her ribs. When Amanda undid her belt and the button of her hiking shorts, Quinn lifted her hips to make it easier for Amanda to get them off.

Amanda stood and unbuttoned her own shorts, sliding them down her legs slowly. The come-hither smile was almost enough to make Quinn haul herself out of bed and toss Amanda on it. She resisted, but barely.

Amanda slinked back onto the bed but stopped halfway up Quinn's body. She locked eyes with Quinn and there was no mistaking her intent. It felt so strange not to please Amanda first, but the strangeness vanished when Amanda slicked her tongue up and over her clit. She arched instinctively.

Amanda pulled her mouth away. "Aren't you always the one telling me to be still?"

She gritted her teeth. She had said that to Amanda on more than one occasion. "Yes."

"Think you can manage?"

Quinn dropped her head again and laughed. "Yes, ma'am."

Amanda's mouth—her sweet, hot, perfect mouth—returned. She let out a moan, but she didn't move. Not to be unfair or anything, but she wasn't sure how much she could take being on the teased end of things.

Fortunately, Amanda didn't tease for long. And when Quinn couldn't stop her body from moving, from seeking the release that felt at once so close and so far away, Amanda didn't stop her. The orgasm took her and she didn't even try to stop it.

When her pulse finally slowed and she was able to catch her breath, she turned the tables. Even though Amanda's teasing had been fairly tame, Quinn gave it back to her in spades. When Amanda came, Quinn barely slowed the movements of her hands and mouth.

When Amanda came a second time, she called out with abandon. Such an incredible sound—pure and visceral—it made Quinn's heart tremble in her chest. She pulled Amanda into her arms, not quite ready to accept what that tremble so clearly signified.

Amanda sank into Quinn's embrace as she came down. As her body and mind stilled, she began to trace circles on Quinn's chest with the tip of her finger. "I have to say, I think I could get used to rustic."

"Could you now?" Quinn kissed the top of her head, making her smile.

"Absolutely. It's so peaceful up here. So relaxing. And clearly, the lack of neighbors makes me more than a little uninhibited."

Quinn shifted, nudging Amanda onto her back and rolling on top of her. "I like you uninhibited."

"You bring out something in me I didn't even know was there."

"Good."

She let out a contended sigh. "I literally can't tell you the last time my body felt this amazing."

Quinn kissed her. "Does that mean you're ready for a hike?"

She closed one eye and made a face. "Yes?"

Quinn kissed her. "I was kidding. I think we've exerted enough."

"Oh, thank God." She would have hiked. She wasn't a wimp.

"I thought we could take a shower, build a fire, start making dinner."

Now they were talking. "Shower?"

"Come with me." Quinn took her hand and helped her up. Without letting go, she went to the lone closet in the cabin and pulled out a pair of towels.

Amanda looked around, realizing the room was a perfect square, save a small water closet that definitely didn't have room for anything besides a toilet. "Wait. There's no bathroom. You promised running water."

"There is. I wouldn't lie about such a thing." Quinn pulled her to the cabin door.

Amanda stopped short. "We're naked."

"And there is no one around for miles and miles."

She frowned. They hadn't seen another soul, or another house, for the last fifteen minutes or so of the drive. Still. "Are you sure?"

Quinn kissed her nose. "Maybe we'll give the bears a show."

"Bears?" It came out more as a squeak than a word, but she didn't care. They most definitely had not discussed bears.

"They're more scared of you than you are of them. Promise."

"Yeah, not helping."

"But I've distracted you from fretting about the shower, right?"

Amanda laughed because she had. "Maybe a little."

"I promise no bears are going to wander up to the cabin in the middle of the afternoon."

She wasn't sure how Quinn could make such a promise, but freaking out about the possibility wouldn't do her any good. And she did want a shower. Sexy weekends required showers. "All right."

Quinn led them out the single door and around the side of the cabin. A tidy flagstone path covered the ten or so steps it took to get from the door to the shower. Even without the threat of being seen, it felt so weird to be outside naked in the middle of the day. Weird, but also kind of freeing. The sun peeked through the leaves and kissed her skin. The breeze was like a full body caress.

The shower was enclosed on three sides by the cabin and a pair of cedar plank walls. There were hooks for their towels and a bench. The floor was done in smooth river stones that massaged the bottoms of her feet.

"And it's warm?"

Quinn smiled. "I promised you hot water, didn't I? There's a small water heater that runs on propane."

Amanda grinned in return. "Doesn't sound rustic at all."

Quinn reached around her and turned on the water. After fiddling with the knob and letting it run for a few seconds, she motioned for Amanda to step under the spray. "I'll be honest, putting the shower outside was more choice than necessity."

She dunked her head and the warm water sluiced over her. Sunlight poured in, along with the breeze. Quinn's arms came around her. She blinked her eyes open and found Quinn staring at her. "You know, I'm coming to see the appeal."

They took turns lathering each other and rinsing off. Quinn pressed a kiss to her shoulder. "We've got a few minutes left before this runs cold."

Amanda glanced down, smiling at the image of their wet bodies. "I think I'm good."

"I'm not. But I will be."

Before she could ask what that meant, Quinn spun her around and placed a hand between her shoulders. She got the hint, bending forward and bracing her hands on the shower wall. But she tossed a defiant smirk over her shoulder. "Is this because I—"

The rest of the question vanished when Quinn's hand moved between her legs, two fingers buried deep inside her. Quinn raised a brow. "Maybe."

There was a cockiness in Quinn's tone, in her eyes. She should have found it a turn off, but she didn't. Maybe because it was such a departure from her usual demeanor. Whatever it was, it was sexy as fuck. "Should I talk back? Test you?"

Quinn slid out of her, then thrust back in with force. "I guess that depends on what you want to happen."

A shocking array of X-rated images and scenarios flashed through her mind. She'd never call herself a prude, but her brain absolutely didn't work that way. She was a mother, a woman pushing fifty.

Quinn tightened her grip around Amanda's waist and filled her again. "Having second thoughts?"

She bit her lip. "Not unless you count 'more' and 'yes, please' as second thoughts."

Quinn started fucking her, slow but deep. "No, I'd say those things put us right on the same page."

"Oh, good," she managed.

"I like you like this, pliant and at my mercy. Is that wrong?"

"Not. Wrong. At. All." Each word came out staccato, matched to the rhythm of Quinn's hand.

"Because I profoundly respect you."

Something about Quinn making that statement with fingers buried deep inside her did wicked things to Amanda. "You should respect me harder."

Quinn let out a groan. "What was it you said about testing me?"

She looked over her shoulder again. "I think I asked if that's what you wanted."

"Right."

Amanda squirmed, not really wanting to break free but enjoying this game they'd stumbled into. "Like this."

Quinn's hand stilled, her grip loosened. "I see."

She wiggled. "Wait. Who's testing who?"

"Does it matter?" Quinn angled her head, the look on her face playful.

"You know, I don't think it does." She liked everything about Quinn and wanted her pretty much any way she could get her.

"So agreeable."

She made a show of batting her eyes. "I try."

Quinn started her movements again and she moaned. Yep, pretty much any way she could get her. Despite coming earlier, she had no trouble climaxing again. Quinn had this way of getting her body to do things she had no idea it could do.

She wanted to have her way with Quinn, but the water had turned cold. Not to be deterred, she hastily wrapped herself in a towel and pulled Quinn back to the house. Inside, she disposed of her towel, then Quinn's. Then she nudged Quinn onto the bed and settled herself right back between Quinn's legs. If the amount of times Quinn could make her come was a surprise, the seemingly insatiable desire she had to reciprocate proved an utter delight. She'd always enjoyed that, but with Quinn, she honestly didn't think she could get enough.

She couldn't remember the last time she took an afternoon nap, but they did that, too, waking up just as the light took on the softness of late afternoon. They got dressed long enough to take a leisurely walk to the lake at the edge of Quinn's property and got back to the cabin with enough daylight left to enjoy a glass of wine on the porch before dinner.

They ate and cleaned up. Quinn opened a second bottle of wine to go with dessert and what turned into an epic game of Scrabble. By the time the last word was played, she was more than a little tipsy and wanted nothing more than to tear Quinn's clothes off again. And since she had nowhere to be and, for the moment at least, not a care in the world, that's exactly what she did.

CHAPTER TWENTY-THREE

Quinn would have been content to spend the entirety of their time in bed, but Amanda insisted on a real hike. She'd been promised a waterfall, after all. They struck out after breakfast and made it back in time for lunch and another shower together.

Amanda pulled on her clothes slowly. "I don't think I want to go back to reality."

"I always feel that way after a weekend in the woods. I'm glad you do, too." She didn't add that she could already imagine a lifetime of weekends spent like this. Or that Lesedi had never shown even a hair of interest in joining her.

"Are you ever tempted to play hooky and stay an extra day?"

Given Amanda's reluctance to spend a weekend off-grid in the first place, the question made her smile. "I have a couple of times, but only when I didn't have anything essential waiting for me."

Amanda laughed. "I'm not sure I'm familiar with that feeling."

"Maybe when Cal and Daniella are both out on their own."

She'd meant it in a lighthearted way, but Amanda seemed to turn the idea over in her mind. "Maybe so."

After loading the car, Amanda stood surveying the cabin while Quinn locked up. She remained that way when Quinn descended the stairs and joined her. "Ready?"

She let out a wistful sigh. "Yeah."

They climbed into the car and Quinn started the engine. "Thank you for running away with me."

Amanda buckled her seat belt. "Thank you for sharing such a special place. I hope we can come back."

"I never need much encouragement, so you just say the word."

When they pulled onto Route 28 heading south, Quinn turned on North Country Public Radio. The Sunday afternoon lineup—more quirky programming than news—always felt like a gentle way to ease back into reality. They laughed over a *Car Talk* repeat and ruminated on the weekly puzzle.

A few miles from Old Forge, Amanda's phone winked to life with a flurry of chirps, pings, and sound bites. Quinn chuckled. "I guess we're back in range."

Amanda didn't respond. She was already frowning at her screen. Quinn tried not to let it bother her. Amanda had owned the fact that unplugging was a rarity for her. Of course she'd be anxious to check in.

Amanda gasped, then swore.

"What? What's wrong?" Quinn stole peeks at her while doing her best to keep her attention on the road.

"Cal's in the hospital."

"What?" Panic gripped her. Realization that it had to be a fraction of what Amanda was feeling quickly followed.

"He had his appendix removed."

"Like, today?" Disbelief warred with the knowledge that an appendicitis could come on and reach emergency status in a matter of hours. That exact thing had happened to her when she was fifteen.

Amanda didn't answer. She'd finished reading messages and had her phone to her ear. "Where are you? How is he?"

She couldn't hear enough to know if it was Daniella on the other end of the line or Mel. Instinctively, she reached over and put a hand on Amanda's knee. Amanda looked her way briefly, but there was misery in her eyes.

"I'll come right there. It'll be three hours at least, but I'm coming." Amanda led out a shaky breath. "I know. Okay. Call me if anything changes."

She ended the call and Quinn gave her a second to settle her nerves before asking, "Is he all right?"

Another shaky breath. "Mel says so, but I won't believe it until I can set eyes on him myself."

Probably not the moment to confess how much she loved Amanda's mama bear instincts. "So, he had the surgery already? He's in recovery?"

"In a regular room, apparently. He felt lousy yesterday. Mel said he called her at five this morning because he hadn't stopped puking and had a sharp pain in his side."

Quinn tried to offer a reassuring smile. "Good thing he knew the symptoms."

Amanda shook her head. "I should have been there."

"How could you have known?"

"I shouldn't have been inaccessible." Amanda poked at her screen, then held up the phone. "He texted me last night and I didn't get it."

"And he called his other mother, who seems to have done the right thing."

She let out an exasperated sigh. "You don't understand. I'm the one who is always there. I'm the one who takes care of everything."

Quinn swallowed the retort on the tip of her tongue. "This is no exception. You'll be at the hospital in a matter of hours and I have no doubt you'll take impeccable care of him until he's back to one hundred percent."

"I need to check on Daniella."

Quinn focused her attention on the road while Amanda called her daughter. The conversation started tense, but Amanda laughed before they finished. That was a good sign. "What do you need from me? What can I do?"

Amanda blinked at her a few times, as though surprised by the question. "Just bring me to Cayuga Medical. I told them I'd be there as quickly as I could."

A small knot of helplessness rooted in Quinn's stomach. "Do you still have your appendix? I had mine out when I was fifteen."

"I still have mine."

Amanda seemed only half focused on the conversation, but she had to believe even minor distraction was an improvement over worrying and beating herself up for the next three hours. "I went from fine to hospital the same day, but I was home the next and back to normal in less than a week."

"I know that's how it works, but it doesn't make me feel the tiniest bit better."

"Would you like me to list all the ways you're an outstanding mother? I'd be happy to."

She'd hoped the comment would at least get her a smile, but Amanda's eyes welled with tears. "My son needed me and I was off playing with my girlfriend like some irresponsible teenager."

The words stung. Even as she rationalized Amanda was upset, that she was in an understandably emotional state, they lodged in her chest. Because, emotional state or not, maybe they were true.

More deflated than she cared to admit, Quinn drove on in silence. Amanda tapped at her phone. She could have been texting her friends or looking up early appendicitis symptoms to torture herself with. Either way, she didn't bother trying to make conversation.

She dropped Amanda at the hospital with a promise to bring Amanda's things over whenever she made it home. She hesitated, then asked for an update whenever Amanda had a moment. Amanda mumbled an "of course," but climbed out of the car without a kiss or even making eye contact.

Quinn headed home, telling herself a hundred times Amanda's actions were completely reasonable given the situation. But when she pulled into the lot of her building, she sat for a long moment. She might be good at telling herself all the right things. Believing them was another matter entirely.

Thanks to her back-and-forth with Mel and Daniella, Amanda didn't have to bother with tracking down where Cal was. She took the elevator to his floor and barely resisted the urge to run down the hall to his room. At the door, she made herself pause for a moment. The last thing her son needed was seeing her all freaked out.

She took a deep breath, then blew it out. She was fine. Cal was fine. Everyone was fine.

She entered the room to the sound of Mel laughing. No, not laughing. It was a guffaw that bordered on a snort. When she rounded the wall, she found her ex-wife doubled over with laughter and both of her kids giggling like, well, kids. It was jarring and sent her already frazzled nerves into orbit.

"What's so funny?" She didn't mean to snap, but it sounded like that. She cleared her throat. Hopefully it passed for surprise.

All three of them froze and looked her way. Like when the kids were little and she'd caught them in the middle of something they knew they weren't supposed to be doing. The funny thing was, Mel had usually been part of the antics then, too.

"Mom." Cal looked both happy to see her and relieved. "You're here."

The familiar twinge of being the killjoy faded and she went to him. She wrapped an arm around his shoulder and kissed the top of his head, just like when he was little. "How are you, baby?"

He leaned into her for a moment, then pulled away. "I'm fantastic now. This morning, I thought I was going to die."

She felt the blood drain from her face and a fresh wave of guilt wash over her. "I'm so, so, so sorry I wasn't here."

"Not literally die. It was fine. I called these two and they took care of me."

Amanda shook her head. "I should have been here."

He gave her a look of exasperation. "Mom, chill. I'm fine. It's not like I'm some five-year-old you left to fend for himself."

"Still." She turned to Daniella, pulling her into a fierce hug. "I'm sorry I wasn't here."

When she let go, Daniella smirked. She angled her head toward Cal. "It's all good. He lived."

It was hard to tell if Daniella really was fine or hiding the fact she'd been scared behind sarcasm. Now wasn't the time to poke at her, but she'd make sure they had a heart-to-heart later. In the meantime, she turned her attention to Mel. "Thank you for swooping in and taking care of everything."

Mel offered her a soft smile. "I'm still part of the team, you know."

She didn't know what she expected Mel to say, but it wasn't that. No, she expected a hint of snark or, at the very least, condescension. How was it that everyone in her family seemed to be throwing her off her game? Maybe the problem was she was already off her game. Unsure what to do with that, she fell back on maternal guilt. "I'm sorry you had to handle this by yourself."

Mel brought a hand to her cheek. "You're here now."

If the gesture gave her a tingle of discomfort, she chose to ignore it. Everyone's emotions were high. Emergency surgery could do that to people. "I am. Where do things stand? What do I need to do?"

Mel let out a chuckle. "I know you struggle with this, but I don't think there's anything to do."

She frowned, although it was hard to know if it was the comment or that there really might be nothing for her to do. "Any word on when he'll be released?"

"Tomorrow. They want to keep him overnight to make sure there's no fever or other signs of infection." And then, as if sensing the question in Amanda's mind, she added, "It's standard practice. Nothing to be concerned about."

She blew out a breath, relieved. But still worried. And suddenly exhausted. "Okay. Good."

"Have you not even been home yet?"

She looked down at her khaki shorts and hiking boots. "I wanted to come straight here."

Mel nodded. "Of course. I'm fine staying if you want to go shower and unpack and whatever."

"Oh, no. I'm not going anywhere." She looked over to the bed. Daniella had perched herself on the edge and she and Cal appeared to be heckling an episode of *Judge Judy*. "Have you both been here all day?"

Another nod.

"Why don't you two take off and I'll stay?"

"They're going to kick you out at nine. We've already been warned."

She imagined a harried nurse reading her rowdy family the riot act. "Well, I'll stay until then."

"How about we all stay and then you let me bring you home. I assume you don't have a car."

She didn't. It hit her how she'd pretty much brushed Quinn off. She'd need to apologize. "I can get an Uber."

Mel raised a brow. "Girlfriend not hovering nearby?"

There was a trace of snark or something similar in Mel's voice, but Amanda didn't have it in her to take her to task. Or attempt to explain. Not that she owed Mel an explanation anyway. "No."

"How about I bring Daniella home and then swing back for you?"

If part of her knew it wasn't the best idea, it was a part that didn't have the energy to put up a fight. "That would be great."

Mel grinned as though she'd been given the keys to the candy shop. "Perfect."

She looked over at the bed again. "He's really going to be okay, right?"

Mel slung an arm around her, much like she'd done with Cal, and pressed a kiss to her temple. "He's going to be perfect."

For just a second, she let herself sink into the comfort of Mel's embrace. She'd known it to be true in an intellectual sense, but only in that moment did the rest of her believe it. "Right."

Mel released her and turned to Daniella. "You ready to get back?"

Daniella looked Cal up and down and sighed. "I guess."

The reluctance to leave told Amanda all she needed to know. Today had been rough on both her kids. She gave Daniella a hug. "Go get some rest. Are you driving back to Rochester tonight?"

She hesitated for a moment but ultimately nodded. "I've got the morning crew of kids and I won't want to get up early enough to get there. I mean, unless you need me."

"You go. I'll text you updates."

Daniella told Cal to stop being so much trouble, then she and Mel left. Since Cal didn't seem to be in significant discomfort, she took the spot on the bed Daniella had vacated. "How are you really?"

He gave her a reassuring smile. "I'm fine. I'm sorry I freaked you out."

She took his hand and gave it a squeeze. "Freaking out is my prerogative."

"Where's Quinn?"

The question caught her off guard. "I had her drop me off."

"Oh." Cal frowned. "Did she have somewhere to be?"

"Um, I don't know. I didn't ask."

"Oh. Okay." He smiled, but his voice conveyed disappointment.

"I mean, she was genuinely worried about you. I think she probably didn't want to horn in on family time." Only in justifying it to Cal did reality sink in. She'd done nothing to make Quinn feel welcome or wanted.

Cal lifted a shoulder. "I guess I've started thinking of her as family."

Leave it to her kid to make her feel two inches tall, but not about the thing she was already beating herself up over. "Really?"

He sighed. "Not like I think you're about to get married or anything."

"Oh, well, as long as it's not that." How did this become the conversation?

"I just mean she's been around a lot and, I don't know, it's kind of nice."

Amanda's shoulders slumped. She'd been so busy thinking about her time with Quinn as a selfish thing, it hadn't occurred to her it might be something her kids actually liked, valued. Her terseness with Quinn on the ride down came back to her. She had been selfish, but not in the ways she'd thought.

"Was that the wrong thing to say? I'm sorry."

She stopped pinching the bridge of her nose and looked over at her son. His color was almost back to normal and, thanks to whatever meds they'd pumped into him, he didn't seem to be in any pain. And yet, there he was, sitting in a hospital bed, apologizing to her. "I'm the one who's sorry. I was so focused on getting to you, I didn't think about anything else."

He shrugged, clearly not inclined to analyze her decisions to death. "It's cool. I'm sure I'll see her soon."

She had to laugh. He made it sound so easy. "I'll let her know you asked about her."

"Did you guys have a good time?"

Amanda took a deep breath. The truth was she couldn't remember having a more relaxing weekend. Even without all the sex. Quinn had this way of getting her to slow down, unplug. She hadn't realized how bad she'd gotten at doing that. "We did."

"Good. You don't have enough fun."

The comment hit home, almost as much as Cal asking about Quinn in the first place. "I have fun."

He gave her an exasperated look. "You know what I mean."

She could argue with him, but he was right. She wasn't uptight, exactly, but between parenting and owning a business, she had a hard time shutting off. "Okay, okay."

"I think it's good for you, that's all."

He didn't say it, but she could tell he meant Quinn was good for her. That hit home, too. Perhaps all the neat little compartments she'd created in her life weren't so neat after all.

CHAPTER TWENTY-FOUR

After storing her camping gear and putting on a load of laundry, Quinn showered and put on fresh clothes. She made a cup of tea and picked up a book but couldn't seem to focus. She set it down and turned on the television, which only made matters worse.

The worst part was not knowing which part of the last few hours made her feel worse—Amanda's comment about their relationship or the fact that Amanda was going through this hugely stressful thing and Quinn wasn't doing anything to make it better. She huffed out a breath and got up to pace. Definitely the latter. Not helping made every helper fiber of her being stand on edge.

She stopped pacing. That was it. She'd help. Surely, there was something she could do. She picked up her phone. After deleting three different versions, she finally hit send.

How's Cal? How are you? Can I do/bring you anything?

Maybe it was overeager, but whatever.

Doing something calmed her nerves. She picked up her book again and managed to read a few pages before checking for a reply. After the fifth or sixth time of doing it, she set her phone down in disgust, only to have it chirp.

He's good, all things considered. I'm going to stay until they kick me out for the night.

She hadn't realized how worried she was until the news sent a wave of relief through her. She reread the message, searching for context that wasn't there. *Can I bring you dinner? A change of clothes?*

Amanda's reply came immediately. *Thanks for offering, but I won't be staying too late.*

Quinn couldn't repress a sigh. Getting confirmation she wasn't needed sucked worse than feeling helpless in the first place. *Ok. Let me know if you think of anything.*

The typing bubble appeared, but then vanished. Seconds ticked by, but no text came through. She went to switch her laundry, purposefully leaving her phone on the counter. It took all of two minutes, but she tapped the screen the second she got back.

You could come visit tomorrow. Cal should be released in the morning and he asked where you were. ;)

She might have preferred if Amanda specifically wanted her there, but Cal was a close second. And while the winky face could have been read any number of ways, she decided to read it as a playful, you're part of the family gesture. *That would be great.*

Amanda didn't reply, so she set her phone aside. She resumed pacing, but more slowly. This time, instead of freaking out, she considered what it would be like to actually be part of Amanda's family. Her kids were beyond the age of needing—or wanting, probably—a stepparent. And given what she knew about Mel, she wasn't eager to be in any sort of competition with her.

Was it possible to carve out a space of her own? She sighed. It might be more fair to ask if Amanda had any inclination to carve out space for her and, if so, what that space would look like. Especially since Daniella seemed so on the fence about her. Or on the fence about her mother dating at all. Hard to say. And not really her place to say.

That was the problem. Even at her boldest and most self-assured, a lot of it wasn't hers to decide. She just had to put herself out there and hope for the best. The prospect, complete with having so little control over the situation, terrified her.

The thing was, she was pretty sure Amanda was worth it. No, that wasn't accurate. Amanda was worth it. It was whether or not their relationship had enough potential to be worth it. It was the first time she'd needed to ask that question since her divorce.

Still. Things with Amanda felt different. For the first time in a long time, she felt inspired. Inspired to be adventurous. Inspired to take a chance. And perhaps most importantly and most terrifyingly of all, inspired to fall in love.

By the time Mel returned, Cal had fallen asleep and Amanda was struggling to stay awake. It had been an exceedingly eventful couple of days. Mel gave her a tender look that she did her best to ignore. "Ready?"

Amanda glanced at Cal. If she hadn't known he'd just had surgery, she wouldn't have guessed it. Oh, to have the resilience of an eighteen-year-old. "I guess so."

"I can tell you don't want to leave, but he's fine. And you'll do him more good tomorrow if you're well rested."

Mel was right. She wasn't about a lot of stuff, but she was about this. "I know."

"Come on." Mel extended her hand.

She took it, but only because she could honestly use the help hefting herself out of the low chair. "Thanks."

Before she could let go, Mel pulled her into a hug. "You doing okay?"

She let herself soak in the comfort it offered, but only for a second. She one hundred percent did not want to give the wrong impression. She took a deep breath and squared her shoulders. "I am. I'm sorry you had to do this alone."

"We're a team, remember?"

Funny how they didn't feel like a team so much of the time they were married. "Are you sure you don't mind driving me? I can call Erin or Julia or take a cab."

The look of mild exasperation felt oddly more comfortable and familiar than the tender one a moment ago. "Could you relax and let me do something nice for you?"

Much like Cal's comment about having fun, the question hit her. When had she become so rigid? "Sorry. Thank you for offering. I appreciate it."

Mel grinned. "That's better."

They headed to the visitor lot. She made a show of opening the passenger door and Amanda slid in, letting herself melt into the leather seat. Mel rounded the hood and got in. She started the car and drove in the direction of Amanda's house. How long had it been since they'd been in a car together, just the two of them?

Surreal or not, Amanda willed herself to relax. They weren't sleeping together or fighting. They were back to what they'd managed to settle into over the years: comfortable.

"How are things at home?" She realized how little she'd asked about the state of Mel's marriage and had a pang of guilt.

Mel shook her head. "I've moved out."

She didn't know why, but she'd expected Mel and Bella to reconcile. "Oh, no. Is it that bad?"

Mel shrugged. "I'm in one of those short-term apartments. We've told each other it's temporary, but I don't know."

"I'm sorry." She was, truly.

"Thanks."

"Was it her idea or yours?" That part was probably none of her business, but she wanted to know.

"Mine. If we have any chance at all, we need to get some space, evaluate our priorities."

Amanda had said essentially the same thing when their marriage tanked. Did Mel remember that? "I hope you can make it work."

Mel glanced at her and lifted a shoulder. "I feel like it's going to work out the way it's supposed to."

She let the cryptic reply sit. It was none of her business if and how things worked out, and she certainly didn't want to give Mel the impression it was. Especially with how things were going with Quinn.

Quinn. She still felt bad about how she'd left things with her. Even if the brief text exchange made it seem like Quinn wasn't upset, it didn't make her behavior okay. She'd flung her own guilt and other emotional nonsense on her and all but said she regretted going away together. Which was uncalled for but also untrue.

Quinn had gotten her—invited, nudged, and inspired her—to unplug from her life and responsibilities and just think about herself.

Yes, the timing of Cal's second ever time being hospitalized sucked. But Quinn had no way of knowing that and neither did she. Yes, she wished she could have been there. But her kids were neither helpless nor dependent on her for their well-being. She'd gone out of her way to raise them to be anything but those things.

She owed Quinn an apology. Not a few words over text, either. Because she needed to do a lot more than apologize. She needed Quinn to understand not only how much fun she'd had—and she'd had plenty—she needed Quinn to understand what the weekend meant to her.

"I'm dying to know what you're thinking right now."

The sound of Mel's voice startled her. She'd almost forgotten Mel was sitting right there next to her. "Just zoning, I think."

"You must be exhausted, between today and all the outdoor rustic stuff." Mel curled her lip, her disdain evident.

"Yeah, must be that." No need for Mel to know the exact nature of her outdoorsy activities, or her indoor ones for that matter. Given the state of Mel's marriage, it would be rubbing salt in the wound. The analogy gave her a flashback of Mel and Bella's wedding. Funny how the tables could turn.

Mel pulled into the driveway and, even though there was no need, cut the engine. She started to say she had her keys, but Mel was already out of the car and coming around to open her door. On another day, she might have poked fun at the gallantry. Today, she was too tired.

"Thank you again for the ride."

"Happy to. It was nice to have a few minutes alone." For a second, she thought Mel was going to attempt to walk her to her door. But she stuck her hands in her pockets and rocked back on her heels. Then she looked up at the stars.

"You okay?" It wasn't like Mel to get overly reflective.

"I'm working on it. Ask me again in a few weeks." She accompanied the second statement with a wink.

Amanda resisted the urge to read too much into it or ask for clarification. Like she'd said, to herself at least: it was none of her business. "Good luck sorting it all out."

Mel gave her a knowing look, paired with a knowing smile. "From you, I'll take it."

The conversation was getting weirder by the second, but she couldn't tell if it was Mel or her own exhaustion. "I can probably handle discharge tomorrow if you have other things you need to do."

Her expression turned serious. "No, I'll be there. I want to be there."

"Okay. I'll plan to see you then." She fished her keys out of her purse and started up the walk.

"Hey, Amanda?"

She turned. "Yes?"

Mel offered her a playful nod. "Those hiking shorts look good on you. You've still got the best legs of any woman I know."

Amanda blinked, at a loss for words. Mel didn't wait for her to come up with any. She smiled and got back in her car and was gone. Amanda stood there for a long moment, staring at the driveway where Mel had been. What the hell was that?

It didn't matter. Mel was no longer hers to figure out or explain, to navigate or fight or anything else with. Which was a good thing, because she didn't have the wherewithal or the inclination to try. Instead, she shook her head and let herself into the house.

She climbed the stairs, peeling off clothes as she went. In the shower, she closed her eyes. It wasn't difficult to push aside all thoughts of Mel as the hot water ran over her tired muscles. Even Cal and the panic that gripped her when she learned he was in the hospital faded to the background.

She lathered her body and gave her mind over to Quinn, to the memories of showering together and every other magical moment of their two days in the woods. And for the first time in a long time, she didn't try to rein herself in or be reasonable or rational. She just let herself enjoy it and maybe, a little, imagine what a whole lifetime of that might look like.

CHAPTER TWENTY-FIVE

Amanda opened the door and sighed. Fewer than twenty-four hours had passed since she last saw Quinn, but seeing her there sent a ripple of calm through her. The potency of that, the immediacy, hit her. "Hi."

"How's the patient?"

"Already annoyed he has to stay in bed for a few days."

Quinn smiled. "That's a good sign, right?"

"It is." She stepped back so Quinn could come inside.

Quinn angled her head. "Is someone else here?"

"Mel's on her way out. I would have made it so you didn't have to overlap, but I assumed she'd be gone by now." She'd assumed Mel wouldn't bother coming to the house after the hospital, then she'd assumed Mel would help Cal get settled and not linger. Her typical assumptions of Mel were backfiring a lot these days.

Not her business. Not her business. Not her business. It was becoming a bit of a mantra.

Quinn's eyes narrowed slightly. Subtle, but Amanda had learned it was one of her few tells when it came to being irritated. "It's totally fine. I'm sure Cal is happy to have both his moms doting on him."

"He is." She put her hand on Quinn's arm. "This isn't probably the best time and I know Cal is anxious to see you, but I'm hoping we could maybe talk later."

Quinn frowned. "Is everything okay?"

She took a deep breath. "I'm hoping so. I mostly want to apologize for being a jerk yesterday."

The frown gave way to relief. "You weren't a jerk."

She lifted a hand. "I'm sure we could debate this. Just know the purpose of the conversation is making nice, not anything bad."

"I'm not sure I'm on board with the idea of needing to make nice, but I won't argue." She made a bowing gesture with her hand. "Per your request."

The comment made her realize how ridiculous she sounded. She could apologize for that later, too. "Deal."

"Mom, is that Quinn? Stop hogging her." Cal's holler carried from the living room.

She angled her head. "Shall we?"

In the living room, Cal sat sideways on the sofa with his feet up and a mound of pillows around him. Mel, who'd been perched on the opposite arm, stood. She offered Quinn a friendly nod. "Quinn. Good to meet you."

"You, too."

She knew Mel well enough to recognize a certain amount of condescension in the friendly tone. Hopefully, Quinn didn't pick up on it. Cal certainly didn't. He just looked happy to see Quinn. "Can you believe I had an appendicitis while you were gone?" he asked.

"Pretty crazy timing. I'm sorry we weren't reachable." Quinn still seemed distressed by the whole thing.

Cal shrugged, still laid-back about the whole thing. "It's all good."

"Can I get you some coffee?" she asked Quinn.

"I'd love some," Mel said before Quinn even had a chance to reply.

She was annoyed with Mel for inviting herself to stay, but didn't want to say so in front of Cal. Or Quinn, for that matter. Mostly, she wanted a few minutes alone with Quinn and that wasn't Mel's fault. "Quinn?"

"Sure." She didn't seem crazy about chumming it up with Mel, but she didn't look terribly offended, either. That was a relief.

She fixed coffee, poured Cal a fresh glass of water, and returned to the living room. Mel was in the middle of telling a story about Cal's childhood exploits. It could have been perfectly innocent, but it felt a bit like an animal marking its territory. She tried shifting the subject to Quinn's nephew being at Cornell and Cal, God bless him, ran with it.

After what felt like an eternity of small talk, Mel noted she should probably head to her office for a few hours. Amanda walked her to the door to make sure she didn't change her mind. She didn't, but she did drop a hint about coming over for breakfast again before the semester started, complete with a line about having a sleepover. Like old times. Amanda kept her answer noncommittal and shooed Mel out the door.

She returned to the living room and found Quinn and Cal engrossed in conversation. It would have made her smile under any circumstances. Today, with Cal a day out of surgery and Quinn with every right to be upset with her, it felt like a much needed balm to her frazzled nerves.

Cal looked up and caught her eye. "Mom, I asked Quinn to stay for lunch. Is that cool?"

It would be cool if there was anything other than teenage boy food in the house. "Of course. I'm not sure there is anything for lunch, but of course."

"I'm happy to run out and get something," Quinn said.

"I couldn't ask you to do that." The refusal was more instinct than anything else, but having Quinn running errands for her was simply too much.

Quinn, who'd taken a seat in the wing chair next to the couch, leaned forward. "You may not know this about me because I'm not one to brag, but I'm really good at takeout."

Cal laughed and even Amanda couldn't suppress a snicker. "You know, I think I might have known that about you. Still."

Cal rolled his eyes. "Since I'm starving and this sounds like the kind of thing adults could argue about for forever, how about Quinn keeps me company and you go get lunch?"

Amanda bit her lip, wanting to call Cal out for being imperious, but knowing he was right. And she'd be lying if she denied liking the idea of her son wanting to spend time with Quinn one-on-one. "Quinn?"

Quinn shrugged. "I really don't mind, but it works for me."

"All right. Requests?"

"I defer to the patient." Quinn made a bowing gesture that was kind of adorable.

"Meatball subs?" Cal looked at her with optimism.

She cringed. "Maybe something easier on the stomach?"

He frowned. "The doctor said I could eat whatever."

"But your stomach is still worn out from puking. How about something a little more bland?"

His shoulders slumped but he didn't argue. "Turkey sub?"

"Better. Quinn, are you cool with subs?"

"Love 'em." She seemed to mean it and not just say it.

"Let me grab a Post-it." She took down their orders, asked one more time if everyone was okay with her running out, and laughed when they gave almost identical exasperated faces. "I'll be back in a few."

After Amanda left, Quinn returned her attention to Cal. She might not be able to say the same about his sister, but she was perfectly at ease spending time with him without Amanda around. She expected conversation to return to the relative ranking of the *Star Wars* movies, but she found him looking at her with a far more serious expression than the admittedly opinionated discussion warranted.

"I hope I didn't ruin the end of your weekend."

She really did like this kid. "Not at all."

"So, you had a good time?" Cal's tone and the angle of his head made it sound like a loaded question.

"We did. I've had the cabin for close to fifteen years. It's peaceful."

"I'm glad." He seemed like he wanted to say more but wasn't sure what, or maybe how.

"I can take you up there sometime if you're into that sort of thing."

"Yeah."

"I'm not sure there's time before school starts, but I don't close it until the end of October. And there's always spring." Only after saying it did the implication—that she and Amanda would still be together come spring—hit her. Too late to take it back now. She picked up her coffee to stop herself from making it worse with caveats.

"Are you in love with her?"

Of course, he chose the exact moment she took a sip to drop that question. She didn't spit all over him, but she choked and coughed. And coughed and coughed.

He waited patiently, drinking his own water, while she struggled to catch her breath. Finally, when she'd cleared her airways and collected her thoughts, she asked, "Did you orchestrate that whole lunch thing just to ask me that question?"

"Maybe."

She appreciated his honesty. "Can I ask first what makes you ask?"

His gaze didn't waver. "Do you think it's an unreasonable question?"

"Uh." How did he go from goofy teenager one minute to making her feel like the teenager talking to an overbearing father the next? "We haven't talked about it."

He blinked. "I didn't ask if you'd talked about it."

From everything she'd gathered, Cal was a pretty laid-back guy. She wondered if the pain medication he'd been given affected his filters. Or maybe if his sister had put him up to an inquisition. "Yes, but you can see how it's a conversation I'd feel better having with her first."

Cal nodded slowly. "I'll concede the point."

Quinn hoped he was speaking figuratively. She didn't want it to feel like a battle. "It's sweet that you're protective of her."

Cal sighed. "She likes you, you know. Like, a lot."

It was clear he didn't make the statement lightly. "I like her a lot, too."

"I know it's cheesy or cliché or whatever, but don't hurt her, okay?"

With that one comment, he went from brooding dad type to little boy trying to look out for his mom. She appreciated it. More, she got it. She'd never had that sort of experience with her own mother, but she'd made a point of sitting down with both Gary and Xinxin before their respective weddings. She reached over and patted Cal's knee. "I'm going to do my absolute best not to."

The answer seemed to satisfy him. He nodded again. "Good."

She didn't want to come across as trying to change the subject, but she was so ready to change the subject. "So, how are you feeling?"

He gave her a bland look. "Really? That's the best you could come up with?"

She shrugged, not really minding that he called her out. It made it seem like they were friends. Even if she and Amanda weren't using words like love yet, she hoped they would. And having a good relationship with her kids was an important part of that. "Okay, then. How about this? Does your sister dislike me or does she dislike anyone who dates your mother?"

Cal laughed. "What makes you think she doesn't like you?"

She merely raised a brow.

"Okay, okay. Fine. She doesn't dislike you in particular."

It was good to have an answer, although she wasn't sure if it made her feel better or not. "So, she doesn't like anyone your mother dates?"

He sighed, like he was trying to decide how to answer. "Here's the thing. Mom doesn't date."

Amanda had said as much, but she'd taken it to mean not extensively. "Like, at all?"

"She did a couple of years after the divorce. Nothing stuck. Honestly, I don't think she found it all that fun. And then she just stopped."

Maybe she shouldn't be asking him such things, but since they were already on the subject, it didn't feel like fishing. "How long has it been?"

"Before you? At least five or six years."

Amanda had alluded to something brief shortly before they got together. Perhaps it didn't last long enough to mention to her kids. "Huh."

"The thing with Daniella is that she hates our other mom's new wife. And so I think she secretly hopes that will explode and they'll end up back together."

"Oh." She didn't see that coming, but it made sense.

"Which is seriously bananas. They've been divorced for like longer than they were married. If it was going to happen, it would have happened by now."

She didn't know why, but his delivery came across like a vote of confidence. It made her worries about being in Mel's shadow seem almost silly. Still, she didn't want to give the impression she had any role in the matter one way or the other. "I'm sure stranger things have happened."

"Truth."

She couldn't put her finger on the exact dynamic she and Cal had going, but she liked it. Not equals, exactly, but a mutual respect. And he genuinely seemed to enjoy her company as much as she enjoyed his. Maybe one day she and Daniella could get to something remotely in the same vicinity. "Any more burning questions before your mom comes back?"

She'd been kidding, but he seemed to take the question to heart. "I don't think so, but I will make another request."

Given the serious nature of his last one, she braced herself. "What's that?"

"Try to get her to go away again. It's good for her."

She laughed. "I don't think I'm the one you have to convince."

"Oh, man. That's so one hundred."

She spent enough time with Jacob and Adam to know that was a good thing. "I mean, I'm not saying you should try to convince her. I'd never ask you to do that."

"But if it's my opinion, there's nothing wrong with me saying so, right?"

She wasn't about to shut him down. "Totally your prerogative."

Cal stuck out his hand and they exchanged a fist bump. Which made her feel like a dork, but she was okay with that.

"What's all the laughing about?" Amanda's voice came from the kitchen even though Quinn hadn't heard her come in.

"Just guy stuff." Cal's reply came with a shrug and a knowing smile.

Well, he wasn't wrong. She got up and headed for the kitchen. "Anything I can do to help?"

CHAPTER TWENTY-SIX

Within a few days, Cal was back to his old self. A relief since his orientation at Cornell started in less than two weeks. Not that he seemed to feel any sense of urgency on that front. Getting him to pack felt like pulling teeth, so much so that Amanda started to worry he didn't want to go.

When she finally asked him as gently and with as little judgment as possible, he rolled his eyes. "Come on, Mom. You know I want to go."

She tried to read his face, whatever it was he wasn't saying. "It's not like you to drag your feet on something so important."

He shrugged. "I mean, the college part is. But I'm not going far. Not even as far as Rochester. You can bring me whatever I forget."

If she weren't so relieved, she'd lay into him for assuming she'd be at his disposal. "Forty-five minutes or not, once the bakery opens, you know better than to think I'm going to play chauffeur for you."

He grinned. "But you're going to be coming to Ithaca to see Quinn, so you'll already be close by."

He had a point. And more importantly, he wasn't getting cold feet about college. "I'm still not doing an emergency run to campus because you run out of clean underwear."

"Mom."

"What?" She was mostly teasing him at this point, but still.

"I have to wear my underwear between now and then."

She laughed, not only because he was right, but because his delivery was so matter-of-fact, it made her feel silly for worrying in the first place. "Fine."

"Besides, I need to get in all the *Fortnight* I can because I obviously won't have time for games when classes start."

"Well played, Cal. Well played. Carry on."

She'd just left him to his own devices when her phone rang. Quinn's face appeared on the screen, making her smile. "Hi."

"Hello, beautiful."

It shouldn't make her heart flip every time Quinn called her that, but it did. "What are you up to today?"

"Calling you with good news."

"Good news? Bakery good news? Is it done?" Amanda chuckled at the disbelief in her own voice.

"It will be. Two more days. But that's not an estimate. I'm saying it with confidence."

She wiggled her shoulders and hips to a nonexistent beat. "It's a good thing we're on the phone because I'm doing a happy dance and it isn't pretty."

"I think I'd prefer to be the judge of that myself. I have a feeling it's a pretty sexy thing to behold."

"You're sweet. Completely wrong, but sweet."

"I could argue with you, but I'd rather celebrate. I also wanted to give you as much notice as possible since I know you're itching to reopen."

She had been. She'd also been going back and forth on whether to do a party or grand reopening or anything like that. This timing was better than she'd hoped for, especially after the flooring debacle. She didn't have major wedding or other event cakes for another two weeks.

"What? Are you really that self-conscious about your dancing?"

She laughed. "Maybe I should be, but no. My mind was racing ahead. Sorry."

"You? Thinking twenty steps ahead? No way."

"Okay, okay. There's no need to poke fun." Although, really, she didn't mind the way Quinn teased.

"You'd rather I make fun of your dancing?"

"At least I don't have any illusions on that front."

"Ah. Well, in that case, I'm totally going to give you a couple of glasses of wine and try to get you to dance with me. But first, we have a bakery to reveal."

She closed her eyes for a second and let herself be nothing but excited. "When can I see it?"

"Well, technically it's your building. You have the keys and can go anytime."

True. Unexpectedly deflating, but true.

"But I'd love to be there with you. How do you feel about staying away for the next couple of days and letting me pick you up for an official reveal?"

Deflation gave way to a bubble of joy. "I'd love that."

"Oh, good. I know I didn't do the work myself, but I feel almost as attached as you do."

The flutter her heart did had nothing to do with the prospect of seeing the bakery, all done and put back together. "I'm really excited."

"I hope I get an invite if there's a party."

Quinn couldn't see her face, but she grinned nonetheless. "You're at the top of the list."

"Fantastic. I won't keep you, but I'll look forward to it."

"Can't wait."

After ending the call, she grabbed a notebook. She didn't start with potential party guests, but she did have about a dozen other lists to get started. At the very top of all of them? Bringing Tanya up to speed and getting her back on the clock as quickly as possible.

Not only did Tanya answer on the first ring, she was at Amanda's doorstep in under an hour. She offered a shrug and a laugh. "What can I say? I've missed the place."

Amanda pulled her into a hug. "Same."

"I've missed you more, for the record, but I've really missed being there."

Over the years, Tanya had become as much a fixture of Bake My Day as Amanda. Maybe more so to the average customer, since Amanda spent so much of her time in the kitchen. "Again, same."

"All right, enough of the mushy stuff. Let's get to work."

Amanda chuckled, but didn't argue. She led the way into the kitchen and poured coffee. A minute later, they sat at the table with matching notebooks, pencils poised. "Okay. You first."

"How grand are we talking?" Tanya asked.

"Not very. I mean, we're throwing it together in a week."

Tanya raised a brow. "We can throw a lot together in a week."

Amanda grinned. "Good point."

"So, grand?"

She did love the idea of something big and loud and celebratory, with people spilling out of the bakery onto the sidewalk. Since they couldn't serve alcohol, the cost wouldn't be anything more than the product they gave away. And given how long she'd had her hands out of the kitchen, she had an itch to bake up a storm. "Grand."

"Where do we start?"

"Invitations, I think. We should get something up on social media and email our existing client list." Given the number of wedding cakes and larger orders she did in an average year, it was a big list.

"Do you want me to," Tanya paused and made a face, "design something?"

Tanya had a pretty solid hate-hate relationship with technology. Even though she teased Tanya about it, she did her best not to inflict it on her. "I'll enlist Julia's help for that."

Tanya's eyes lit up. "Oh, she's fantastic at that stuff."

She was. Her artistic eye and penchant for detail had made the grand opening of Rustic Refined a smashing success. And since she'd helped with the catering for that event, she had no doubt she could rope Julia in. "How do you feel about starting on the menu?"

"Now you're speaking my language."

In under an hour, they'd sketched out a full menu. The sweets came easy—a smattering of their most popular items scaled down in size. The savory fare took a bit longer. Amanda had been brainstorming the lunch menu, but she couldn't get past the feeling she was missing something. Tanya huffed. She shifted in her chair and sighed. And then she rattled off half a dozen ideas Amanda would have paid a chef to come up with.

"You've been holding out on me."

Tanya sniffed. "I've had too much time on my hands."

They settled on three items to be part of the party menu, but she had plans to incorporate them all into the rotating offerings. They spent a few minutes strategizing drinks and setup, then theorized how many people might actually come. With a four-hour window and an open house format, she hoped several hundred would work their way through. That might be wishful thinking since school was starting, but she'd rather over plan than under.

"Close your eyes." Quinn didn't expect Amanda to obey, but thought it would be cute. When she did, without hesitation or a word of protest, Quinn's breath caught in her throat. Did Amanda have any idea the power she held?

"How long are you going to make me wait?"

Her tone was playful and her eyes remained closed, but it yanked Quinn back to the moment. "Sorry."

Amanda chuckled. "In case you hadn't noticed, I'm a bit eager."

Amanda's eagerness—about her bakery, when she was trying something new, in bed—was one of Quinn's absolute favorite things about her. "You have every right to be."

She took Amanda's hands and led her slowly forward. "Okay, I'm going to take you up the new ramp."

Even with her eyes closed, Amanda beamed. "I love that you made this happen."

"I love that it was important to you." Enough to take on the expense even though the building was old enough to qualify for an exemption.

"It will allow for strollers and walkers as much as wheelchairs. It's a win all around."

They moved up the ramp and to the new entrance. They'd been able to salvage both original doors and set them in a single frame to create French doors. Not only did they look great, it would make it easier for customers to come and go at the same time. Of course, Amanda had seen those already.

She stepped to the side and placed one of Amanda's hands on the handle. "I'll let you do the honors."

Amanda turned the handle but didn't immediately open her eyes. She pushed the door open and stepped over the threshold. "Now?"

"Now." Quinn smiled and maybe held her breath.

Amanda gasped, then let out an, "Oh."

The cases stood empty and nothing hung on the wall except the massive chalkboard Amanda wanted for the menu. Still, the new counter gleamed and the furniture had been arranged. It looked, not wholly unlike the original, but significantly different.

Amanda stepped farther inside. Her hands went to her heart, and she turned a slow circle. On the second time around, she stopped so they were face-to-face. "Quinn."

"Do you like it?" She didn't really need to ask. Amanda had been deeply involved in the decisions and had seen much of the work in progress. But for some reason, Quinn needed to hear the words.

Amanda did another sweep of the space. This time, when she looked back at Quinn, her eyes glistened with tears. "I love it."

A strange mix of relief and pride spread through her. Not unheard of when she got to unveil a completed project, but this feeling was unlike anything else. Because it wasn't the project making her heart beat erratically and her head almost dizzy. This particular feeling had nothing to do with the project and everything to do with the woman standing in front of her. "I love that you love it."

Maybe part of her wanted to say I love you, but the timing wasn't right. That shouldn't get caught up and potentially confused with the emotional intensity of the day. Soon, though. The thought of it might terrify her, but she wanted—needed—Amanda to know how she felt. And, if she was being honest, she needed to know if Amanda felt the same.

"It's so much better than I imagined. Is that silly to say, given I was here only a week ago?"

"Not at all. There's nothing like seeing it all put together for the first time."

Amanda took a step toward her. "It wouldn't have happened without you."

Despite having a healthy confidence in her work, her instinct was to deflect the compliment. To assure Amanda that the heart of the design came from her own wishes for the bakery. But the truth of the matter was the final design was so perfect because it had come from both of them. And maybe it was overkill to hang too much on that, but she didn't care. "I could say the same about you. That's why it's so great. We did it together."

Amanda nodded and smiled, even as a tear made its way down her cheek. "You're right."

Realizing how close she was to spilling her heart at Amanda's feet, Quinn grabbed her hand. "Come on. I want you to see the rest."

She led Amanda behind the counter and through the kitchen. In the new decorating space, Amanda clapped her hands in delight. They finished in the expanded eating area, complete with the hodgepodge of antique tables and the chairs they'd scouted together. "I have no words for how perfect it is."

Quinn's heart felt like it might not stay in the confines of her chest. "I got you a little something. A bakery warming of sorts."

Amanda dropped her head to the side. "You didn't have to do that."

"But I wanted to." She went over to where she'd tucked the package behind a table and pulled it out. "It's nothing fancy."

Amanda accepted the gift and gently tore the paper away. "Are these the plans?"

She didn't usually frame project plans. It always seemed a bit egotistical. But these, complete with pencil marks and eraser smudges and Amanda's handwritten notes, felt special. "You don't have to hang them, but I loved how the design evolved and I thought you'd appreciate remembering the process."

"Oh, I'm hanging it all right. I just have to decide whether to put it out here where the customers can enjoy it or in the decorating room so I can."

Quinn's heart melted at the statement. "I'm so glad I got to work on this with you. It's been one of my favorite projects in a long time."

"I'm glad, too. But I feel like I should confess something."

"What's that?" She tried to ignore the tiny hitch in her chest.

"The bakery isn't my favorite part of this." Amanda moved her hand back and forth to indicate the two of them.

"No?" She knew what Amanda meant, but like before, she wanted to hear her say it.

"No." Amanda closed the distance between them. "You are my favorite part."

She cleared her throat and reminded herself to keep things light. "Well, yeah, but I was afraid saying so would have been unprofessional."

Amanda laughed. "I wouldn't have minded."

"Oh, good. Then you are absolutely my favorite part. Well, you, us, this whole thing." She mimicked Amanda's gesture.

"I'm glad we're in agreement."

"Total agreement."

Amanda's mouth came to hers. The kiss started playful but quickly turned into anything but.

"Are we running that kind of establishment now?" Tanya's voice cut through the haze of Quinn's thoughts.

Amanda took her time pulling away. "If you mean blissfully happy, then yes. That's exactly the kind of establishment we're running."

She would have expected Amanda to be a bit more of a prude. Maybe she and Tanya were closer friends than she'd realized.

Amanda offered her a sheepish smile. "Sorry. I forgot I told Tanya to come by."

Quinn chuckled. "It's fine. It's your bakery after all."

Amanda beamed. "It is. And it's perfect." She turned to Tanya. "What do you think?"

Tanya nodded slowly as she looked around, apparently unfazed by walking in on her boss making out with someone. "It's so perfect. Like a whole new space, but with the same personality."

"Yes, that's exactly what I was going for."

Tanya lifted her chin in Quinn's direction. "Nice work."

She got the feeling that was high praise in Tanya's book. Even if it wasn't, it was good enough for her. "I should probably leave you two. I hear there's a party in a couple of days."

Amanda winced. "We're not going to regret that, right?"

Tanya shrugged. "When do supplies arrive?"

"Tomorrow."

Tanya waved a hand dismissively. "We got this."

"If there's anything I can do to help, let me know." Since they'd already been caught making out, Quinn braved giving Amanda a kiss on the cheek before taking her leave. "Anything that doesn't involve baking, of course."

Tanya laughed. Quinn offered them a parting wave and let herself out. She was looking forward to the party, and to the bakery coming back to life. Even if it meant Amanda would be a hell of a lot busier. As fun as it had been to spend so much time together, she was in it for the long haul. And that meant making it work along with both their careers, family obligations, the whole nine yards. It might be weird to admit, but she was looking forward to the realness of that.

No, it wasn't weird. It meant she was in love. And the realness managed to be both exhilarating and calming. And maybe just a tiny bit terrifying.

CHAPTER TWENTY-SEVEN

Quinn arrived at the party early, so she headed for the back door of the bakery and let herself in. Music wafted through the kitchen, along with the aromas of chocolate, butter, and vanilla. Her stomach rumbled in a mixture of appreciation and longing.

Amanda's back was to her, so she took a moment to appreciate the view. The dress Amanda wore hugged her curves, but then flowed to her knees. The gray fabric, complete with pale pink polka dots, didn't match the bakery exactly, but complemented it. Quinn couldn't help but smile at the choice. "You look as beautiful as one of your cakes."

Amanda turned. She had a pink Bake My Day apron on over her party dress and a piping bag of frosting in her hand. "Hi."

Quinn's breath caught in her throat. "What can I do? I'm at your disposal."

"Um."

She pointed at the frosting. "Except that. You do not want to see what happens when frosting and I mix."

Amanda gestured with the tip of the bag. "Is it as cute as powdered sugar on your nose?"

She flashed back to their first meeting, the one where she'd been caught mid-donut. "Well, I might look adorable covered in frosting, but sadly, I'd probably wind up wearing more of it than the cupcakes would."

Amanda's gaze traveled down her body and back up. "There are worse things."

Quinn tipped her head. "Noted."

"I wouldn't want to ruin that gorgeous suit you're wearing, but perhaps we should experiment later."

The comment—silly and playful but laced with innuendo—sent a stab of lust through her. It still struck her how immediately and intensely Amanda could have that effect on her. "You should save some frosting."

Amanda licked her lips and she seriously considered tossing the pastry bag aside, pushing her up against the table, and kissing her, despite her declared intention of helping. Unfortunately, or maybe fortunately, Tanya pushed through the swinging door before she had the chance.

Tanya lifted a chin in her direction. "Aren't you looking sharp?"

She gave the hem of the jacket a tug and angled her head toward Amanda. "I can't look like some two-bit chump next to my date here."

Amanda gave her an exasperated look. "I told you you didn't have to dress up."

"Kidding." She lifted her hands defensively, then turned to Tanya. "Kidding. I'd be playing the part for any opening I had a hand in."

"Well, it suits you." Tanya nodded her approval. "But I'm still going to put you to work. Jack and Erin are setting up drinks and could probably do with a little adult supervision."

Amanda looked around the kitchen, then at Quinn. "Do that. Things are under control here."

She made to leave the kitchen but stopped. She might not devour Amanda in front of Tanya, but there was no reason she couldn't give her at least a little kiss. She crossed the space—the space that had nearly doubled in size—and took Amanda's face between her hands. She planted a very reasonable kiss on her mouth and said, "Holler if you need me."

She grinned at Tanya's low whistle, then headed to the front of the bakery. Despite Tanya's teasing, Jack and Erin seemed to have everything under control. A coffee and tea station had been set up where the register would normally be and matching glass dispensers of pink lemonade and iced green tea sat on a table off to the side.

She was about to commend them on their handiwork when the bell hanging from the front door jingled cheerfully. Cal walked in, followed by Daniella and Mel. She got that now familiar mixture of delight and apprehension.

"Hey, Quinn." Cal strode right over to her and gave her a hug. "You look like such a grownup."

She chuckled. "I kind of am a grownup."

He made a face. "Overrated."

Daniella offered her a polite nod and Mel extended her hand. "Good to see you."

It was entirely possible she was imagining it—her own mild discomfort laced with uncertainty—but she got a strange vibe from Mel. Not challenging, exactly, but something close. Smug, maybe. Like there was a competition Quinn didn't even know about and Mel had just won it.

She brushed off the feeling and turned to Cal, who was raving about the new design and asking her a string of questions about how and why she'd come up with this or that. Mel and Daniella put their heads together and whispered to each other. At this point, she was perfectly happy to let them keep to themselves.

Amanda emerged from the kitchen and a flurry of hugs and compliments and enthusiasm ensued. She took that as her cue to fade into the background, at least for the moment. She joined Erin and Jack and chatted with them about the bakery and the weather and whether or not Amanda would manage to hold on to some of the more laid-back lifestyle she'd embraced over the last month.

Julia and Taylor arrived with a bakery warming gift—a photo of Seneca Lake in a frame made with wood salvaged from the renovation. Amanda cried and asked Quinn to hang it in the seating area where a more generic piece of art had been.

Guests started to arrive in earnest and Quinn slipped into architect mode. She chatted about the project and handed out business cards. She talked up Joss and pointed her out to anyone and everyone who expressed interest in any kind of reno work. As much as she wanted to be at Amanda's side, she was content to do her own thing and let Amanda shine.

And shine she did. Every time Quinn had a free moment, she searched the room for Amanda. She talked. She laughed. She positively glowed. And when Mel sidled up to her and whispered something in her ear, Quinn hardly even minded. Because when the party was over, Amanda was going home with her.

❖

"I bought you a gift." Mel's face was sly.

"You did?" Amanda's mind went to the framed plans she'd ultimately decided to hang in her decorating room, making her smile.

Mel winked. "I couldn't let such a big day pass without something."

No point telling her the smile was for Quinn. Mel might not give her the flutters anymore, but the fondness remained. Always would, she supposed. "Are you giving it to me now?"

"That was the plan."

If a small part of her was annoyed Mel chose the middle of the party to give it to her, she brushed it aside. That was Mel's way. "All right."

"It's out front."

A warning bell sounded in her brain. "It is?"

"I arranged to have it delivered."

The warning bell grew louder and words like danger flashed through her brain. Whatever it was, it was going to be showy. "You didn't go overboard, did you?"

Another sly smile. "What's overboard, really?"

Without waiting for a response, Mel took her hand and led her through the crowd toward the door. She searched for Quinn, relieved to find her deep in conversation with Erin and Julia. She resisted the urge to yank her hand free.

On the sidewalk, topped with a giant red bow, sat a dough sheeter. And not any dough sheeter. No, it was the kind of high-end, free-standing model she'd lusted after for years. The kind that cost ten grand. "Mel."

"I think it's about time you have one of these, don't you?"

Whether she did or not was beside the point. It was expensive, extravagant, and completely inappropriate. "You shouldn't have."

Mel slung an arm around her shoulder. "But I wanted to."

She shouldn't accept it. Couldn't. Though, God, it was beautiful. "It's too much."

Mel released her shoulder and turned to face her. "There were so many years I wasn't as supportive as I should have been. Let me do this for you now."

There was no answer because the first part, at least, was true.

"And don't pretend you don't want it. Daniella assured me this was the thing you've been most pining for."

"That's not the point."

Mel grinned. "Of course it is. I'm giving you what you want."

She realized they weren't talking about a piece of kitchen equipment or how often Mel did or didn't show up while they were together. They were talking about something much more in the moment. Embarrassment was suddenly the least of her problems. "Mel—"

"It's here. Do you love it?" Daniella's enthusiastic voice interrupted her train of thought. Which maybe wasn't a terrible thing because she had no idea what she was going to say.

Mel's arm went around Daniella. "She's getting there. You know how she feels about gifts she thinks are over-the-top."

Daniella rolled her eyes. "Seriously."

The fact that they'd commiserated over this gave her pause.

"What's going on?" Cal appeared, Zoe in tow. "Whoa. What's that?"

"M got Mom the dough roller of her dreams." Daniella seemed to take satisfaction in knowing something Cal didn't.

Tanya emerged next, followed by Erin and Jack. Then Julia with Olivia and Joss. The exact thing she didn't want to happen was happening. The only thing worse than becoming the center of attention was having Mel right there with her, part of the spectacle.

Mel lifted an arm. "No need to stop the party, folks. I was just giving Amanda her bakery warming present."

Amanda closed her eyes and wished she could simply melt into the pavement. And maybe reappear in the kitchen all by herself. Or home. Or maybe in Quinn's cabin, preferably with Quinn. Anywhere but here. With Mel. And an audience.

She braved a look around, not wanting to see Quinn, but needing to know if she was among the onlookers. It was a silly question. Of course she was. And if the look on Quinn's face was anything to go on, she'd have been better off not knowing. She turned back to Mel. "You really, really shouldn't have."

"Sure she should have," Daniella said and started to clap.

As it so often did in this sort of situation, people started to join in, and the next thing she knew, everyone was applauding. It would have been sweet if it hadn't been so humiliating. She waved her hands in a futile attempt to make it stop. Eventually, it did. Only everyone continued to look at her and Mel and the large and shiny dough sheeter. Daniella stepped forward with two glasses of champagne. She handed one to each of them, like the whole thing had been perfectly orchestrated.

"Since we're all out here, what do you say we raise a glass to the return of Bake My Day? And, of course, its beautiful owner." Mel lifted her glass. "To Amanda."

A chorus of "to Amanda" enveloped her. Much like the applause, she appreciated the sentiment, even as being the center of attention made her cringe. She looked back to where Quinn had been, only Quinn was no longer there.

She was pretty sure things couldn't get any worse.

"All right. All right. I think I've officially exceeded my capacity for being in the spotlight."

That earned her a good laugh from the crowd. She gestured to the bakery and people shuffled inside. A few used it as their cue to offer congratulations and head out. Inside, guests continued to help themselves to snacks. She looked around for Quinn but didn't see her. Great.

"Could we talk for a minute?"

Mel's voice behind her made her jump. "Really? You didn't get enough attention outside?"

"Please."

She should say no on principle. She should also go find Quinn. But she wanted to give Mel a piece of her mind while her irritation was still fresh. "Fine. Come with me."

She led them through the kitchen to the decorating room, quiet and removed from the bustle of the party. "You shouldn't have bought me such a lavish gift."

"I stand by what I said. You deserve it. But I'd be lying if I said that was the only reason I bought it for you."

The embarrassment of before gave way to a sprouting seed of dread. "I don't know what you're talking about."

Mel took a step toward her. "Surely you do."

Part of her did. Part of her knew deep down exactly what Mel was getting at. But she'd be damned if she was going to own it. Or give Mel even the slightest hint of encouragement. "I do not. And I'm pretty sure anything you have to say on the matter will turn out to be something we both regret."

"I've ended it with Bella. Amanda, I'm in love with you." Mel made it sound like a declaration of victory.

Victory for whom was the question. "Mel, we're not doing this. I've told you that. Several times, in fact."

"But you thought I was trying to play both sides. I'm not doing that anymore."

Amanda rubbed her hands over her face. She wondered if Mel's use of "anymore" even registered. "That isn't the reason. If you actually listened to me instead of fixating on what you want, you'd know that."

"Is this gesture not grand enough for you? Is that the problem? I can go grand." Mel squared her shoulders and patted her chest, like it was a point of pride.

"Jesus Christ, Mel. No." She couldn't keep the irritation from her voice. Even now, Mel pulled out the same old bag of tricks. And with it, that same old way of making everything about her.

"What will it take then? I'm prepared to do whatever you ask."

She couldn't come up with an honest answer that didn't feel at least a little bit cruel. "There's nothing. It's not about that."

Mel's brow creased, like she heard Amanda's words but they didn't compute. "I don't understand."

"I'm not in love with you. I haven't been in love with you for a very long time." It was the first time she'd ever had to say such a thing. As much as she didn't want to, especially right now, it hit her how significant it was to say it out loud.

"So, the last few months meant nothing to you?"

She shook her head. "You say that like we've had this whole affair."

Mel looked genuinely confused. "Didn't we?"

As much as she didn't want to rehash the specifics, it seemed like that was the only way she was going to get anywhere. "We slept together twice. One of those times was a drunken accident. That's it."

"But we had dinner, we hung out."

"And we planned one date and you stood me up."

Mel pounced. "You're still mad about that, I can tell. I've said I'd make it up to you."

Her patience snapped. "You're not listening to me. You never listen to me."

That seemed to catch her attention. "I listen."

"Then it's worse because it means you hear what I'm saying and choose to ignore it." How could she not see that?

Mel offered a playful smile. "Is it so bad if I want to convince you I'm right?"

"I'm not a target market, Mel. I'm not some coveted demographic you're trying to sway to your product." She'd never used that analogy before, but it struck her how much it resonated. Now, but also during their marriage. Even when it came to matters of the heart, Mel never stopped thinking like a marketing professor.

Mel didn't answer right away. Amanda could tell her words had landed hard. What she couldn't decide was whether they were sinking in or if Mel was putting together her counterpoint.

Eventually, she said, "I don't think of you as just some consumer. I love you."

Amanda sighed. "I know. I love you, too. As the parent of my children and the first person I ever really fell in love with. But we can't be together. Please, please believe me when I say that."

"You're a very stubborn woman." Mel put a hand on Amanda's cheek.

Finally, she'd managed to convince her. Amanda leaned into it slightly. "Thank you."

The next thing she knew, Mel's mouth was on hers. It caught her so by surprise, she stood there for a moment, stunned.

"Oh, my God."

Cal's voice yanked her back to the moment. She pulled free and took a giant step back. "Not what it looks like."

"So, you weren't kissing?"

"So, maybe it was a little bit what it looked like," Mel said.

Amanda glared at her. "You are not helping."

Because things weren't bad enough, Daniella appeared in the doorway. "What's going on?"

"Nothing," she said, but it was drowned out by Cal's reply of, "Our moms were kissing."

"Oh." Daniella seemed neither bothered nor surprised.

"Your mother and I have been seeing each other," Mel said.

"No, we haven't." Her tone was sharper than she would have liked but, seriously, what the hell was Mel thinking?

Mel didn't miss a beat. "Okay, perhaps that's a little bit of an exaggeration."

Cal stuck both hands out in a show of confusion. "Well, you either have or you haven't."

Amanda blew out a breath. As much as she did not want to be having this conversation with Mel, she wanted to be having it with her kids even less. Especially as a party—a party she was hosting no less—went on mere feet away. Still. She didn't trust Mel to do the explaining. "We had a moment. Maybe a couple of moments. But one of us came to our senses and ended it before things got out of hand."

"Out of hand?" Cal asked.

"Moments?" Mel and Daniella said, both in disbelief.

Oh, dear God. Could this get any worse? "Yes. And it's over and done and we all need to accept that and put it behind us."

She glared at Mel, who finally seemed to be getting the picture. "I'm sorry," she said.

Amanda closed her eyes for a second. When she opened them, Mel looked both sad and defeated. "I think you should go."

Mel nodded. She sighed. She offered Cal and Daniella what seemed like an apologetic look. And then she was gone.

Chapter Twenty-eight

Amanda remained in the room with Cal, who still looked more confused than anything else, and Daniella, who seemed to be on the verge of throwing something or crying. She started with Daniella. "Honey—"

"Don't honey me. I can't believe you won't give M another chance. She left Bella for you." Daniella's tone was sharp.

"I can see you're really upset by this, but I'm not sure what gave you the impression we were—"

"She told me, okay? She told me you got together the night of my concert and she told me she still had feelings for you."

"What?" Cal sounded even more bothered by that than the fact she and Mel had hooked up in the first place.

Daniella planted her hands on her hips. "She still loves you, more than she ever loved Bella."

She was pretty certain Mel mostly loved what she couldn't have, but she wasn't about to say that to Daniella. "But there's a reason we broke up. Probably a hundred or more reasons. Those don't just go away because enough time has passed."

Daniella lifted her chin, defiant. "Some of them did. M got tenure. You're not working as many crazy hours as you used to. And Cal and I aren't needy little kids taking up all your time."

"You were never needy little kids." She looked at both Daniella and Cal, hoping they didn't doubt that for even a second.

Daniella sighed. "You know what I mean."

"Honey, I'm sorry if Mel telling you about us made you think there was some chance we'd end up back together." Apologizing for Mel's behavior while at the same time wanting to throttle her felt like a cruel irony.

Another sigh, this one laced with a groan of frustration. "It was my idea, okay?"

Even without knowing exactly what Daniella meant, she knew it wasn't good. "What was your idea?"

"The dough sheeter, the grand gesture, everything. I convinced her to go for it." Her voice cracked at the end and she swiped away tears with the back of her hand.

"Oh, Daniella." Her frustration with Mel remained, but her heart ached for her daughter.

"It was stupid. I get it. You're in love with Quinn now and M doesn't stand a chance."

For as mature as Daniella was when it came to a lot of things, her take on love and relationships and her parents wasn't one of them. At least not yet. "It wasn't stupid. It's perfectly reasonable to want your parents to be together."

Daniella shook her head and rolled her eyes. "I thought I was over it, you know? Like, I haven't spent the last ten years pining to be a family again. It's just, I don't know. When it seemed like there was a chance it might happen, I guess I got excited."

This was exactly the reason she didn't want to tell the kids in the first place. But of course Mel wouldn't see it that way. For as much as she loved her children, her own needs and desires always came first. "I'm sorry."

"It doesn't matter. It's too late." Without waiting for a reply or anything else, Daniella shook her head and left.

Amanda was torn between chasing after her and giving her space. Since Cal remained—looking completely shell-shocked—the latter won out. Since the first apology had been directed at Daniella, she decided to lead with, "I'm sorry."

He shook his head. "I don't get it."

"It was a bad idea, but sometimes we get caught up in things and we don't make the best choices." This one might top her all-time list of terrible decisions.

"But I thought you were with Quinn. I thought Quinn made you happy."

"She does." It struck her how much Cal had picked up on that, especially given the extent to which Daniella refused to.

He frowned and continued to shake his head.

"What M and I had was brief and then it ended before Quinn and I even started dating. I thought we were both clear on that, but I was wrong." And even in her anger, part of her felt terrible about that.

"Yeah, okay."

She blew out a breath. "I'm sorry she misunderstood, and I'm even sorrier you and Daniella got caught up in the mess."

"Caught up?" He stuck out his hands with exasperation. "I'm just finding out about it today."

"Do you want to know more?" Not that she wanted to talk about it. But it wouldn't be fair to let him be the only one in the dark.

Just as quickly as his hackles were raised, he slumped his shoulders in seeming defeat. "Is it really over? There's no chance you're getting back together?"

She shook her head. "No chance."

"Then I don't think I do. Is that okay?" The worried look on his face made her want to hug him.

"Completely okay. I think it would be for the best if we could put it all behind us."

"Yeah." This yeah had more feeling than the first.

"Are you okay?"

He nodded, then rolled his eyes. "Better than Daniella, apparently."

Ugh. That was the truth. "She'll be okay. Eventually."

"I'll go try to find her."

He'd probably have better luck than she would at this point. "That would be great. And I really am sorry for this, for keeping it from you."

He crossed the room and gave her a hug. "You're a grownup, Mom. You don't have to tell your kids everything."

And just like that, he made everything a tiny bit better. "Thank you."

"Maybe go find Quinn, though. She looked kind of freaked last time I saw her."

A whole new wave of panic swept through her. "I will. I just need one second to pull myself together."

He hugged her again, then he was gone. She covered her face with her hands for a second and tried to take the kind of slow, deep breaths that were supposed to be calming. How much had Quinn seen? Heard? As much as part of her didn't want to know, to face it, she needed to find out. Maybe more importantly, she needed to explain. And there was only one way to do it.

Every instinct in Quinn's body told her to flee, but her feet remained rooted to the floor. Like an accident on the side of the road, she couldn't tear her eyes away. Not from Mel when she emerged from the room. Not from Daniella and Cal when they followed and looked at her with something resembling disdain and pity, respectively.

Part of her wanted to go to Amanda. Whether to have it out or reassure, she didn't know. But she remained fixed in the kitchen. Waiting.

After a long moment, Amanda came out. She looked exhausted and, maybe, defeated. Quinn's heart broke a little more, for completely different reasons than before.

When Amanda caught sight of her, she came to an abrupt stop. "How much of that did you hear?"

Quinn blew out a breath. "Enough."

Amanda winced.

"I heard raised voices and I was worried."

"I'm so sorry."

Quinn nodded without being sure why. No, that wasn't true. She had no doubt Amanda did feel sorry. What she was sorry for was another matter. Quinn couldn't even begin to settle on what, exactly, Amanda was regretting. She had even less of an idea about her own feelings.

"I wanted to find you, to talk, after Mel pulled that stunt with the sheeter."

She thought about her own gift to Amanda and laughed. It sounded hollow and brittle in her own ears. "Quite the statement."

"It was presumptuous and extravagant and—"

She lifted her hand and Amanda stopped speaking. "You don't need to downplay it for my benefit."

Amanda shook her head. "I'm not. The whole thing made me uncomfortable, but I didn't want to cause a scene."

Even as her heart wrenched, she understood. "I think I should go."

Amanda's expression was pained. "Please don't."

"I'm not saying we can't talk, but you still have a bakery full of guests and I'm sure people are looking for you." And there was the matter of not trusting herself to have a rational conversation.

"I don't want to leave things like this."

"I think we have to. Go take care of what you need to take care of." To think she'd been on the verge of telling Amanda she was in love with her.

"Are you sure?"

She wasn't sure of much at this point, save the pressing need to go hole up far, far away from this moment. "I'm sure."

"Tonight, maybe? After all this is over?"

Quinn nodded, relieved but also a bit devastated Amanda was so quick to agree. "Of course."

"I really am sorry."

Again, the apology offered little in the way of clarity or reassurance. "Me, too."

Amanda looked at her with confusion but didn't press. Instead, she took a deep breath and squared her shoulders. "Thank you."

She strode out of the room with purpose, leaving Quinn standing there all alone. Despite the wish to escape, she lingered. Memories of being in that exact spot—during the initial walk-through, during construction, with Amanda that very morning—played through her mind. She'd gone from being unsure about ever falling in love again to setting herself up for another broken heart. The irony of both playing out in a few short months made her ache.

"Quinn?"

She turned at the sound of Cal's voice. "Hey."

Cal looked at his feet, then back at her. "You okay?"

"Yeah. Thanks." He didn't need to hear the voices and questions swirling around her brain. And to be honest, the fact that he thought about her, came and checked on her, helped in quieting those voices.

"You're not going to break up with my mom, are you? Because of this?"

It still caught her how much people his age could sound like total grownups one second and little kids the next. "I wasn't planning to, but I'm not sure where it leaves us."

She desperately wanted to ask if he'd prefer his parents get back together, but she wouldn't do that to him. Not because he wasn't mature enough to have a meaningful answer, but because it was an unfair question in the first place.

"Good." He looked at his feet again and Quinn couldn't decide if there was something else he wanted to say or if he didn't know how to leave the conversation gracefully. Eventually, he looked up. "She's happier than she's been in a long time and I'm pretty sure it's because of you."

She knew enough from her relationships with Jacob and Adam that teenage boys didn't say things like that just to say them. Not that she'd descended to hopelessness, but his words fortified her. "The feeling is mutual."

"Good." He nodded this time, as though confirming something he'd hoped was true.

"I am going to take off, though. I think there's been enough excitement for one day."

He nodded again, but his face was sad. "Yeah."

"Good luck next week with orientation and classes starting and everything. You're going to do great."

"You say that like I'm not going to see you."

She had absolutely no idea what was going to happen with Amanda, but she offered him an encouraging smile. "Of course you will. But probably not before you move in."

He sighed. "Right. Yeah."

She was in love with Amanda, but she was also kind of in love with her kids. Well, one of them at least. "Once you're settled, I'll come take you to lunch."

That seemed to cheer him up. "Yeah, okay. Cool."

"I'm sure your parents have everything covered, but if you need something, text me. Okay?"

"I will." He nodded with more enthusiasm.

"Good."

She started to leave, but he put a hand on her arm. "I don't know how much of that you heard, but my sister is out of her mind. Our moms should not get back together. Like, at all."

She laughed in spite of the hollowness in her chest. "Thanks."

He offered her a half smile, like they were in on some sort of secret together. "Anytime."

She did leave then, feeling perhaps a shred less hopeless than a few minutes before. On the drive home, she tried to shut off the questions and fears. She failed spectacularly.

CHAPTER TWENTY-NINE

The knock on Quinn's door startled her. Moping, it seemed, could be quite engrossing. She got up, half hoping it was the Chinese food she wished she'd ordered an hour ago. When she opened the door and found Amanda, looking hesitant and exhausted, on the other side, her heart nearly stopped. "Hi."

"Hi."

Breathe. "I wasn't expecting you."

"I was worried that if I texted, you might not answer." Amanda sighed. "Or tell me not to come."

If she only knew. "I would have answered."

"Oh. Well. I'm sorry for showing up unannounced then."

She shook her head. "Don't ever apologize for showing up."

A faint glimmer of hope came into Amanda's eyes. "Does that mean I can come in?"

She opened the door wide. "Always."

She came in and Quinn closed the door behind her. She hesitated for a moment, then set down her purse. "I hope you know I ended it a while ago. Before you and I ever slept together. Even before our first date."

Quinn nodded, but she couldn't quite muster a reassuring smile. "I know."

"I don't want to be with her. I'm not even remotely tempted."

"I believe you."

Amanda's eyes narrowed. "Your words say that, but your eyes don't."

How could she explain without laying each and every one of her insecurities at Amanda's feet? "I do believe you. Everything I overheard reinforces that."

"But something's wrong. I can tell. Is it that I slept with her in the first place? Does that seem like a bigger deal now?"

"No." She wasn't thrilled with the idea, but it wasn't like she would hold something against Amanda that happened before they got together. No, this was about the role Mel played—would always play—in Amanda's life. She didn't know if she could be in a relationship where she was always overshadowed. "I…"

"Yes?"

"We should sit down. Can I get you a glass of wine? Something stronger than wine?"

That broke the tension slightly and Amanda chuckled. "Wine would be great."

Quinn escaped to the kitchen. She poured two glasses, but before going back to the living room, she braced both hands on the counter. Just breathe.

She found Amanda on the sofa, feet tucked under her. She accepted the glass of wine Quinn offered, but set it on the coffee table. She sat up straight and squared her shoulders. Quinn imagined it was her standard serious talk posture, honed through years of parenting.

"So," she said.

Quinn joined her and took a deep breath. "So."

"I think I need to know what you're feeling. Are you mad? Disappointed? Wanting more details about what happened?"

She wasn't expecting Amanda to start with her. She scrambled to organize her thoughts into words. "Unsure, I guess."

"Unsure about my feelings for Mel? Or for you?"

"Neither." Not entirely true. She desperately wanted to know how Amanda felt about her. But something about this moment muddied the waters. She didn't want any declarations tainted by Amanda's attempt to reassure.

"Oh." Amanda's shoulders dropped. "Unsure about what, then?"

She should have thought more about how to articulate this instead of spinning one wretched scenario after another. "How all the pieces fit, maybe. Whether your life has room in it for me, for us."

That only seemed to confuse Amanda more. "Do you feel like we don't spend enough time together?"

Great. She'd managed to make herself sound needy and clingy. "No, no. It's not that at all. Please don't think I'm one of those women who wants no life outside of a relationship."

It came out more vehemently than she intended, but Amanda smiled. "I've never gotten that impression from you."

"It's more—" Ugh. Why was this so hard? "When I was married, it was pretty clear I was the boring one."

"What?" Amanda looked genuinely confused, which proved a small consolation.

"Lesedi was a star—in her work, in our social circles. Everyone is drawn to her. I never minded being in her shadow. To be honest, I'm probably more comfortable out of the spotlight anyway."

Amanda nodded, but looked no less confused. "I know what you mean. Truly. But I'm struggling to follow what this has to do with us."

"I was happy to be in the background until my wife fell for someone with as much flash as she had."

"Oh." The word dragged out as realization dawned.

"I get that your kids come first. I'd never want it to be otherwise, but they mean you're always going to have this connection to Mel. And if she's still in love with you…" she trailed off, not wanting to finish the thought.

Amanda took a deep breath. "She's not. She just thinks she is."

Quinn let out a chuckle, but there was no humor in it. "I think you're underestimating her."

"She wants what she can't have. It's a competitive thing." Amanda rolled her eyes as she spoke and shook her head.

"Even if that's the case—"

"Even if that's the case, I'm not in love with her. I don't want to be with her. And that isn't going to change."

Quinn believed her. She believed her the first time she said it. But she was failing epically at explaining the difference between that and her real fears. "I'm sorry I seem to be sending us in circles. I'm truly not worried you're going to get back together with her. It's whether I'm actually what you want. What if I'm appealing right now because I'm different? What if I'm just a rebound, some experiment?"

Amanda smiled then. Her brow arched. "Rebound? I've been divorced, like, five times longer than you have."

"But you considered getting back together with her. It says something about that kind of person still having a certain appeal."

"My brief..." she hesitated, "affair with Mel reminded me of why we broke up in the first place."

"Wasn't it because she fell in love with someone else?"

Amanda tipped her head back and forth. "On the surface, yes. But that was only the catalyst. Mel takes up all the oxygen in the room. Mel is..." another pause, "always about Mel."

She'd gotten that vibe but chalked it up to her own predisposition to dislike the woman. Having Amanda say it, and use those words, went a long way. "I appreciate you saying that."

"I'm not just saying it for your benefit." Amanda looked down at her hands, then at Quinn. "I like that you're subtle."

Quinn offered her a rueful smile. "That's a kinder word than boring."

"And completely different. You're not boring. You're low-key but still adventurous. You have such empathy and such care for the feelings of others. You're honest and open-minded and have such a deep sense of integrity."

She squirmed. This was exactly how she didn't want this conversation to go. "You don't have to stroke my ego."

"What if I'm not trying to stroke your ego? What if I mean it?"

"Maybe you do. But I'm not sure I'm in a place to hear it, if that makes any sense."

Amanda frowned. "I'm sorry, but it doesn't."

"I think you feel bad about how things went earlier and you want to make me feel better."

"Both true."

"Which I appreciate, but I can't, or I guess I don't want, you telling me how you feel about me as part of trying to make me feel better."

"Oh." She let the word hang.

"That might not be fair of me, but I'm trying be honest and not just say the things that will make us feel better in the moment."

Amanda took a deep breath and Quinn braced herself. "I respect that. It makes sense. It makes me sad, but it makes sense."

It made her sad, too. "Thank you."

"So, where does that leave us?"

She so wasn't the expert. "Well, you're going to be crazy busy the next couple of weeks, between getting Cal moved in and the bakery back up and running. What if we took a breather? Let the dust settle."

"Is that your gentle way of breaking up with me?"

She scrubbed her hands over her face. "No. If I didn't think there was any hope, I'd say so."

"But there's a chance you are going to in the end."

The look of anguish on Amanda's face slayed her. It took every ounce of restraint she had not to gather Amanda in her arms and ask if they could just put the whole mess behind them. "I mean, I think there's a chance either of us could end up there. I don't think you want to get back together with Mel, but I don't think it's as resolved as you want it to be. And Daniella doesn't, either."

"You're right." Amanda blew out a breath and her whole demeanor took on a look of defeat. "But promise me we are going to talk."

The request gave her a dose of reassurance. "We will."

Amanda untucked her feet and set them on the ground. "Okay. I won't outstay my welcome now."

It wouldn't be fair to take Amanda's hand, tell her how badly she didn't want her to go. But, God, did she want to. "It's not like that. I hope you know it's not like that at all."

Amanda nodded but didn't speak. She stood. Quinn followed her to the door. She picked up her purse. Quinn opened the door.

Amanda stepped outside, but turned. "I'll be thinking about you."
She nodded, not sure of what else to do.

Amanda left and Quinn closed the door behind her. She slumped
against it and let her head tip back. She'd think about little else.

❖

Mel pulled into the driveway just after eight and Amanda
braced herself. They'd discussed the logistics of moving Cal into
his dorm over text but hadn't seen each other since the party. The
cloud of the day and how it ended still loomed.

Cal finished shoveling eggs into his mouth and polished off his
orange juice. "Two minutes."

She laughed as he bolted from the table and headed upstairs. It
was a good thing he was such a serious student or she'd worry about
him ever getting to class on time. "Take your time."

She took a steadying breath and headed to the front door. She
opened it just as Mel lifted a hand to knock. She offered Amanda a
sheepish smile. "Hi."

The body language went a long way in helping her relax. "Hey."

"Big day."

"It is." She was prepared for it, but it didn't make it any less
significant. "How did yesterday go?"

She'd initially hesitated to take a wedding cake order the day
Daniella was due to move back into her dorm, but given everything,
she wound up relieved to have the conflict. And since Daniella was
allowed a car on campus this year, there really wasn't a need. It did
make her feel like a coward and a terrible parent, but it was the truth
of the matter. At least she could point to wanting to avoid Mel as
much as Daniella.

"Perfectly uneventful. Nadia says hi."

That made her feel better, as did the mention of Daniella's
roommate. And Daniella had responded to her text last night. She
knew it was residual awkwardness and not an irreparable rift, but
the evidence helped. "Oh, that's nice."

"Cal?"

"Brushing his teeth, I think. Otherwise, ready."

Mel folded her arms and leaned forward. "Are you as freaked out by all this as I am?"

She chuckled. "A state of general disbelief is all."

"You always were the levelheaded one."

"For better or for worse." She blew out a breath. "Coffee?"

"I'd love some."

Mel followed her to the kitchen. She poured a fresh cup and refilled her own. Cal came bounding down the stairs looking at once completely grown up and like her little boy about to take on the first day of school. "Hey, M."

"Ready to load up?" Mel asked.

He nodded affably. "Ready as I'll ever be."

It took less than an hour to load both vehicles and about the same to drive to Cornell. They unloaded his things with the help of a slew of move-in volunteers, then left him to his first day of orientation. She and Mel went through family orientation sessions, just as they had at Rochester the year before. The emotional magnitude of dropping her baby off at college was mitigated by having a better sense of how it all worked.

Mel opted to head to her office for a bit when things wrapped up, making their good-bye quick and tidy. For some—or perhaps many—reasons, the drive home felt about twice as long as the drive there. She pulled into the driveway dirty, sweaty, and exhausted. And alone. She hadn't expected the alone part to bother her. She liked the quiet and there were already plenty of nights she had the house to herself. Something about this, though, felt permanent.

Inside, she climbed the stairs and headed straight for the shower. Being clean, and in a pair of loose fitting cotton pants and a tank top, made her feel better. As did pouring a glass of wine and flopping on the sofa. Even if it was barely six in the evening.

She picked up her phone. A text from Cal about the horrors of ice breakers and one from Mel about being glad they could have the day together, all things considered. She sent a cackling GIF to Cal, but pondered her response to Mel for a long minute.

I'd like to go back to how things were before. She hit send before realizing the multiple possible interpretations of "before." *Before we slept together.*

The reply bubble appeared, then vanished. Minutes ticked by and she felt like an idiot waiting for a response. Instead, she switched over to her thread with Quinn. Other than a message that morning wishing her luck and Cal the best, there was nothing. No request to get together. But also no assertion she didn't want to get together.

She needed to give it some time. Erin had said as much. Jack, too. Julia was more for hashing it out, but not communicating—and the power of the grand gesture—were still fresh in her mind. She shook her head. Quinn had basically asked for space, so that's what she was going to give her.

I want to agree, but I can't bring myself to regret what happened between us.

She stared at Mel's words. It was easier for her to say. Her life was already imploding when they hooked up.

Not the showy scene that embarrassed us both. The reconnecting. Appreciating who we are now in new ways.

Tears pricked her eyes, not because Mel was wrong, but because she was right. Hooking up with Mel woke her out of a hibernation she hadn't even realized she was in. In some ways, it put her in the mindset to open her heart to Quinn. Even with the havoc the whole thing had wreaked, she couldn't bring herself to regret it. *Yeah.*

Is there anything I can do to make it right?

She had this mental picture of Mel showing up at Quinn's office and pleading her case. *Try to get Daniella back to a good place.* Send. Sigh. *I think the rest is mine to deal with.*

I have a good feeling it's going to work out. You're a catch and Quinn isn't an idiot.

The assertion—the closest thing to complimenting Quinn Mel had managed—made her chuckle. *I just need to convince her that taking a chance on me doesn't make her one.*

Mel replied with the laughing emoji, then the crying one, and finally a heart. She reiterated her opinion and wished Amanda a good night. Amanda thanked her and set her phone aside. She should probably eat dinner, but food was the last thing she wanted.

She padded into the kitchen to refill her wine glass and grabbed a sleeve of crackers. A hangover after her first night as an empty nester would be rather pathetic. She returned to the sofa, picked up her phone, and once again contemplated texting Quinn.

She messaged Erin instead, her only other single and potentially home by herself friend. But the text went unanswered. Given her luck, and Erin's, Erin was on some hot date who would turn out to be the love of her life.

God, that smacked of bitterness. Enough. She got up and physically shook herself. Whatever happened with Quinn, she had a full and happy and satisfying life.

Only, for some reason, telling herself that had tears threatening.

The thing was, she did have all that. It was more than a lot of people had and she was grateful. But she missed Quinn. It had only been a few days, but she missed her company, her body. And, truthfully, it was more than that. She missed the sense of optimism Quinn seemed to bring into every room she entered, her unflappable sense of adventure. And perhaps most of all, she missed who she was with Quinn—a braver and more carefree version of herself.

What was worse, being bitter or pathetic? Since it felt like she was pushing the limits of both, probably better not to ask. She carried her empty glass to the kitchen and headed upstairs. Maybe she could read herself to sleep.

In bed, she managed a chapter before giving in. She picked up her phone. *You don't need to respond, but I wanted you to know I'm thinking about you.* She added and deleted *I miss you* at least five times before sending the message without. No pressure. That was the point.

She went back to her book. By midnight, she turned the last page and her eyes finally felt heavy. She turned off the lamp, pulled the blankets up, and did her best not to think about the fact that Quinn hadn't texted her back.

Chapter Thirty

Short of a message from Mel herself, getting an email from Daniella was pretty much the last thing on earth Quinn expected. The fact that it included a request to talk only intensified the feeling. Still, she didn't hesitate for a second before accepting. Because as much as she didn't want to be in the business of seeking Daniella's approval or blessing or whatever, she couldn't imagine a future with Amanda without it.

When she pulled onto the University of Rochester campus the next day, she realized it was the first time she'd ever done so. After stopping at the visitor booth, she navigated to a parking lot and found a spot. A smaller campus that Cornell, but it had the same mix of old brick buildings covered with ivy and more modern designs. The student union was especially striking, triggering a vague memory that it had been designed by I.M. Pei.

She chuckled to herself. Once an architect, always an architect.

She was fifteen minutes early, but Daniella was already waiting for her in the coffee shop where they'd agreed to meet. Despite Daniella's assurances it wasn't going to be a bad talk, a tingle of apprehension worked its way down her spine. Daniella stood. "Hey, Quinn."

"Hi." She tried for a friendly smile. "How's the semester going so far?"

The question seemed to relax her. "So far, so good. I'm pretty sure organic chemistry is going to be the death of me, but otherwise…"

She trailed off and Quinn laughed. "I felt that way about my second semester of physics."

Daniella shook her head. "Don't tell me that. I've got physics next year."

It seemed unlikely Daniella had invited her all this way to discuss her course load, but Quinn wanted her to steer the conversation. "I'm sure you'll be great."

Daniella smiled. "Thanks. Um, can I get you a cup of coffee?"

"Coffee would be great, but let me get it."

The smile turned into a smirk. "Did my mother tell you to say that?"

"No, it's a rule of adulthood that when you hang out with college students, you treat." She hesitated, not sure whether to disclose the rest. "I didn't tell your mom I was meeting you."

That seemed to give her pause, but eventually she nodded. "I appreciate that."

Even without her anxiety over this meeting, simple curiosity would be screaming for an explanation at this point. "So, what are you having?"

A few minutes later, they sat with matching mochas, topped with whipped cream and drizzled with chocolate. If it had been Cal, she could have joked about having similar tastes. But it wasn't Cal. And she had no sense of whether she was in friendly territory or enemy.

Daniella took a deep breath and squared her shoulders. The gesture reminded her so much of Amanda when she'd set her mind to something. "First, thank you for driving all this way. I could have met you—"

Quinn waved a hand. "No worries. I like the drive and I rarely make it up to Rochester."

"Still. Thanks." She stared at her coffee and chewed the inside of her lip for a moment, then looked up and made eye contact with Quinn. "I owe you an apology."

Maybe a small part of her thought—hoped—this meeting would be about making peace, but she'd not allowed herself to expect it. "If you've been hoping your parents would get back together, I'm sure it was difficult to see your mom dating someone else. You don't need to apologize for that."

"But I do need to apologize for giving M reasons to think that's what Mom wanted when those reasons didn't exist."

Daniella seemed to be owning a much bigger role in the recent brouhaha than Quinn had believed. "What do you mean?"

Daniella huffed out a breath. "You know, I never really thought about them getting back together. Mom and M, they never gave off that vibe. And then they did and I found out they'd hooked up and I don't know, I got all caught up in the possibility."

Even if it unraveled her chances with Amanda, she could empathize with that longing. Or, at least, she could separate the reality of her broken heart from the kid who wanted her family to be together. "I can see how that might happen."

"Yeah. Well," she paused and frowned. "I shouldn't have interfered and maybe I ruined everything, but I wanted to try to make it right."

"I don't think you should blame yourself. Grownups get into plenty of trouble all on their own."

"But I'm the one who told M she had a chance, should try. I told her Mom said things she didn't." She shook her head. "It was stupid and it so backfired."

Quinn's mind raced, wanting to press for enough details to piece everything together. "Does your mom know that?"

"Not yet. I, uh. I wanted to start with you."

It didn't make sense. "Why?"

"Because if I can convince you to give her another chance, the whole situation will be a lot less shitty."

She wanted a full explanation, but it felt weird being privy to things Amanda didn't know. Her desire for answers, for hope, won out. "I'm not trying to make you relive it or feel worse, but do you think you could tell me the whole story?"

Daniella smiled, looking suddenly grownup. "I suppose it's the least I can do."

Quinn sipped her mocha, glad she'd gone for the comfort drink and not the stoic black coffee. "I don't want you to feel you owe it to me, but I'd like to understand."

"For starters, I never liked Bella. To be fair, the feeling is mutual. She might teach college, but I'm pretty sure she doesn't like kids, much less teenagers."

Quinn tried to swallow a snicker. She knew firsthand being a professor at an Ivy League institution did not require such trivial things as liking students. "I'm sure that was hard."

Daniella shrugged dismissively. "It was fine. She mostly steered clear of us."

The comment made her realize she had no idea what the custody arrangement was when Cal and Daniella were too young to come and go as they pleased. "Were you at their house a lot?"

"M had every other weekend and dinner once a week. More routine than a court-ordered thing."

It hurt her heart to think about kids even knowing language like court-ordered, but this wasn't the time to indulge those feelings. "Did they get along, Amanda and Mel?"

Daniella let out a snort, then schooled her expression. "Sorry. It was, uh, iffy at first. Like, tense conversations in the driveway at drop-off kind of iffy."

Amanda had said as much, but given the sleeping together, she'd assumed it was an exaggeration for her benefit. "Wow."

"Yeah. So, when M started acting kind of crushy, it was so weird. And then she told me about the affair and asked for my help to win Mom back."

"Oh." She let the word hang, but it failed to capture the extent of her feelings.

Daniella rolled her eyes. "Exactly."

Half an hour later, everything made sense. Well, as much sense as such a convoluted situation could make. And it changed, not everything, but a lot. For the first time in weeks—or if she was being honest, maybe ever—she didn't worry that being with Amanda would be a source of friction with her family. Mel had overplayed her hand, at the encouragement of her daughter who now seemed to genuinely regret her role in the whole thing. She'd thought things were complicated. And now that word felt almost painfully inadequate.

But even with all the explaining, one question loomed large in her mind. "So, what are you hoping happens?"

Daniella sighed. "I guess I hope you two do the happily ever after thing."

It was a big statement, much bigger than she needed to make if her goal was simply to make peace. "That's a tall order."

"I mean, if that's what you want. It's up to you." She lifted both hands. "I'm officially done with interfering."

The assertion made Quinn think of her sisters, her friends, and all the well-meaning meddlers in her life. "If that's a lesson you can learn at your age, you're ahead of the curve."

"Does that mean you're going to take her back?"

She smiled at the choice of phrase. "I think it's a little more complicated than that."

Daniella grinned. "It won't be by the time I'm done with her."

If part of her wanted to point out the contradiction in that logic, it was eclipsed by her very real longing to win Amanda back. Or take her back. Whatever. The prospect of having another chance made her giddy. She reined it in. She and Amanda still needed to have a very long talk if they had any hope of making things work. Still, it felt like maybe they were going to get the chance to have that talk. "Thank you."

She rolled her eyes. "I'm just trying to fix what I broke in the first place."

Daniella's machinations had certainly made things more difficult, but they hadn't been the sole reason for the current state of affairs. She'd allowed her own insecurities about being interesting enough, exciting enough, get in the way. Even Amanda played a part, omitting details that had the potential to rock the boat. She shook her head. "You didn't break anything."

Daniella gave her an incredulous look, once again looking so very much like Amanda.

Quinn raised a hand. "I'm not saying you didn't make them messier. But it wasn't all your doing."

"Thanks for saying that. I feel better."

She reached across the table and gave Daniella's hand a squeeze. "Thanks for being such an adult and owning you made a mistake."

Daniella took a deep breath, rolling her shoulders and then letting them drop. "Do you want a tour of campus while you're here? There are some really cool buildings."

Almost more than the apology, the invitation made her think there was hope for them after all. "That would be fantastic. And then I'd be happy to do a Wegmans or a Target run or whatever if you need anything."

Daniella lifted her chin. "You're getting good at this."

Quinn didn't know if she meant spending time with college students or something else, but she didn't care. The prospect of spending time together, just the two of them, made her happy. "I try."

By the time she was alone in her car and driving south, she and Daniella had wandered campus and gone to dinner together. The only thing giving her pause was the fact that Amanda had no idea what was going on. But Daniella promised to call her immediately and fill her in. Quinn wanted to ask for a report, but it felt like maybe too much to ask. Well, that and a bit insecure. Since the whole point was not to let herself be ruled by that, she refrained. She'd talk with Amanda soon enough and, hopefully, clear the air once and for all. But first, groceries.

You should call Mom. Or go over. :)

The text from Cal came just as she got in line with her basket of coffee, cream, and a frozen pizza. *Is everything okay?*

Yes. D wanted to text you but didn't have your number.

Oh. That meant Daniella had spoken with Amanda. She tamped down the jolt of nerves. If Cal and Daniella wanted her to go to Amanda's, it had to be good, right? Before she could logic her way through that, her phone rang. Amanda's smiling face appeared on the screen. She stepped out of line, not wanting to be that person, and answered. "Hi."

"Hi." Despite the uncertainty in Amanda's voice, the sound sent a warm tingle through her. Only a week had gone by without hearing it, but the effect was like a drink of water after days in the desert. "I hear you spent the day with Daniella."

"I did. She's quite a remarkable young woman."

"That's generous of you, all things considered."

"I might not love what she did, but I understand why she did it." She paused, wondering if Amanda was going to ask her over, but decided not to wait. "Are you free now? I think we should probably talk."

She could hear Amanda take a deep breath on the other end of the line. "I'd like that. Do you want to come here? Or I can come to you?"

"I'm already out and about. I'll come to you." She looked down at her basket. "I'm at the store, actually. Do you need anything?"

"Just you."

Short of I love you, she couldn't think of words she'd rather hear. "I'll be there in half an hour."

Chapter Thirty-one

Amanda drummed her fingers on the kitchen island, then gave in to the urge to pace. Again. After a couple of minutes, she sat. Again. How long could thirty minutes take?

This was ridiculous. She was ridiculous. Or, at the very least, dramatic. Quinn was coming over to talk, not have a knock-down, drag-out fight. If anything, this might be their chance to make up.

Not that they were fighting, really. They'd just not spoken in a week. And the whole situation made her feel as precarious as her first attempt at a wedding cake.

The problem was that Quinn was so unlike Mel. Yet, Mel was her only real frame of reference when it came to relationships. Quinn's quiet resignation left her uneasy and unsure.

Now she had to navigate Daniella's revelation. It didn't make any difference in how her heart leaned, but it might influence Quinn. But would it ultimately make Quinn more inclined to give them a chance, or less?

She'd just stalked away from the front door when the knock came. She spun around and hurried to open it, as if a second of hesitation might send Quinn running in the opposite direction. She yanked open the door, half expecting to have to chase her down the sidewalk.

But instead of a hasty retreat, Quinn stood there, perfectly still. Not statue stiff, but with that aura of calm about her. Only in that moment did she realize how used to Quinn's energy she'd become. A sigh escaped her.

"That bad, huh?"

"Oh, my God. No. I didn't mean it like that. I was—"

"I'm kidding."

Cripes. She was wound tighter than a, well, something wound really tight. "Sorry."

"May I come in?"

She nodded more vigorously than was probably necessary and stepped back. "Please."

"So, Daniella called you?"

Based on what Daniella had said, she had every reason to be hopeful. But rational thought stood little chance against anxiety in full bloom. "She did."

"It was quite the day." Quinn smiled, but shook her head.

"I want to hear everything or, at least, everything you're willing to share. Can I get you something? Tea? A glass of wine?" Part of her wanted a drink to smooth out the edges, but her stomach wanted nothing to do with it.

"I'm okay. Do you want to sit?"

She nodded again, feeling like a bobble head doll. "Sure. Yes."

They settled on the sofa, close but not quite touching. Quinn gave her a sideways look. "How much did Daniella tell you?"

How much Daniella told Quinn felt like a more relevant question, but she resisted turning it around before giving her own answer. "I think pretty much everything she told you."

Quinn shifted on the couch to face her. "Good."

"I'm sorry for all this. It isn't what you signed up for and it isn't—"

Quinn lifted a hand. "You don't need to apologize. Other than your kids, you never did anything to make me believe you had priorities or entanglements elsewhere."

It wasn't untrue. Even though she hadn't told Quinn about it, she was done with Mel before they'd had a real date. "Still, I could have been a lot more direct with Mel and maybe prevented some of this."

"Maybe." Even as she conceded the point, Quinn sighed. "But if I'd been less worried about being in her shadow, I could have prevented some of this, too."

Amanda frowned. "What do you mean?"

"I think I alluded to it before, when Cal had his appendicitis. I'm not the big personality who commands attention the second I walk in the room."

But Mel was, in spades. "I don't find that attractive. It isn't what I want."

"I believe you. It's just..." she paused, making Amanda wonder if she didn't know what to say next or how to put it nicely. Eventually, she continued with, "Mel is that person. And I know you don't want to be with her, but she—"

"Swoops in and sucks up all the oxygen." How could she have not seen that?

Quinn lifted a shoulder and angled her head. "I don't like to think I'm one to constantly compare myself to other people."

"But the last few weeks have made it pretty impossible not to."

She offered a half smile. "Something like that."

"What can I do to make it up to you? Or to make it so you don't worry about that anymore."

Quinn sat up straighter. "I've realized I've been an idiot, so there isn't anything you need to do."

"You haven't been an idiot." If anyone had, it had been her.

"I have, because I let insecurity get the better of me. But I'm not that person. I know what I have to offer."

She couldn't help but smile at that. "I like what you have to offer."

"I know. And same, for the record. I like everything about you."

"Even the fact that I have an obnoxious ex and a tendency to be bossy?"

"Your ex is of no consequence and I like that you're bossy." Quinn angled her head slightly. "I like it even more when bossy you lets me boss you around."

The comment sent a burst of heat right through her. It settled somewhere south of her stomach. Something about Quinn had changed. Not changed, maybe, but shifted. Something she'd gotten glimpses of here and there—when they were hiking, or in bed. It took her a moment to find the right word, but when it hit her, there was no mistaking it. Quinn Sullivan was confident. So different from Mel's self-assured charm, this was subtle, like Quinn herself. But it was there and it was clear and it was sexy as fuck.

"What?"

They were supposed to be having a heart-to-heart. Admitting her mind had steered in the direction of bed probably wasn't the best course of action. "Nothing."

"Come on. We just cleared the air. You can't hold out on me now." She said it in kind of a joking way, but not. That confidence again.

She cleared her throat. "I was thinking how much I like this side of you. How good it looks on you."

Quinn merely raised a brow. She seemed to be enjoying watching Amanda squirm. How delightful was that?

Amanda shook her head. She was going to have to own it. "It's sexy, okay? This side of you is sexy."

Quinn's smile was slow, and it upped the sexy factor about tenfold. "Is that so?"

"I know. I know. We're talking about relationships and making it work and I'm thinking about getting in your pants. It's terrible."

"I wouldn't say terrible." Her eyes danced with humor.

"You can stop making fun of me anytime."

"Who's making fun? An interesting and robust sex life is an essential component to a healthy relationship. At least in my book."

"Right." Maybe being teased about how much she wanted Quinn wasn't the worst thing.

"I mean, since we sorted out the emotional details, it seems like we should probably tend that part of our relationship, too."

Amanda swallowed, her desire ratcheting up in earnest. "Well, if it's for the good of the relationship."

Quinn stood and extended her hand. "Let me take you to bed?"

She'd phrased it as a question, but there was no question about her intention or who was going to be in charge. A seemingly impossible mix of emotions swirled through her: desire, love, but also something more. Quinn somehow managed to make her feel safe but bold, reckless even. A heady mix for someone so used to playing by the rules and worrying about everyone and everything but herself.

Maybe one day she'd find the right words to explain it, to let Quinn know what a magical gift she'd given her. For now, words weren't necessary. She tucked her hand in Quinn's and allowed herself to be led upstairs.

❖

With Amanda nestled in the crook of her shoulder, Quinn felt about a thousand times better than she had a few hours before. But there was still something hanging between them. Something she'd not been brave enough to say. "I didn't say something earlier that I should have."

Amanda's hand, that had been stroking her chest, stilled. "What's that?"

She shifted and rolled over so she could look Amanda in the eye. "Before I do, I need you to know it's not the afterglow talking."

Amanda laughed and shook her head. "Noted."

She took a deep breath. "The reason I asked for a break, said that I wanted us both to sort things out, was because the stakes felt so high."

"I get that. I really do. And I hope you know I backed off because I wanted to respect what you needed, not because I didn't love you."

"Um." All the ways Quinn imagined telling Amanda how she felt, having Amanda beat her to the punch hadn't been one of them.

Amanda's eyes narrowed but she didn't speak.

"Oh, God. I'm sorry. I said 'um' because I was about to tell you I love you and you saying it first totally caught me off guard." So much for being smooth and confident. Since the ship of saying the right thing had sailed, she took a deep breath and prepared to keep going. Only Amanda didn't let her finish. Instead of answering with words, she placed a hand on either side of Quinn's face and pulled them together.

Amanda's lips felt like sunshine and promise and happily ever after.

The kiss, more a statement than anything else, stopped the inane flow of words. She was as grateful for that as much as the kiss. But when Amanda's mouth angled, taking them deeper, all she could be grateful for was Amanda.

When Amanda eased back, she looked at Quinn with expectant eyes. Right. Because in all her drivel, she'd neglected the three most important words. Or, since Amanda had gone first, four. "I love you, too."

"Oh, good. I was worried there for a second you were rethinking the whole thing."

Quinn laughed. "I love you. I love you. I love you. I think I started falling in love with you the moment you approved my plans."

Amanda laughed, too. "Don't be silly."

She shook her head. "I mean it. You enchanted me from the beginning, but connecting with you like that, sharing a vision. I was a goner."

"I was so worried I'd messed everything up." Despite laughing a second before, her eyes shone with tears.

"You couldn't possibly."

"Don't try to downplay it now. You had serious doubts." A tear spilled over. "Because of my actions. Or maybe inactions."

How had she managed to make such an amazing woman fall in love with her? Even now, it hinted at magic. "I did have doubts, but they were as much my doing as anything else."

"I'm glad you didn't give up on us."

"You're not something I wanted to lose."

Another smile. Another tear. Quinn kissed this one away. "You'll stay, right? Tonight?"

"Well, if you insist."

Amanda angled her head. "I'd prefer it if you stayed tonight, tomorrow, and the day after that. And maybe the weekend."

God, she loved this woman. "So bossy."

This time, Amanda lifted her chin. "You knew what you were getting yourself into. I'm pretty sure we literally just discussed it."

"No complaints, merely an observation."

"Right, right. And you like bossy me."

Quinn shifted, bracing herself over Amanda. "I do."

Amanda bit her lip and looked at her with as much desire as their first night together. "Because then you get to turn the tables."

She kissed Amanda's neck, her jaw. "This is true."

"I love when you do. Really, I love all the things you do. In bed, out of bed. All of it."

"Well, that's convenient."

Amanda arched beneath her, pressing their bodies together in the most perfect way. "How so?"

"Because I love everything about you."

"I'm a very lucky woman."

She thought about all the bad dates and misfires, the lonely nights and wondering if she'd fall in love again. She hadn't used the term unlucky, but it had certainly felt that way. And now all that had changed. "No luckier than me."

"I love it when we agree."

So far, they didn't disagree about much. She wasn't naive enough to think it would always be that way, but she had a good feeling about their ability to navigate whatever came up. "Agreed."

"Hey, Quinn?"

She also loved how Amanda said her name. "Yes?"

"I love you."

"I love you, too."

Amanda smiled. "I'm really glad."

Quinn kissed her lightly. "So glad."

And then she kissed her with all the care and longing and passion and playfulness Amanda had awakened in her. Things she'd lost sight of, forgot she possessed. Things she never wanted to be without again.

EPILOGUE

The following spring.

Quinn drummed her fingers together. "Are we ready?"

Amanda buckled her seat belt and gave Quinn a questioning look. "I'm not sure. I don't know where we're going and you seem really stressed."

She blew out a breath. "Sorry."

Amanda reached over and squeezed her hand. "Don't apologize. Talk to me."

Amanda's concern went a long way in calming her nerves. "I'd rather show you. Is that okay?"

Amanda moved her hands up and down, indicating herself. "I'm here. Completely in your hands."

The trust gave Quinn the shot of courage she needed. She put the car in gear and pulled out of Amanda's driveway. "It's not far."

"All right." Amanda's smile was a mixture of encouragement and amusement. She probably thought Quinn was a little off her rocker.

In some ways, she was. She and Amanda had talked about moving in together, about the appeal of finding a place they could make their own. But the idea of starting from scratch added a whole extra layer of complexity. And time. And possible disagreement. Still, she'd not been able to shake the idea. And when this piece of land came on the market—only a couple of miles outside Kenota, in the direction of Ithaca—it felt like a sign from the universe.

Taking Amanda there, suggesting they build a house from the ground up, would have been a pretty big deal. The ring burning a hole in her pocket? That was another matter entirely. But in some ways, the two were inseparable. She wanted to build a life with Amanda, in every sense of the word.

She turned off Route 96 onto Otter Creek Road. Corn field gave way to forest on one side. The road pitched upward, opening up a view of rolling hills. They were too far from either lake to have a glimpse of water, but she didn't mind. Everything else about the location was perfect.

"Are you taking me to see a house?" Amanda turned to her and beamed. "Is that the surprise?"

"Not exactly." It wasn't a question, but her voice did a lilt at the end like it was. She cleared her throat. "Not exactly." There. That was better.

Amanda frowned, but more confused than irritated. "What does that mean?"

She was spared having to answer by their arrival. She pulled into the gravel driveway that had been started, but only went for about ten feet. "You'll see."

She cut the engine and tilted her head, indicating they should get out. She rounded the front of the car and took Amanda's hand. Amanda smirked. "Now I see why you told me to wear practical shoes."

They picked their way through tall grass and low brush. About fifty feet from the road, trees gave way to the large clearing that would be more than enough room for a house. Quinn stopped walking but didn't let go of Amanda's hand. "What do you think?"

"It's beautiful." Amanda looked around, then at Quinn. "Do you get to build a house here?"

"Maybe. If I play my cards right."

Amanda frowned again. "Is this one of those super intense and demanding clients who's making you jump through hoops even before you get the job?"

Quinn bit her lip and resisted the urge to laugh. "I wouldn't categorize her that way."

"Why are you being so weird today? What's going on?"

Amanda's cluelessness was about to make this whole hare-brained scheme either a lot more fun or horribly awkward. "I was hoping you might be my client."

"Me?"

"Well, technically we."

Finally, realization dawned. "You want to build a house for us."

"I'll hire experts to do the heavy lifting, of course, but I do want to design it and I'm hoping we can both get our hands a little dirty along the way. Makes it so much more personal, don't you think?"

"You bought this property for us."

She'd been sorely tempted, but she'd resisted. "Not yet. I think it's perfect, but it's also the kind of decision we should make together."

Amanda brought both hands to her cheeks and looked around again. "You want to build me, us, a house."

She swallowed and reminded herself to breathe. "I do."

"I can't think of a better way to start the rest of our lives together."

Okay. This was it. Now or never. "I don't entirely agree on that front."

"What—"

Quinn got down on one knee. She'd not done that when she and Lesedi decided to get married, but something about Amanda made her want to go the traditional route. It had the added bonus of being closer to the ground and making it less likely she'd keel over and pass out. "I want a future with you—a home and a life and a forever. But I'd be so much happier if you would do it as my wife."

Amanda didn't move. She didn't speak, either. She just stared at Quinn. Then the ring, the antique emerald cut diamond Daniella had helped her pick out. Then Quinn again. "I…"

Waiting for her reply was utter torture. Probably fewer than ten seconds passed, but each one felt like an eternity. "I'm not sure if it will influence your answer, but I feel like I should tell you I talked to both Cal and Daniella about this. Not that you need their permission, but I wanted them to know I was hoping for the whole family, not just you."

Amanda nodded. It started slowly but picked up steam. "Of course you did."

It wasn't a no, but it wasn't a yes, either. And being on her knee only exacerbated the ticking seconds and the fact that Amanda had yet to answer. "It seemed like the right thing to do, but please don't think for a second it's anyone but you I'm proposing to. I love you, Amanda, and I want to spend the rest of my life with you."

"I love you, too. More than I thought possible. And I love who I am when I'm with you. That's been maybe the most magical part of all this."

Quinn's heart, already at a persistent thud, began to race. "That, too. Absolutely."

"I can't imagine wanting to spend my life with anyone else."

"So, is that a yes?" Please, let it be a yes.

"Oh." Amanda's eyes got huge. "Yes. A thousand yeses. A million."

For as sure as she'd been Amanda would say yes, she'd never been so relieved in her life. She freed the ring from the cushion in the box and slid it onto Amanda's finger. "Just to be clear, you can say yes to this and no to the land. I want you to love where we end up."

Amanda took a second to admire the ring before grabbing Quinn's hands and pulling her to her feet. "Yes to all of it."

"It's really okay to think about it for a couple of days."

Amanda placed a hand on each of her shoulders and looked her in the eyes. "Are you trying to talk me out of it?"

She laughed. "No. Absolutely not. But they're two separate decisions and I don't want the excitement of one taking over the significance of—"

"Quinn."

She'd been rambling. She'd promised herself she wouldn't ramble. "Sorry."

"Do you trust me?"

"Utterly."

Amanda took a deep breath and looked around before returning her gaze to Quinn. "I love it. And you. I want it all."

Quinn let Amanda's words sink in. "I want to spend the rest of my life making you as happy as you make me."

Amanda smiled and angled her head ever so slightly. "Well, you're off to a pretty good start."

She thought about breaking ground, picking out furniture. Trips to the cabin and going with Amanda on wedding cake deliveries to interesting places. Big family dinners and quiet mornings on the porch. She wanted all of it, too. "I'd say we're just getting started."

About the Author

Aurora Rey is a college dean by day and award-winning lesbian romance author the rest of the time, except when she's cooking, baking, riding the tractor, or pining for goats. She grew up in a small town in south Louisiana, daydreaming about New England. She keeps a special place in her heart for the South, especially the food and the ways women are raised to be strong, even if they're taught not to show it. After a brief dalliance with biochemistry, she completed both a BA and an MA in English.

She is the author of the Cape End Romance series and several standalone contemporary lesbian romance novels and novellas. She has been a finalist for the Lambda Literary, RITA®, and Golden Crown Literary Society awards but loves reader feedback the most. She lives in Ithaca, New York, with her dog and whatever wildlife has taken up residence in the pond.

Books Available from Bold Strokes Books

Best Practice by Carsen Taite. When attorney Grace Maldonado agrees to mentor her best friend's little sister, she's prepared to confront Perry's rebellious nature, but she isn't prepared to fall in love. Legal Affairs: one law firm, three best friends, three chances to fall in love. (978-1-63555-361-1)

Home by Kris Bryant. Natalie and Sarah discover that anything is possible when love takes the long way home. (978-1-63555-853-1)

Keeper by Sydney Quinne. With a new charge under her reluctant wing—feisty, highly intelligent math wizard Isabelle Templeton—Keeper Andy Bouchard has to prevent a murder or die trying. (978-1-63555-852-4)

One More Chance by Ali Vali. Harry Bastantes planned a future with Desi Thompson until the day Desi disappeared without a word, only to walk back into her life sixteen years later. (978-1-63555-536-3)

Renegade's War by Gun Brooke. Freedom fighter Aurelia DeCallum regrets saving the woman called Blue. She fears it will jeopardize her mission, and secretly, Blue might end up breaking Aurelia's heart. (978-1-63555-484-7)

The Other Women by Erin Zak. What happens in Vegas should stay in Vegas, but what do you do when the love you find in Vegas changes your life forever? (978-1-63555-741-1)

The Sea Within by Missouri Vaun. Time is running out for Dr. Elle Graham to convince Captain Jackson Drake that the only thing that can save future Earth resides in the past, and rescue her broken heart in the process. (978-1-63555-568-4)

To Sleep With Reindeer by Justine Saracen. In Norway under Nazi occupation, Marrit, an Indigenous woman; and Kirsten, a Norwegian resister, join forces to stop the development of an atomic weapon. (978-1-63555-735-0)

Twice Shy by Aurora Rey. Having an ex with benefits isn't all it's cracked up to be. Will Amanda Russo learn that lesson in time to take a chance on love with Quinn Sullivan? (978-1-63555-737-4)

Z-Town by Eden Darry. Forced to work together to stay alive, Meg and Lane must find the centuries-old treasure before the zombies find them first. (978-1-63555-743-5)

Bet Against Me by Fiona Riley. In the high stakes luxury real estate market, everything has a price, and as rival Realtors Trina Lee and Kendall Yates find out, that means their hearts and souls, too. (978-1-63555-729-9)

Broken Reign by Sam Ledel. Together on an epic journey in search of a mysterious cure, a princess and a village outcast must overcome life-threatening challenges and their own prejudice if they want to survive. (978-1-63555-739-8)

Just One Taste by CJ Birch. For Lauren, it only took one taste to start trusting in love again. (978-1-63555-772-5)

Lady of Stone by Barbara Ann Wright. Sparks fly as a magical emergency forces a noble embarrassed by her ability to submit to a low-born teacher who resents everything about her. (978-1-63555-607-0)

Last Resort by Angie Williams. Katie and Rhys are about to find out what happens when you meet the girl of your dreams but you aren't looking for a happily ever after. (978-1-63555-774-9)

Longing for You by Jenny Frame. When Debrek housekeeper Katie Brekman is attacked amid a burgeoning vampire-witch war, Alexis Villiers must go against everything her clan believes in to save her. (978-1-63555-658-2)

Money Creek by Anne Laughlin. Clare Lehane is a troubled lawyer from Chicago who tries to make her way in a rural town full of secrets and deceptions. (978-1-63555-795-4)

Passion's Sweet Surrender by Ronica Black. Cam and Blake are unable to deny their passion for each other, but surrendering to love is a whole different matter. (978-1-63555-703-9)

The Holiday Detour by Jane Kolven. It will take everything going wrong to make Dana and Charlie see how right they are for each other. (978-1-63555-720-6)

Too Hot to Ride by Andrews & Austin. World famous cutting horse champion and industry legend Jane Barrow is knockdown sexy in the way she moves, talks, and rides, and Rae Starr is determined not to get involved with this womanizing gambler. (978-1-63555-776-3)

A Love that Leads to Home by Ronica Black. For Carla Sims and Janice Carpenter, home isn't about location, it's where your heart is. (978-1-63555-675-9)

Blades of Bluegrass by D. Jackson Leigh. A US Army occupational therapist must rehab a bitter veteran who is a ticking political time bomb the military is desperate to disarm. (978-1-63555-637-7)

Guarding Hearts by Jaycie Morrison. As treachery and temptation threaten the women of the Women's Army Corps, who will risk it all for love? (978-1-63555-806-7)

Hopeless Romantic by Georgia Beers. Can a jaded wedding planner and an optimistic divorce attorney possibly find a future together? (978-1-63555-650-6)

Hopes and Dreams by PJ Trebelhorn. Movie theater manager Riley Warren is forced to face her high school crush and tormentor, wealthy socialite Victoria Thayer, at their twentieth reunion. (978-1-63555-670-4)

In the Cards by Kimberly Cooper Griffin. Daria and Phaedra are about to discover that love finds a way, especially when powers outside their control are at play. (978-1-63555-717-6)

Moon Fever by Ileandra Young. SPEAR agent Danika Karson must clear her werewolf friend of multiple false charges while teaching her vampire girlfriend to resist the blood mania brought on by a full moon. (978-1-63555-603-2)

Quake City by St John Karp. Can Andre find his best friend Amy before the night devolves into a nightmare of broken hearts, malevolent drag queens, and spontaneous human combustion? Or has it always happened this way, every night, at Aunty Bob's Quake City Club? (978-1-63555-723-7)

Serenity by Jesse J. Thoma. For Kit Marsden, there are many things in life she cannot change. Serenity is in the acceptance. (978-1-63555-713-8)

Sylver and Gold by Michelle Larkin. Working feverishly to find a killer before he strikes again, Boston Homicide Detective Reid Sylver and rookie cop London Gold are blindsided by their chemistry and developing attraction. (978-1-63555-611-7)

Trade Secrets by Kathleen Knowles. In Silicon Valley, love and business are a volatile mix for clinical lab scientist Tony Leung and venture capitalist Sheila Graham. (978-1-63555-642-1)

Storm Lines by Jessica L. Webb. Devon is a psychologist who likes rules. Marley is a cop who doesn't. They don't always agree, but both fight to protect a girl immersed in a street drug ring. (978-1-63555-626-1)

The Politics of Love by Jen Jensen. Is it possible to love across the political divide in a hostile world? Conservative Shelley Whitmore and liberal Rand Thomas are about to find out. (978-1-63555-693-3)

All the Paths to You by Morgan Lee Miller. High school sweethearts Quinn Hughes and Kennedy Reed reconnect five years after they break up and realize that their chemistry is all but over. (978-1-63555-662-9)

Arrested Pleasures by Nanisi Barrett D'Arnuck. When charged with a crime she didn't commit, Katherine Lowe faces the question: Which is harder, going to prison or falling in love? (978-1-63555-684-1)

Bonded Love by Renee Roman. Carpenter Blaze Carter suffers an injury that shatters her dreams, and ER nurse Trinity Greene hopes to show her that sometimes love is worth fighting for. (978-1-63555-530-1)

Convergence by Jane C. Esther. With life as they know it on the line, can Aerin McLeary and Olivia Ando's love survive an otherworldly threat to humankind? (978-1-63555-488-5)

Coyote Blues by Karen F. Williams. Riley Dawson, psychotherapist and shape-shifter, has her world turned upside down when Fiona Bell, her one true love, returns. (978-1-63555-558-5)

Drawn by Carsen Taite. Will the clues lead Detective Claire Hanlon to the killer terrorizing Dallas, or will she merely lose her heart to person of interest, urban artist Riley Flynn? (978-1-63555-644-5)

Death Overdue by David S. Pederson. Did Heath turn to murder in an alcohol induced haze to solve the problem of his blackmailer, or was it someone else who brought about a death overdue? (978-1-63555-711-4)

Entangled by Melissa Brayden. Becca Crawford is the perfect person to head up the Jade Hotel, if only the captivating owner of the local vineyard would get on board with her plan and stop badmouthing the hotel to everyone in town. (978-1-63555-709-1)

First Do No Harm by Emily Smith. Pierce and Cassidy are about to discover that when it comes to love, sometimes you have to risk it all to have it all. (978-1-63555-699-5)

Kiss Me Every Day by Dena Blake. For Wynn Evans, wishing for a do-over with Carly Jamison was a long shot, actually getting one was a game changer. (978-1-63555-551-6)

Olivia by Genevieve McCluer. In this lesbian Shakespeare adaptation with vampires, Olivia is a centuries old vampire who must fight a strange figure from her past if she wants a chance at happiness. (978-1-63555-701-5)

One Woman's Treasure by Jean Copeland. Daphne's search for discarded antiques and treasures leads to an embarrassing misunderstanding, and ultimately, the opportunity for the romance of a lifetime with Nina. (978-1-63555-652-0)

Silver Ravens by Jane Fletcher. Lori has lost her girlfriend, her home, and her job. Things don't improve when she's kidnapped and taken to fairyland. (978-1-63555-631-5)

Still Not Over You by Jenny Frame, Carsen Taite, Ali Vali. Old flames die hard in these tales of a second chance at love with the ex you're still not over. Stories by award winning authors Jenny Frame, Carsen Taite, and Ali Vali. (978-1-63555-516-5)